INVERCLYDE LIBRARIES

Gu 1

| PORT GLASGOW | | |
|---|---|---|
| 2 6 AUG 2015 | 2 0 FEB 2016 | 2 3 APR 2016 |
| 2 8 JUN 2016 | | |
| GOUROCK | | |
| - 8 SEP 2018 | | |
| | | 2 9 AUG 2019 |
| 1 9 SEP 2019 | | |
| 2 0 SEP 2022 | | |
| | | |
| | | |
| | | |
| | | |
| | | |

## INVERCLYDE LIBRARIES

**This book is to be returned on or before
the last date above. It may be borrowed for
a further period if not in demand.**

*For enquiries and renewals Tel: (01475) 712323*

WITHDRAWN

Inverclyde Lib

D1342248

34106 003282400

## Hard Feelings
'a tale that reads like James M Cain modernised by Bret Easton Ellis. It will make you squirm'– *Guardian Unlimited*

'Starr has plumbed the shallows of his brittle characters and their selfish lives, depicting them in a hard-edged style that is clean, cold and extremely chilling' – *New York Times*

'Jason Starr is the first writer of his generation to convincingly update the modern crime novel by giving it provocative new spins and *Hard Feelings* is his most accomplished thriller yet. It might be new-school noir but like the classics of the genre it has a brutal escalation of tension, pungent dialogue, a hardboiled simplicity and grace, and a whopper of an ending. It's also darkly funny and a pure pleasure to read. As you race through it you realize that Jim Thompson has just moved to Manhattan'
**– Bret Easton Ellis**

'Convincing and entertaining... *Hard Feelings* dances a mesmerizing tango between reality and its menacing shadow' – *Time Out New York*

'a gripping novel of paranoia and obsession that's damn near impossible to put down' – *Time Out*

'a powerfully written, thoroughly involving novel of paranoia, obsession and revenge' – *Crime Time*

'one of the best things about a Jason Starr novel is the ending: it never quite goes the way you think, and this novel is no exception' – *Barcelona Review*

## Tough Luck
'a hard-knuckled writer' – *New York Times Book Review*

'From the first page of this noir thriller, you know things are only going to get worse, but you can't stop reading'
– *Newsweek*

'*Tough Luck*, an enthralling character study, is perfect car-crash literature; spiritual sustenance for the "inner rubberneck" in all of us' – *New Mystery Reader Magazine*

'Starr delivers a wild ride through a mob-saturated Italian-American community in 1980s New York, keeping the surprises coming up to the last sentence'
– *Publishers Weekly*

'a noir world that is not only bleak, but painfully funny'
– *Mystery Ink*

### Twisted City
'Jason Starr is terrific and *Twisted City* is one of his best. Starr knows what James M. Cain knew: that a whole world of evil lies right on the edge of the everyday world and you can cross the border in a city minute. His stuff is tough and real and brilliant' – **Andrew Klavan**

'Jason Starr is one of the new voices of noir fiction, a writer capable of taking noir from what it has always been toward whatever it can become. He's got his own slant, his own slashing style, and the moral honesty true noir requires. I could go on, but just look at the proof, *Twisted City*'
– **Daniel Woodrell**

'Demonic, demented and truly ferocious and a flat out joy to read. In other words, a total feast. Like it? … I plain worshipped it' – **Ken Bruen**

'Streamlined as a model's hips, dark as the inside of a dog's gut, *Twisted City* is a hip, white collar update on the James Cain, Jim Thompson style novel with a seasoning all its own. Jason Starr is a unique talent, and *Twisted City* is one unique book' – **Joe R. Lansdale**

Also by Jason Starr

# COLD CALLER

## Jason Starr

**NO EXIT PRESS**

INVERCLYDE LIBRARIES

This edition published in 2014
by No Exit Press,
an imprint of Oldcastle Books
P.O.Box 394, Harpenden,
Herts, AL5 1XJ, UK

noexit.co.uk
@NoExitPress

© 1997 Jason Starr

The right of Jason Starr to be identified as the author of this work
has been asserted in accordance with the Copyright, Designs
and Patents Act 1988.

All rights reserved. No part of this book may be reproduced, stored
in or introduced into a retrieval system, or transmitted, in any form
or by any means (electronic, mechanical, photocopying, recording or
otherwise) without the written permission of the publishers.

Any person who does any unauthorised act in relation to this
publication may be liable to criminal prosecution and civil claims for
damages.

This is a work of fiction. Names, characters, places, and incidents either
are the product of the author's imagination or are used fictitiously, and
any resemblance to actual persons, living or dead, businesses,
companies, events or locales is entirely coincidental.

A CIP catalogue record for this book is available from the
British Library.

ISBN
978-1-84344-511-1 (print)
978-1-84344-512-8 (epub)
978-1-84344-513-5 (kindle)
978-1-84344-514-2 (pdf)

Typeset by Avocet Typeset, Somerton, Somerset TA11 6RT
Printed in Great Britain by Clays Ltd, St Ives plc

For more information about Crime Fiction go to @CrimeTimeUK

*For Sandy and Chynna*

# 1

ON MOST DAYS, I wouldn't have said anything. Like the typical New Yorker, I'd have given her a couple of dirty looks, maybe grunted a little, and minded my own business. But that morning was different. Maybe things were already building up in my life, pushing me to the brink. Or maybe I was just having a bad day. I'd had a fight with my girlfriend the night before and she'd left for work that morning without saying goodbye.

"Excuse me," I said irritably. "Excuse me."

She didn't answer. I thought she didn't hear me so I said it again, a little louder, then I noticed she was wearing a Walkman. I tapped her on the shoulder and she turned around as if I'd pinched her.

"There's plenty of room over there," I said, motioning toward the middle of the subway car.

"Get your hands off me!" she screamed. Because of the Walkman, her voice was especially loud.

"I was just asking you to –"

A thick, heavy hand arrived on my shoulder.

"Leave the lady alone, will ya?"

He was a young, muscular guy, wearing the plain gray uniform that plumbers and electricians wear.

"I was just asking her if she could move inside a little," I said.

"You were grabbing her," the guy said. "I saw you grabbing her."

"I didn't grab her," I said. "I was just trying to get her attention."

"You were grabbing her," he insisted. "I saw you. You've been kicking and grabbing people ever since you got on this train. You stepped on my foot before and you didn't even say excuse me."

"Look, what's your problem?"

I don't remember what else he said to me, or what I said back to him, or who pushed who first. All I know is that within a few seconds I was wrestling with a man twice my size in the middle of a crowded subway car. He was so much bigger than me, I don't know if you can even call it a fight. He got me in a headlock and punched me in the face a couple of times and then squeezed my head and neck. People on the train were screaming – some begging for us to stop, others cheering us on. The doors opened and somehow our wrestling match moved onto the Seventy-seventh Street platform. That's when the guy got his best shot in, connecting with a solid upper-cut above my left eye. Finally, a Transit cop came over and separated us. People had formed a circle, staring at me. I had a flashback to junior high school in Bainbridge Island, Washington, when Johnny McGuiness beat the hell out of me and a crowd of kids gathered around laughing. These people weren't laughing but I felt just as embarrassed as I'd felt eighteen years ago.

The cop asked us who had started the fight. The man said I did, which was a lie, and I said so. But when the cop asked if I wanted to press charges I said no.

"I just want to get to work," I said.

"It's up to you," the cop said. As I was walking away, he added, "I'll get you to a hospital if you want me to. That cut looks pretty bad."

I kept walking.

With some crumpled up old napkin I found stuffed inside my back pocket, I put pressure on the wound. I got on the next train to Grand Central.

*

I was working at a company called American Communications Association. I made appointments for sales
representatives to sell discount long-distance phone
services to businesses. It was a part-time job, just four
hours a day, but I worked full-time shifts three days a
week. After I'd lost my real job as V.P. of Marketing at
Smythe & O'Greeley, a big New York ad agency, I'd
only intended to work at A.C.A. temporarily, to make
some extra cash after my unemployment benefits ran
out. But two years had gone by and I was still at
A.C.A., no closer to finding another job in advertising.
Of course I'd interviewed at plenty of agencies, but the
story was always the same – I was either over-qualified, or they said I'd been out of work too long. I was
beginning to think that I'd be a telemarketer for the
rest of my life.

The A.C.A. office was on Forty-third Street, near
Eighth Avenue. When I got off the elevator on the
seventh floor, Eileen, the receptionist, was chewing gum
and polishing her nails. She'd never said a word to me
or to any of the other telemarketers before, but today
she dropped the nail polish when she saw me.

"My God, what happened to you?" she asked.

"Nothing," I said casually. "A little accident, that's
all."

As I headed along the corridor, I realized the cut
might be worse than I thought. I felt the napkin and
discovered blood seeping through.

I went into the call center, where the telemarketers
worked. The large square-shaped room had four rows
of three-foot-wide cubicles. Surrounding the room were
the managers' offices with windows facing the telemarketing floor. Mike Peterson, the Floor Supervisor, came

over to me while I was punching in at the time clock.

"Bill, there you are. I didn't think you were going to make it in today."

"Well, here I am," I said.

"Why didn't you call? Did you oversleep? I mean you know how it is here in the summer. We have a full staff and we need to –"

I turned around. Mike saw the cut on my face. He looked like he was going to vomit.

"Jesus Christ, you're bleeding!"

"Really?" I said. "I was wondering what all that red stuff coming out of my head was."

"What the hell happened?"

"I had a rough ride in on the subway."

"The subway?"

"What difference does it make? I'm here now, aren't I?"

"You should really get stitches for that or something."

"It's all right," I said. "I just have to wash it out."

In the bathroom, I finally got the bleeding to stop. I put on a couple of Band-Aids I'd found in the cabinet under the sink, then went back out to my cubicle and prepared to work.

I hated my job, but I was good at it. I averaged two or three appointments a day, which was better than most people in the office. I earned sixteen dollars an hour, while most people were making ten or eleven. I was the second-oldest telemarketer, in seniority and age. Only Harry Pearlman, who was fifty-two years old, had been with the company longer than me. I think I was better on the phone than Harry though. I was very confident and relaxed and people always seemed to trust me. Even when people didn't really need our service I could sweet talk them into an appointment. Like this one time, a guy hung up on me while I was in the middle of my pitch. I called him right back and said, "I'm sorry, sir, we must have been disconnected," and I wound up getting him.

I got off to a hot start on the phone, making two appointments in the first fifteen minutes. During the eleven o'clock break, I went to the concession machines in the back and bought a can of Pepsi. Greg Brown was there talking to a girl who'd just started at the company. Later, I found out her name was Marie Stipaldi.

"Man, you know they're ripping us off," Greg was saying. "Just because the salesman makes the sale, you think he's giving us credit for making an appointment? I know for a fact them motherfuckers ripped me off for three appointments. That's fifteen dollars, man. That shit adds up after a while."

"I don't care about commissions," Marie said. "I'm just working here for the ten dollars an hour."

"Well, I care," Greg said. "And if they keep fucking with my shit I'm gonna go in there and do something about it."

"What are you gonna do?" I said. "Sue them?"

"Fuck the lawyers, man," Greg said. "I'll go into Ed's office and tell him the way it is."

"A lot of good that'll do," I said. "You know how easy they can replace one of us?"

"They can't replace me, man. I've been making ten appointments a week. I'm the king of A.C.A. I'm the most important employee at this company."

"Believe me, nobody's important at this company," I said. "I've been here a long time, too long, and I never saw one guy go into that office and get what he wanted."

"He's right," Marie said to Greg. "You can't treat this

job like it's serious. You have to expect to get ripped off."

"That's easy for you to say," Greg said. "A white man can go in and get anything he wants, but a black man's gotta take what he can get. I bet one of you guys could go up to the biggest company in America, IBM or Texon or Exico or whatever the fuck it's called, and you could get whatever job you wanted. But if I walked in there they'd give me a mop and tell me to start cleaning the toilets. And I know for a fact that if I was white, I'd be getting my commission money here."

"I disagree," I said. "Look at me. They owe me two hundred dollars in back commission."

"I don't care what you say," Greg said. "The people who run this place are a bunch of racist motherfuckers. I don't know about you, but I wouldn't be too upset if I showed up here for work one day and the whole place burned down – with all the people in it."

"That's terrible," Marie said.

"I'm not talking about you," Greg said. "Just them managers, you know. I know if they was sittin' in a fire, beggin' for me to help, I'd just let their asses burn."

Greg started to laugh. I started laughing too, partly because I liked Greg and partly because I agreed it would be nice to watch Mike and Ed burn. As we were laughing, Mike poked his head into the room.

"Break's over, guys. Let's get back on those phones now."

"I been meaning to ask you," Greg said to me as we were walking back to our desks. "Who fucked you up like that?"

"Fucked me up?" I said like I was confused. "Oh, you mean *that*," I said touching my forehead. "It was just an accident."

"Yeah, right," Greg said laughing. "You got your ass kicked. Who was it? Did you fuck him up bad?"

"I got a few whacks in," I lied.

"But he looks like he got a few more whacks in," Greg said laughing.

As I was about to sit down at my cubicle, Mike came over and said he wanted to talk to me in his office.

"What about?" I said.

"I'll tell you in private."

I followed him, wondering what he could possibly want to talk to me about. Had he been listening near the concession machines and heard the things Greg had said? If so, I decided I'd stand up for Greg and deny everything.

Mike closed the door and told me to sit down. He went around to his desk and brought up a file on his computer screen. Mike was thin and wore a white shirt with a black tie and black suspenders every day. He always looked nervous and insecure and I often wondered if he was gay. Not that it would've bothered me if he was, but I think it bothered Mike that I wondered about it. He always treated me like I somehow disapproved of him.

"I really hate to do this," he said, not making eye contact with me. "But I'm afraid I have no choice."

"You're firing me?"

"Of course not," he said. "It's nothing that drastic. I know you're one of the best people here, which is what makes this so hard. It's just that...well, you know we have certain rules around here. They're not my rules, of course. They're Ed's rules and it's just my job to enforce them. You know you were late this morning."

"I thought we discussed that already."

"I just didn't want to say anything until I checked my

records and made sure, but you realize this is the third time you've been late this month."

"I know that," I said. "But as you can see something happened this morning that was beyond my control."

Mike was nodding his head.

"I'm sorry about that, I really am, but we have a rule, and that's why we have the rule, so we don't punish you for your first infraction. On July first you were eight minutes late to work, on the eleventh you were fifteen minutes late, and today you were late an hour and ten minutes."

"I don't believe this," I said.

"I'm sorry, but there's nothing I can do about it," Mike said. "After your first infraction, I gave you a verbal warning, then I gave you a written warning, and now I have to send you home without pay."

"This is ridiculous," I said, raising my voice. "Do you think I wanted to be late this morning?"

"It's not a question of what you wanted or didn't want –"

"This is a joke, right? You're not serious."

"I'm afraid I'm very serious," Mike said. "Maybe you didn't mean to be late this morning – I mean of course you didn't mean it – but there's the fact that you've been late two other times this month, and you didn't call one of those times either."

"Do you know how long I've been working here?"

Mike moved the cursor to a new spot on the screen.

"Twenty-six point five months."

"That's over a year point five longer than you've been working here," I said bitterly, "and I think that entitles me to a few privileges."

Mike's cheeks had turned pink. I could tell he was upset that I wasn't respecting his authority. Or maybe it was the gay thing coming out again.

"I don't care how long you've been working here," he said. "You're still a telemarketer and you have to go by the same rules that the other telemarketers go by."

I stood up.

"Excuse me, but where do you think you're going?"

"Back to work."

"I already clocked you out for the day."

"You did *what*?"

"I'm sending you home, Bill. If you don't go, I'll have to do something drastic."

"Are you threatening my job now?"

"I don't *want* to threaten your job, but you're giving me no choice."

"I'm going back to work. I've already made two appointments today and I plan to make a couple more. In other words, I'm going to continue doing my job."

"Bill, you're making a big mistake."

"I want to speak to Ed."

"Ed won't talk to you."

I stormed out of Mike's office and headed across the telemarketing floor. The argument had caused a scene. Almost everyone had stopped making phone calls, and when I passed Greg's cubicle, I saw he was fighting to hold back his laughter. This made me smile, but I was too furious to laugh.

Ed was on the phone and motioned for me to sit down. He was the typical guy from Long Island you might see any weekday night in his shirt and tie at a strip club or a sports bar. He was balding and had a bushy mustache and a beer-drinker's gut. He quit drinking a few years ago, but he was one of those recovering alcoholics who imposed their newfound wisdom on everyone around them. Sometimes people joked and called the company A.A. instead of A.C.A. because Ed ran the Telemarketing Department like it was a Twelve-Step program. He was constantly telling us about "our responsibility to ourselves as telemarketers" and how "what we learn at this job will reflect on the rest of our lives." He had created a long list of rules and regulations that read like a manifesto. Besides lateness, there were penalties for drinking or eating at the workstations, cursing, making personal phone calls, and violating the dress code. Even laughing was illegal, if it reached "a disturbing volume." I don't think I ever saw Ed smile or tell a joke, and he rarely said anything directly to the telemarketers. We said hello when we passed each other in the hallway, but this was the first time I had ever been inside his office. The telemarketers were supposed to air their grievances to Mike because Ed was "too busy" to deal with our problems. To me, it looked like Ed was never busy at all. Sometimes I overheard him talking on the phone and his conversations were always about football or hockey or the size of some woman's tits.

Today it sounded like he was talking to his girlfriend, or someone he wanted to be his girlfriend. I was getting impatient listening to him go on and on in that pseudo-nice voice he put on only when he was talking to women – *Really? That's very interesting. I love museums too. Which is your favorite museum in New York?* – but at least it gave me a chance to calm down and figure out exactly what I wanted to say. It was comfortable in Ed's office, a lot more comfortable than where the telemarketers worked. I was sitting in a padded vinyl chair, breathing air that must have been about twenty degrees cooler than on the telemarketing floor.

Finally, Ed hung up. I was expecting him to be upset

that I had barged into his office the way I had, but he was surprisingly cordial.

"Bill Moss," he said as though he enjoyed saying my name. "What happened to you this morning?"

At first I thought he was talking about my lateness, then I remembered the cut on my forehead.

"It's actually the reason why I came in here," I said. "As you can see, I had a little mishap on the subway this morning."

"I'm sorry to hear that. Did you go to a doctor?"

"I don't think it's that bad," I said. "I'll take care of it when I get home. Anyway, what I'm here about, I was late this morning – over an hour. It was the third time I was late this month and Mike wants to send me home without pay."

Ed was looking at me closer now. He had a dazed, stumped expression. This would be the most complicated decision he made all day, I realized, and he didn't want to blow it.

"Let me get this straight," Ed said. "This was the third time you were late, and the other two infractions were brought to your attention?"

"Yes," I said, "but there was an extenuating circumstance."

"I get it," Ed said. "You think you're entitled to an exemption."

"Well, yeah," I said. "I mean it's not like I slept through my alarm clock or anything like that. I've already made two appointments today and I was telemarketer-of-the-month last month. I think I'm entitled to some sort of break."

"But you understood that the rule existed?"

"Of course," I said. "But I've been working here a long time, and as you can see I had an accident this morning."

Ed continued to stare at me, in deep thought, then he stood up.

"Wait right here."

He left the office. Through the windows, I saw him talking to Mike in Mike's office. Mike did most of the talking and I thought he looked angry and defensive. Ed nodded his head a lot with his arms crossed in front of his chest. Then Ed left and started back toward me with his usual humorless expression.

"Well, I discussed the situation with Mike," he said, sitting down at his desk, "and I've decided you're right – he shouldn't have sent you home without pay."

"Thank you," I said.

"However, I'm going to have to back up his decision."

"What?" I said.

"Although I agree with your position," Ed continued, "Mike is your supervisor and if I let you stay today I'd be showing him up in front of the other employees. If you hadn't argued with him and made such a scene, maybe we could've worked something out."

"I don't get it," I said. "You're sending me home without pay – me, one of the best telemarketers in the office, a guy who's already made two appointments today. You're just going to let me walk out of here?"

"I have no choice," Ed said. "I have to respect Mike's decision."

"Fine," I said bitterly. "But if I leave here now, there's a chance I might not come back tomorrow."

"That's up to you," Ed said. "Personally, I hope you stay on with us. Obviously, I don't know you too well, but you seem to have a degree of intelligence, at least more intelligence than most people we hire here, and I'd like to keep you on board. But if you decide to leave, I wish you luck."

I left Ed's office, closing the door hard behind me, but not slamming it. I went to my cubicle and gathered some papers I had in my desk. Greg came up behind me and said in a low voice:

"I told you, man. The guy's a motherfucker, ain't he?"

"What can I say?" I said. "You were right."

"You outta here, man?"

"Looks that way."

"If I don't see you again – peace."

"Peace," I said.

Without saying goodbye to anyone else, I left the office.

On Eighth Avenue, a beggar in front of a triple-x video store asked me for change, a drug dealer offered me crack, a tourist asked me for directions to Times Square. I ignored everyone. My forehead hurt and the heat was unbearable. It must have been a hundred degrees already and it wasn't twelve o'clock yet.

I thought about stopping at a phone booth and calling Julie at work and telling her about my morning, but I figured she'd still be angry at me because of our fight last night. I didn't feel like making up with her, not yet anyway. I crossed Forty-fourth Street with a crowd of people, wondering what to do with the rest of my life.

# 2

I WENT TO the movies. To be honest, I can't remember the name of the movie I saw, but that doesn't mean it wasn't good. I was so busy thinking about work that I hardly remember being in the theater.

Work had always been extremely important to me. When I was six years old my father had dropped dead of a heart attack. Two months later, my mother killed herself, overdosing on sleeping pills. My parents weren't wealthy and they didn't have insurance policies. I had no brothers or sisters and my grandparents were dead, so I was sent to live with my father's brother and his wife who also had a house on Bainbridge Island. My new parents didn't have any children of their own and they always made it very clear to me that after I finished high school I'd have to fend for myself. In junior high and high school I had part-time jobs – delivering newspapers, washing dishes, mowing lawns, walking dogs – and I saved most of my money for my future. I wasn't one of those kids who dreaded work. I preferred work to playing with my friends, and I tried to work as often and as hard as I could. The more I worked and the more money I earned, the more I felt I was protecting myself from my aloneness in the world. I never considered the possibility of not working.

It must have been about three or three-thirty when the movie let out. I wandered crosstown, still feeling depressed. August rent was coming up and I only had a few hundred dollars in the bank. I still had about ten thousand dollars in student loans to pay back from grad school and college and the credit card companies had taken away my Visa and American Express cards. I knew I had to find something fast – maybe work at a bookstore or get a job waiting tables – or making next month's rent would be impossible.

At Fifty-first, I took the number 6 to Ninety-sixth Street. Julie and I lived on the fifth floor of a renovated walk-up on East Ninety-fourth between First and Second Avenues. Technically, this was the Upper East Side, but the best parts of the neighborhood started five or six blocks downtown or west of Park Avenue. Our block was a mix of tenements and small factories. Some yuppies lived on our block, but there were also a lot of working-class black and Puerto Rican families. I liked the area, but Julie thought it was too dangerous, especially at night, and this had become a major conflict in our relationship. Julie always made comments about how her friends were living in such nice doorman buildings in the Seventies and Eighties, and how nice it would be to live in a place where you don't have to walk up five flights of stairs every day. Of course I was sensitive to this, because I knew the implication was that we could be living in a better place if only I was making more money. So I would blow up, accuse Julie of resenting me because she had a higher salary, and she would say that she didn't mean that at all, that she just didn't feel safe in our neighborhood, and then we'd both start screaming, calling each other names, forgetting of course what the argument was about in the first place.

Julie and I had met at a laundromat on Columbus Avenue a few months after I'd moved to New York from Seattle. After two dates, we started spending practically every night together. During the first year we lived together, we were even talking about marriage. Then something happened. I guess there are an endless number of reasons why a relationship can turn sour, but with us there was one big reason – I was Catholic and Julie was Jewish. This was never an issue for me, but it was a big issue for her. My aunt and uncle had sent me to Catholic schools, but I hadn't set foot in a church since college. Julie wasn't religious either, but her parents were, and I always felt she secretly resented me for being what her father called a *shagetz*. She didn't have to say anything specific for me to get offended; sometimes it could just be a subtle comment – "Oh, did I tell you, my friend Lori, she met this great guy Saturday night – he's Jewish and everything." She even asked me once if I would consider converting, but I told her that since I was basically agnostic, that would be hypocritical. She gave me one of her looks – she could look right through me – and I knew she wouldn't bring up the subject again.

When I got out of the subway it was about five o'clock. I knew Julie wouldn't be home from work for another hour and, feeling guilty about our fight, I decided to do something nice for her. I stopped at the Korean grocery on the corner and bought a bouquet of pink roses. I couldn't remember exactly what we had argued about last night, but I knew it was probably my fault. I can be a pretty difficult guy to get along with sometimes, and it was amazing that Julie had the patience to put up with me at all.

I didn't realize how exhausted I was until I'd walked up the first of the four flights of stairs. Living on the fifth floor was good exercise, I always told Julie, but the truth was I hated it as much as she did. When I got into the apartment, I immediately undressed and put on the air conditioning. The landlord had installed French doors to screen off the space near the windows and this was "the bedroom." There was another space where we kept the couch and the T.V., and beyond that was a small kitchen and a bathroom big enough for one person at a time. The apartment would've been fine for a single person, but for two people, especially two people who weren't always on the best terms, it was like living in a walk-in closet.

When Julie came home, I was sitting in front of the T.V. in my underwear, eating some pasta. She was holding a tall bag full of groceries and looked exhausted.

"My God, what a day," she said, out of breath from the walk upstairs. She put the groceries down near the door, then went into the bedroom to get undressed. I stayed on the couch. When we first moved in together, I'd get up and give Julie a warm kiss hello whenever she came home from work, but now we were like a married couple who had been together too long to get excited about each other's comings and goings.

Julie came out of the bedroom wearing a long T-shirt and started unpacking the groceries. Her hair was dyed blond, but not phony-blond; it looked nice, especially when she blew it dry or wore it up with a clip. She had a small, pretty face and light-brown eyes that looked green in the sunlight. She carried some extra weight on her thighs and her hips, but I thought it was sexy. I usually felt proud to be with her, especially when I saw other guys looking at her on the street. But other times – like now – I saw her as a chubby thirty-two-year-old with wrinkles under her eyes and low self-esteem who hated me for not being Jewish and I wondered what I was still doing with her.

"You wouldn't believe what happened to me at work

today," she said. "My boss comes in and he's like, 'Did you mail that letter to Mr. Jacobs yesterday?' I said I didn't mail it to him personally, I put it in the mail room and Jose was supposed to mail it. So he starts going off on me. He's like, 'It's your responsibility to make sure my mail goes out on time. I told you to mail the letter, not Jose.' Can you believe that? Like he thinks I'm going to take the letter to the post office for him or something. Jenny told me it's probably because he's going through a divorce. But I don't see why that has to be my responsibility. If he's angry at his wife, he should take it out on her, not on me. So what do you think? Do you think I – my God, what happened to your face?"

She sat down next to me on the couch.

"It's nothing," I said. "Just a little cut."

"It looks terrible. Let mommy see the boo-boo."

She peeled back the bandage and her eyes widened.

"Bill, that's awful," she said in a serious tone. "What happened? Did somebody hit you?"

"I'd rather not talk about it."

"You have to do something. We have to go to the emergency room."

"I'm not going to any emergency room."

"You have to. If you don't do something you'll get a scar."

"I don't want to talk about it, all right?"

"Fine," she said angrily.

She went back to the kitchen and started putting away the groceries. The sports report came on the news. I watched highlights of the Yankees-Mariners game and saw Hundley hit one out for the Mets. I don't know why I was angry at Julie, I just was. After the announcer read off the other baseball scores, I said:

"I got some flowers for you over there."

"I saw. Thank you."

She leaned against the refrigerator, eating a container of fat-free yogurt, while I watched the beginning of *Jeopardy*. Finally, she said, as if we were in the middle of the conversation:

"And I don't understand why I have to deal with this, after I come home from a hard day at work. I'm just trying to help you and you start up again, snapping at me. And then you think it's no big deal, that you can just give me some flowers and everything's going to be all right. It's not fair, Bill. We have to be able to communicate. All the books I've read, the shows on T.V., say that's when a relationship gets in trouble, when you can't talk to each other anymore. You can't just sit there watching baseball games on T.V. when I'm trying to talk to you."

"They weren't games."

"What?"

"They weren't games, they were highlights."

"You know what I mean, stop changing the subject. I hate when you do that. It's like I can't have a simple conversation with you."

"What makes you think my day wasn't hard?"

"I have no idea how hard or not hard your day was. You won't talk to me about it."

"Maybe it was so hard I don't want to talk about it."

"Did somebody mug you? Is that how you got that cut on your face? I told you this neighborhood is terrible, but you wouldn't believe me."

"I wasn't mugged."

"Then what happened? *Please* tell me."

The Double Jeopardy round was starting. Julie came over and muted the television.

"Who is Edward Albee?"

"What?"

"That's the answer. Put the sound back on, you'll see."

Julie sat next to me, gently rubbing my back.

"What happened?"

"I got sent home from work early today," I said.

"Oh no," she said. "Why?"

I told her the whole story, an abbreviated version. When I finished, she looked confused.

"But what's that have to do with the cut on your face?"

"Forget about the cut. I walked out of my job today. I'm unemployed."

"It's okay," she said, holding my hand. "There's no reason to get upset. I mean you didn't care about that job anyway, right?"

"That's not the point," I said. "It was my job. It was paying rent."

"It's all right. I have plenty of money. I can pay the rent next month if I have to."

"I'm not letting you pay my rent."

"Why not? I love you. I mean we're in love, aren't we?"

"That's not the point," I said, wriggling my hand free from hers. "The point is I need money, I need a job. What am I gonna do, just hang around in this fucking apartment all day?"

"There are plenty of telemarketing jobs out there," she said. "I'm sure you can find one like that. If not, you can always temp."

"What is Nagasaki?"

"Are you listening to me?"

"Yeah," I said. "And then what?"

"Eventually you'll find another ad job."

"Eventually! I've waited two fucking years for eventually!"

"Don't yell at me."

"I'm not yelling at you!"

"You're acting like a total baby now."

"Oh, so now you're gonna start calling me names?"

"What are you talking about?"

"You know exactly what I'm talking about!"

"Lots of people lose their jobs, William. It's just a bad time, that's all. Besides, maybe there's a bright side to all this. Maybe if you could get on unemployment you could use the time to blitz all the agencies again. You could spend every day, nine-to-five, looking for work."

I went to the kitchen and opened the refrigerator. I wasn't hungry, I just needed something to stare at. William, I thought. I hated it when people called me William.

"I can't get unemployment. I wasn't fired, remember? I quit. At least I'm going to quit tomorrow."

"Maybe you shouldn't," Julie said. "Maybe you should just go back there tomorrow."

"There's no way I'm gonna go back there. To beg on my hands and knees to those assholes? Fuck that."

"Then don't go back," Julie said from the couch. "I don't understand why we have to argue about this."

I stood motionless, staring at a carton of milk. I realized Julie was crying. I went over to the couch and sat down next to her. She buried her face in my chest, her body convulsing every couple of seconds. I wiped her tears away with my fingers.

"I'm sorry," I said. "I know you're only trying to help. Stop crying, okay?"

She continued to cry and shake.

"You were yelling at me," she said.

"I know," I said. "I was wrong."

"Are you angry at me for something?"

"Of course not. This has nothing to do with you."

"Then I don't get it. And I don't understand why you won't tell me what happened to your face."

"I didn't tell you because I was embarrassed," I said. "I was mugged on my way to work."

"Oh my God, that's terrible!" She sat up. "Where did it happen?"

"On the subway. Well, not on the subway, Grand Central Station, in the tunnel going to the subway. One guy hit me and the other guy took my money, just a few dollars. There were people around everywhere, but nobody helped me."

"Did you see the guys that did it?"

"They were wearing baseball hats."

"*Shvartzas*," Julie said bitterly. "Are you sure you're okay? Do you want to go to the emergency room?"

"I really don't think it's necessary," I said. "The bleeding's pretty much stopped. But now you can see why I got so pissed off at those assholes at work. It was bad enough getting mugged, but then getting sent home because of it! And then I had to sit there quietly while Ed went on and on about how 'I seem to have a degree of intelligence!' I mean I have an M.B.A., I was a V.P. at a major company, and I have to be patronized by some moron who probably barely made it through high school."

"I know how you feel," Julie said. "Look what happened to me at work today. It's very frustrating when you can't talk back to your boss."

"No, it's different for you," I said. "You're working in publishing, that's your career. When your boss yells at you or puts you down you have to put up with it. But these guys mean nothing to me. On days like today, when they're talking to me like that, I just feel like killing them. I'm not kidding. I actually want to murder them."

"I think you need a drink," Julie said. "Why don't you open that wine Robert and Jennifer brought us?"

"I don't want any goddamn wine!"

"All right," Julie said. "Then forget it."

"I'm just trying to talk to you," I said. "Isn't that what you wanted?"

"Of course I –"

"You think I'm making a big deal about nothing, don't you? You don't see why I'm so upset."

"Of course I know why you're upset."

"You think I should just go back there and ask for my job back like nothing happened. You think I'm secretly glad this all happened because I didn't want to work there anyway. You think I want to sit home all day and do nothing like some kind of bum!"

"Bill, I honestly don't understand what you're talking about."

"I'm an embarrassment to you. You can't stand all your friends married to doctors and lawyers while your boyfriend is a telemarketer."

"First of all, you're not a telemarketer."

"You're right – I'm not a telemarketer. I'm an out-of-work telemarketer! How humiliating is that?!"

"This isn't fair," Julie said. "You had a bad day and I had a bad day and now you're taking it all out on me."

"Fine," I said. "Let's not discuss it anymore."

I went back to the couch and turned up the sound on the T.V. *Wheel of Fortune* was coming on.

"You can't do that," Julie said. "You can't just start all this, then walk away."

"You said you didn't want me to take it out on you."

"That doesn't mean I don't want to talk."

"The argument's over."

"The argument is not over. I didn't even get a chance to say anything yet."

Julie tried to grab the remote from me. I stiff-armed her, trying to keep her away. She fell backwards over the coffee table. The way she landed, hitting the back of her head against the floor, I thought she was dead, or at least seriously injured. But she must have braced the fall with her arms because she sat up on her knees almost immediately.

"Jesus," I said. "Are you okay?"

"Why did you push me?"

"I didn't push you. At least I didn't mean to. I just – are you okay?"

"I hate you!" she said. "I hate you so much!"

She ran into the bedroom, slamming the French doors. The glass rattled for a few seconds afterwards.

"Open the door!" I said squeezing the knob. "I want to talk to you! Come on, open up!"

For several minutes, I tried to convince her to let me in, but nothing I said worked. I must've said "I'm sorry" a hundred and fifty times. I felt terrible for pushing her and I decided this might be the most pathetic day of my life.

"Fine," I said. "If you won't talk to me now, maybe you'll talk to me later."

I couldn't get my clean clothes from the bedroom, so I put on some sweats and a T-shirt I had in the closet and left the apartment. I didn't know exactly where I was going, but I knew I had to go somewhere. Julie was right – I'd been taking my problems out on her and I resolved not to come back until I'd calmed down.

I wound up at a bar on First Avenue and Eighty-seventh Street. I'd never been to the place before, but it was dark and empty and I thought it would be a good place to get drunk. During my third glass of Bud, I was starting to feel better. Julie was right, I decided – I just needed a few drinks to calm myself down.

"Another Bud," I said to the tired-looking barmaid.

I'd been so deep in thought, I hadn't looked around much. I'd never been to this bar before – I hadn't been to any bars the past few months. It was a Tuesday so the place was pretty much dead. A fat guy was playing bar basketball, and at the end of the bar two guys were hitting on these two women. I envied the guys for being single, for not having angry girlfriends waiting for them at home. I wondered if I missed being single, or if I had simply been going out with Julie for too long.

I tried to figure out if the guys were going to score with the women. One woman seemed interested in one of the guys, but the other one had turned her stool toward the bar and was trying to ignore the guy who wanted to talk to her. Definite negative body language. The first woman, the one talking to the guy, was the more attractive of the two by far. She had long, straight brown hair and she was wearing a white T-shirt tucked into faded blue jeans. She was probably about five-two – it was hard to tell with her sitting down – and she couldn't have weighed an ounce over one-oh-five. She was about twenty-five years old, and judging by the lack of any rings on her fingers and the way she kept fidgeting nervously with her hair, I decided she was almost certainly single.

When my other beer came, I noticed her looking at me. I thought she might just be glancing in my direction, trying to ignore the other guy, but her stare was a little too long to be casual. Instinctively, I smiled and she smiled back at me. I felt a buzz down my spinal cord and my face got hot, feelings I hadn't experienced in a very long time.

I started drinking my beer again. It had been so long since I had been in this situation, alone in a bar with a woman looking at me, that I didn't know what to do. Should I smile again? Should I ignore her? I looked over a few more times and our gazes met again. I wondered if she was looking at me because she was attracted, or because she was repulsed. I mean I wasn't exactly a candidate for the next *GQ* cover. I was going bald on top and I was definitely carrying a few extra pounds. And with the bandage on my head and wearing an old sweat suit, I must've looked like an escaped mental patient.

Finally, when she smiled and raised her glass at me, I decided to go over to her. I didn't know what I was expecting to happen – if I was expecting *anything* to happen – but I knew I had to speak to her.

When I sat down next to her and introduced myself, I could tell that the guy standing behind me wasn't exactly thrilled. He gave me a few dirty looks, but finally he got the hint and went to play a game of pinball.

Her name was Lisa. This was her first time at this bar. She was from Philadelphia. This was about the only conversation we had before an awkward silence came between us. She fiddled with her hair and I sipped my beer as I remembered how hard it was to strike up a conversation with a woman in a bar.

"So," she said. "What's with the Band-Aids?"

"I was hoping you wouldn't notice," I said nervously. "I had a little accident getting out of the shower."

"Slippery floor?"

"Tub," I said, smiling.

"You're lucky you didn't die," she said. "My grand-father slipped in the tub last year and it caused a stroke."

"I'm sorry," I said.

"Oh, I don't care," she said. "He was an asshole anyway. He used to curse and complain all the time. And he didn't leave me a dime in his will."

There was another period of awkward silence. She whispered something in her friend's ear and they both laughed, then she looked back at me.

"So what do you do?"

"Me?" I said.

"No, the other guy who's trying to pick me up. Yeah, you."

"I work in advertising."

"Just like everybody else in this city," she said rolling her eyes.

"What is that supposed to mean?"

"You know how it is in New York, or at least how it is on the Upper East Side. Every guy's either a lawyer, a stockbroker, or he works in advertising. I swear to God, I've never met anyone up here who didn't fit into one of those categories."

"Then why do you go out around here?" I said, wondering if she was trying to insult me.

"Good question," she said. "Maybe because there's nowhere else to go. I don't want to hang out in the Village and meet some grunge guy and the Upper West Side's all college students. So I guess it's either the Upper East Side or I dyke out." She looked at me deadpan. "Don't get your hopes up, I'm not a lesbian. I haven't even thought about being a lesbian. Not seriously anyway. What about you?"

"I haven't thought about being a lesbian either."

She didn't laugh.

"I mean are you gay?"

"Yes," I said deadpan. "I'm gay."

"Good answer," she smiled. "I'm starting to like you already."

Lisa started telling me about the differences between Philadelphia and New York and about a movie she saw on T.V. last night, but I wasn't really paying attention. I was looking at her blue eyes and full lips and clean white teeth, wondering what it would feel like to kiss her – just once. I didn't know if I really wanted to pick her up, but when you've been involved with the same woman for five years and things start to go bad, you start to appreciate attention from other women more than you ordinarily would. And there's also the ego factor – any guy, whether he's single or involved, wants to know he still has what it takes.

"You haven't even told me your name yet," she said.

"Bill," I said, shifting on my stool.

*"I'm just a bill on Capitol Hill –"*

"Ha, ha," I said.

"I guess you get a lot of that."

"Not since sixth grade. Can I get you something to drink?"

"I don't think so," she said, looking at her watch. "My friend wants to leave soon and I don't usually let guys buy me drinks anyway."

"I hope I didn't offend you."

"Don't worry, you did. So where do you live?"

"Ninety-fourth Street," I said.

"Do you have a roommate?"

I hesitated.

"I live alone."

"A swinging bachelor, huh?"

"Not quite," I said, anxious to change the subject. "What do you do?"

"Editorial Assistant."

"Really? My...I have a friend who works in publishing. Doubleday. Trade division."

"I'm in the trade division too at Warner. What's his name?"

"Her name. Julie."

"Don't know her," she said. "But I don't know why I should. I mean it's not like everybody in publishing knows everybody else in publishing. Like every truck driver knows every other truck driver, and every farmer knows every other farmer. Somebody, please stop giving drinks to this girl."

Lisa's friend had stood up and was waiting to leave.

"I better go," Lisa said. "It was nice meeting you."

"Why don't you give me your number?" I said. "Maybe we can get together some time."

"I don't like giving out my number at bars, especially when I'm drunk."

"You don't seem that drunk to me."

"I don't know," she said. "I mean how do I know you're not a serial killer or something?"

"I guess you'll just have to take your chances."

She looked over at her friend who was waiting by the door.

"I'll tell you what, I'll give you my work number," she said. "But if I don't hear from you in two days, forget about it."

She wrote her number for me on a napkin, then left the bar with her friend. I stayed at the bar for a few more minutes, finishing my beer, then I started home. I doubted I'd actually call Lisa, but I was glad that she had given me her number anyway. I had proved something to myself and that's all I'd really wanted to do.

I didn't even notice climbing the five flights of stairs and entering the apartment. Julie was asleep, but the French doors were unlocked. I stripped to my underwear and got into bed with her. When I kissed her on her cheek, she turned over.

"Come on," I said. "Wake up. I don't want you going to sleep angry at me. We have to have this out."

She resisted at first, saying she was still furious at me, but I finally coaxed her into sitting up.

"I want to apologize," I said. "For everything. I was a real asshole tonight and I know it. Forgive me?"

"You pushed me onto the floor really hard."

"It was an accident. I'd never do something like that intentionally. I've never pushed you before, have I? Have I?"

She hesitated, staring at me with wide open eyes.

"No," she finally said. "I guess not."

I kissed her gently on the lips.

"Are you drunk?" she said.

"A little," I said. "You were right, I just needed a few drinks to calm down. I was a real mental case before."

We kissed and hugged for a couple of minutes, then she said:

"I was so scared before. When you pushed me, then when you left, not even telling me where you were going, I thought that was it – our relationship's over."

"Don't ever think anything like that, honey. We're just going through some tough times right now, but we're never going to break up."

"Do you really mean that?"

"Mean what?"

"That we're never going to break up. Because that means that some day we'll, you know..."

"I know," I said. "Of course I know."

"But are we going to?"

"I want to," I said. "I mean it's what I'm hoping for."

"I have to know," she said frowning. "I was talking to my friend Katey at work today. She's forty and she's still single and she's afraid she's never going to be able to have kids. I know I'm only thirty-two, but it's like time's going so fast and I don't want to wind up like Katey."

"Don't worry," I said. "You won't."

"But I might. I know we have problems, but I still love you. I don't even care if you convert or don't convert. I still think you'd make a great husband."

"Thanks," I said. "And I think you'd make a great wife."

"Does that mean you want to –"

"It doesn't mean anything. I've told you a hundred times that I don't want to get married until I get my career off the ground again. Maybe if I didn't lose my ad job we'd be married by now, but I lost my job and there's nothing we can do about that now."

"So I'm just gonna have to wait until you find a job?"

"That's right," I said. "And I'm gonna have to wait too. But I'm going to get an ad job soon – somehow I'll make it happen. And until then I've decided to go back to my telemarketing job tomorrow. So what about swallowing my pride? It's just a job, a way to make money. And some day I won't be there anymore and then we'll get married. Besides, I know neither of us want to do it like this. It's late at night and I'm drunk. When we do it I want it to be special. I want to be able to give you a ring and get on my knees and be romantic."

"I guess you're right," she said. "I mean if I've waited this long, a little while longer isn't gonna kill me, right?"

"Right," I said. "It's not gonna kill you."

I turned onto my side and she pushed up behind me, sliding her hand slowly down my chest. We hadn't made love in over two weeks and I didn't feel like it tonight either.

"Tomorrow," I said. "It's been a long day."

Her hand continued past my belly button and I rolled onto my stomach, moaning, "Tomorrow, tomorrow."

# 3

JULIE WAS DRESSED by the time I woke up.

"Remember," she said, checking her lipstick in the mirror. "You have to promise to go to a doctor today. If you don't get stitches you're gonna have an ugly scar there for the rest of your life."

"I promise I'll take care of it," I said.

She bent over the bed to kiss me goodbye. I turned my cheek.

"Bad breath," I said.

"I don't care," she said. "I want to kiss you."

She kissed me again, this time on the lips.

"Got you," she said. "Now you have lipstick all over."

After Julie left, I stayed in bed for a few minutes, thinking about Lisa, wondering if I should call her after all. I glanced at the clock and saw that I'd been day dreaming longer than I thought – it was already past eight o'clock. I showered and got dressed as fast as I could. The last thing I wanted was to be late again.

I was at my office, sitting in my cubicle, by ten to nine. Like every morning, I prepared my stacks of call backs and other papers I needed on my desk, then I went to the bathroom. When I came out, Mike was waiting for me in the hallway.

"Go to Ed's office right now," he said seriously.

I knew I'd have some explaining to do, and I'd prepared for it. I went to Ed's office and sat in the same seat I had sat in yesterday, and waited for him to arrive. Finally, he showed up, holding a mug of coffee.

"Bill Moss," he said, sitting at his desk. "We weren't expecting you here today."

"Why?" I said. "I didn't quit."

"Yes, I know, and we weren't expecting you here today."

He set the coffee on the desk and gazed at me disappointedly. I felt like a delinquent kid in a principal's office. What was he going to do, hit me with a ruler?

"What are you trying to say," I said, "that you're firing me?"

"What do you think I should do?" Ed said.

"You can do whatever you want. You're the boss."

He took a long sip of coffee, then rested the mug on the table and stared at me for a few more seconds.

"You've put me in a very difficult situation, Bill. I can either give you another chance and let you go back to work, or I can tell you to get the hell out of here. If you can't give me a good reason why I should keep you on, I'm afraid I'll have to go with plan B."

It took all my strength not to leap up from my chair and attack Ed. I had to keep reminding myself that this was just a temporary job, a way of making money, that my pride didn't matter. The important thing was that I come up with the rent next month, and the month after that, and that some day this would all seem like a big joke.

"I think there are a lot of reasons why you should keep me here," I said tensely. "First of all, I'm one of your best workers. I won telemarketer-of-the-month last month and I've won the award at least five times since I've been here. Plus, I don't think I really did anything wrong. I mean I've been late a few times before, and I apologize for that, but it's not like I did anything to harm the company."

"What about your behavior yesterday?" Ed said accusingly. "Do you think that harmed the company?"

"No," I said. "I...I don't think so."

"You cursed out Mike to his face and embarrassed him in front of your fellow employees. Do you know what kind of example that sets? I'm asking you a question. Do you know what kind of example that sets?"

"I was upset," I said. "I know I probably said a few things I shouldn't've, but –"

"If I let you get away with that, the telemarketers will start to lose respect for their supervisors," Ed said angrily. "They won't make as many appointments and sales for the office will start to fall. And if sales fall eventually the company will go out of business. Then everybody will be out of work, including me. Do you think I should jeopardize my job by letting you continue to work here?"

I was about to get up and leave right then. Sometimes I think about how different my life would've turned out if I left, how much pain I could've avoided for myself and the people around me. And I would've left too if Ed hadn't said:

"But there is one way out of it. I don't know if you're willing to do this, but if you are then perhaps we can salvage your job here without harming the future of this company."

"What do you want me to do," I said, "get on my hands and knees and beg?"

"Not at all," he said, missing my sarcasm. "I want you to apologize."

"Fine," I said. "I'll apologize to him right now."

"Not to Mike," Ed said. "I want you to apologize to everyone, at the morning meeting."

"Why do I have to do that?" I said. "Why can't I just –"

"No deals," Ed said. "You either apologize to everyone or you walk out that door. Believe me, I won't try to stop you."

"Fine," I said. "I'll apologize to everyone."

I left Ed's office and went back to my cubicle. I was still thinking about walking out on the job and if it wasn't for the rent coming up next week I probably would've done it. But I couldn't find another part-time job in a week. If I had two or three weeks maybe, but not one.

At nine o'clock, Mike came around and called everyone into the conference room. There were only about ten chairs in the room so some people sat on the floor against the wall, and others stood in the back. I stood near the door, hoping that Ed would forget about our agreement.

After he gave the same sickening Twelve-Step program speech I'd heard dozens of times before, about "the professionalism of telemarketers" and how "a positive attitude breeds success, in both sales and life," he said, "There's one last piece of business I want to attend to this morning. Mr. Moss, would you care to step forward?"

I went to the front of the room, trying not to make eye contact with anyone. My plan was to get this over with as fast as possible.

"Yeah, I just want to apologize for what happened here yesterday," I said. "I'm very sorry."

I'd started away when Ed said:

"Wait one moment, Bill. Don't you want to tell them why you're sorry?"

"Why I'm sorry?" I said, gritting my teeth.

"The things we discussed – your unprofessionalism, your disrespect for a supervisor."

"Right," I said, looking down. "I'm sorry I disrespected Mike by cursing at him the way I did, and I'm sorry I was unprofessional. I shouldn't have done those things."

"I hope this sets an example for all of you," Ed said. "If you follow all our rules here and act professionally you'll be a successful worker and a successful human being. Meeting dismissed."

People headed toward the door and I lagged behind, merging with the back of the crowd. I don't know if I've ever felt more humiliated.

Before I made my first phone call, Greg came over to my cubicle and crouched next to me. He was wearing a Walkman and I could hear the loud, pulsing beat of the music.

"I thought you was outta here yesterday," he said.

"What can I say?" I said. "I changed my mind."

"I don't know how you got up there and said all that shit, man. If that was me I'd be out that motherfucking door, you know what I'm saying?"

"I needed the money," I said. "My bank account's looking pretty small these days."

"I hear you, man, but that shit was *humiliating*. I mean I don't say I'm sorry to nobody except my pops, and sometimes I won't say I'm sorry to him neither. Ed can threaten my ass all he wants, but if he fires my ass he better have a good reason, 'cause I don't take no shit from nobody around here."

Ed was walking past my cubicle and said to Greg:

"No Walkmans in the office."

"What?" Greg said like he was offended.

"We have a policy in the office," Ed said, "no Walkmans. Wasn't that explained to you when you started working here?"

"Nah, nah nobody told me that," Greg said.

"Well, I'm telling you now. Take off the Walkman."

Ed continued toward his office. Greg kept the head phones on and made a fuck you gesture with his middle finger.

"Careful," I said. "If he sees you doing that, he'll fire you."

"Fuck that," Greg said. "If he wants to fire me, let him fire me. As long as he gives me that back commission money he owes me, he can do whatever the fuck he wants."

Greg went back to his cubicle, still cursing under his breath. He sat back in his chair with his arms folded for a while, then he took off the Walkman reluctantly and started working. I started working too, hoping it would take my mind off how awful I felt. It took a while for me to get comfortable with my pitch, but then I made three appointments on consecutive calls. During the ten o'clock break, I stayed at my cubicle and took out the napkin from my pocket where Lisa had written her work number last night. The ink was smudged, but I could still read it clearly. I debated whether I should call her. I didn't know exactly what I would say, or what the point of the call would be. But the idea of calling her, just to see what would happen, was incredibly appealing.

My pulse pounded as I dialed the number. I wondered whether she had given me a wrong number intentionally, whether I was going to be calling the city morgue or a kennel club, when her voice mail picked up. After listening to her voice – I decided it was very sexy – I hung up. My heart was still racing, my palms were wet. I decided I'd call back later, at the end of the shift.

I had one of my best days on the phone. Every call I made seemed to lead to an appointment or a promising call back. By the end of the shift, I had made nine appointments, one shy of my personal record, and well more than any telemarketer had made in months. It felt satisfying to have such a good day and to watch the expression on Mike's face when I dropped the stack of appointments on his desk. I didn't say a word, just turned and walked out of the office.

Before I left for the day, I tried Lisa once more. Again her voice mail answered and again I hung up nervously without leaving a message. Remembering that she had been drunk last night, I decided that maybe she didn't come into work this morning. Or, I considered, maybe she regretted giving me her number and she was screening her calls, hoping I'd eventually forget about her.

I walked outside into the hot, humid afternoon. It was by far the most uncomfortable day of the summer. What with the humidity, the smog, and the low ozone layer, it was almost impossible to breathe. After a minute outside, my shirt was a sweaty rag. Squinting in the glare, taking short, economical breaths, I walked toward Eighth Avenue. The streets were mobbed with business people, walking with their suit jackets slung over their shoulders. Some men were walking bare chested, and some people were pouring bottled water onto their heads to cool off. At the corner, I turned toward Forty-second Street. I started to feel light headed, like I was going to pass out. In the past I'd had anxiety attacks when I was hot or in confined places, and I felt like I was going to have one now. I was dizzy, short of breath. I bought a bottle of water from a street vendor and drank the whole thing in one gulp, but I still felt dazed and anxious. Afraid to get on the crowded subway, I decided I'd better kill some time in midtown before I went home.

I went into one of the triple-x video stores on Eighth Avenue.

I'd gone to these stores a few times before, but I never bought anything. It was just a way of killing time and, I have to admit, I liked looking at the erotic video boxes. I went into the bondage section and browsed through the video boxes and magazine covers of women in chains having sex with men in masks. After a while, I got bored, but it was air conditioned in the store and I didn't feel like going back outside into the oppressive weather.

I noticed in the back of the store men coming in and out of the "Live Girl" booths. I had never gone into one of these booths before, but I had heard stories about them from guys at work. I knew that for twenty-five cents you could go inside a private booth and, for a few seconds, watch naked women dance on stage. The idea of actually going into one of these booths had always disgusted me, but for some reason I felt compelled to try it one time, just to see what it was like.

I exchanged a dollar for four tokens, feeling strangely embarrassed, like a teenager buying his first box of condoms. The Pakistani man behind the counter didn't seem to care, however, as he casually instructed me to go into booth number four.

A man was busy mopping in and around the booths that weren't being used. Surprisingly, the place was very clean and there was no discernible odor except the ammonia from the mopping fluid they used to clean the stalls after each customer. I shut the wooden door and sat carefully on the stool. I put a coin in the slot and a piece of wood slid up, revealing a small window, about the size of a porthole. A lethargic, heavy-set Puerto Rican woman was in the middle of a strip tease. She had already taken off her bra, and now she was spinning slowly around a pole, holding on with one hand as she pulled at the elastic of her panties with the other. She wasn't attractive – in fact, she was downright ugly. Her stomach stuck out farther than her breasts and she had the beginnings of a mustache and beard. Her thighs were filled with thick varicose veins and she had the bloodshot, baggy eyes of a drug user. After a few minutes, the covering slid back down over the window. I deposited another token. When I ran out of tokens, I changed two more dollars and fed the new tokens into the slot. I couldn't get enough of it. The woman didn't arouse me, but it was incredibly refreshing to see a new naked body, *any* new naked body. There was no doubt that Julie was much more attractive than this woman, but I had seen Julie naked thousands of times and I hadn't seen another naked woman live, in person, in years.

After about a half hour and five dollars later, I decided to go home. Rather than going down to the hot subway, I took the Eighth Avenue bus uptown. It wasn't until I got off at Ninety-sixth Street that an intense feeling of guilt set in. I felt disgusting for getting excited watching the Puerto Rican woman. I knew another woman wasn't the answer. The answer was getting a good job in advertising and getting my career off the ground again.

When I got home I took a long shower with the coldest water possible.

## 4

I SPENT THE rest of the afternoon sending out resumes. I answered several advertisements in the *Times* classified for marketing positions, and I sent out several resumes to head hunters and to a few agencies I hadn't contacted in over a year. Although most of these places had already rejected my applications, I decided it was worth taking a chance that a new person had been hired in the personnel or marketing divisions, or that the timing was right and they had a position that needed to be filled.

In my updated resumes I exaggerated my job at American Communications, writing that I had been working as a "sales and marketing executive for a national telephone company" and that my duties included, "soliciting and maintaining a new client base, and organizing and conducting a sales campaign in the New York City area." I knew that if I was called in for an interview I'd have to explain that I'd really been working as a ten-dollar-an-hour telemarketer, but I thought I was better off lying than having a two-year, unexplained gap in my career.

It was about five-thirty when I returned home from the post office. It was still unbearably hot outside and I felt like I needed another shower. Instead, I collapsed on the couch and put on the air conditioner and television. When I woke up, Julie was in the kitchen, pouring a glass of orange juice.

"When did you get home?" I said, sitting up. "I didn't even hear you come in."

"A few minutes ago. Go ahead, sleep. I want to get out of these clothes anyway."

"What time is it?" I said.

"Six, six-thirty. Did you go to the emergency room today?"

"The emergency room?"

"Don't tell me you didn't go!"

"I went," I said. "Of course I went."

"Where are your stitches?"

"They said stitches weren't necessary."

"Not necessary! You look terrible. That cut's going to leave an ugly scar if you don't do something. If it's not too late already."

"I'm telling you what the doctor said. I went to the emergency room – New York Hospital. A doctor saw me and he said I didn't need stitches. I was surprised too, but that's what he said. He said the wound's a lot less serious than it looks."

"I don't believe it," Julie said. "Are you sure this man knew what he was talking about?"

"He was a doctor. He was wearing a white jacket and he had a stethoscope around his neck. I guess he knew what he was saying."

"I don't know," Julie said skeptically.

I walked by Julie and went into the bathroom. After I splashed water on my face, I looked at myself in the mirror. The wound still looked pretty nasty. A purple scab had formed over it, but there were still areas in the middle and around the edges where it was bright red.

When I came out of the bathroom Julie was waiting near the stove.

"I don't care what you say," she said, "I'm going to make an appointment tomorrow for you to go see Dr. Goldman, the plastic surgeon who gave me my nosejob."

"A plastic surgeon? What the hell for?"

"With a wound on the face like that, you want to make sure they put the stitches in right. I still can't believe they sent you home like that."

"I'll be fine," I said, walking into the living room. "It probably just needs a few days to heal."

"In a few days you'll have a permanent scar. Please go see the plastic surgeon, just to see what he says. The worst thing that can happen is he'll say nothing's wrong with you."

"Yeah, and I'll have a five hundred-dollar bill to pay."

"Won't your insurance pay for it?"

"I don't have any insurance. Remember? I let it run out a few months ago because I couldn't afford the payments anymore."

"Then how did you pay for the emergency room?"

"I paid cash – a hundred and fifty bucks. If I have to shell out any more money, there's no way I'll be able to pay rent next month."

"I'll pay for the doctor."

"No way. I told you, I'm not going to take any money from you."

"Well, you have to go to the doctor. What if I lend you the money? You can pay me back whenever you want, I don't care. Just go, Bill. You have to go."

I didn't answer her until about a minute later, after I'd put on a pair of jeans and a T-shirt.

"All right," I finally said. "But it's just a loan. I'm going to pay you back in full as soon as I have the money."

She came over and kissed me. Then she started hugging me tighter.

"I'm a little hungry," I said, trying to put her off. "I haven't eaten all day."

"I missed you today."

"I missed you too."

"I was feeling bad about the way I acted last night. I know you didn't mean to push me and I shouldn't've locked you out of the bedroom like that."

"It was my fault," I said. "I was a real asshole."

"Oh my God, I can't believe I forgot to ask you," Julie said, "did you get your job back today?"

"Yeah," I said, walking into the bedroom, "but I really had to humiliate myself to do it. I sent out a new batch of applications today and something better come through."

"Don't worry, it will," Julie said. "I read your horoscope today at work. It's supposed to be a good week for Scorpios."

"Horoscopes are bullshit."

"It doesn't matter if you believe in it or not. You're still going to get a job."

She came up behind me and put her arms gently around my waist. She kissed the back of my neck, then turned my head slowly and started kissing my cheek. I felt her warm tongue making circles as it moved closer toward my lips. Her breasts bulged against my chest as, with a free hand, she squeezed my buttocks. When she started to slide her other hand below my belt, I said:

"Hey, I have an idea. When was the last time we went out drinking together? Come on, let's go to a bar or a club."

"Tonight?"

"Why not? Maybe we can grab some dinner first, try out that Italian place on Second Avenue."

"We can't tonight," Julie said. "Don't you remember? We're meeting David and Sharon for dinner."

I'd completely forgotten about the plans until that moment. I didn't like Julie's friends from college, but I especially disliked David and Sharon. The idea of having dinner with them was about as appealing as spending a night in prison.

"Oh come on, just call up and make some excuse," I said. "Tell them I'm sick or I died or *something*."

"I can't, Bill. Me and Sharon have been planning this for weeks. Besides, she can't get in touch with David. He's working in New Jersey today and he's coming right to the restaurant to meet us."

I complained for a while longer, then I finally gave in.

"I don't understand what's so painful about this," Julie said. "You like David and Sharon, don't you?"

"Of course I like them."

"So what's the problem?"

"Nothing. Really, nothing. I'd love to go out with them, on any night but tonight. Tonight I was just looking forward to spending some quiet time together alone. Then I thought we'd come back and, you know, get a little romantic together."

"Oh, Bill, that's so sweet," Julie said. "I wish we could get out of it too, but we have no choice. We have to meet them."

I heard the prison gates clanging shut. Julie took a shower while I finished getting dressed. After she put on her makeup, did her hair and put on a tight T-shirt and jeans, she was as good looking as any woman in New York. I had flashbacks of being in the peep-show booth hours earlier, watching the Puerto Rican woman dance naked. I couldn't believe I'd enjoyed looking at that pear-shaped drug addict when I was living with such a beautiful lady.

As soon as we went outside, it started to pour. Then the thunder and the lightening and the wind came and we had to run to Second Avenue to hail a cab. We met

Sharon and David at Blue Moon, a Mexican restaurant on First Avenue and Seventy-fifth Street. The place was dark and noisy and the food was no better or worse than a hundred other Mexican places in New York. But Sharon and David always said it was their "favorite restaurant in New York," and it seemed like we wound up eating there every time the four of us got together. It was one of the many trendy Upper East Side restaurants where people loved to sit at the tables on the sidewalk, not because they enjoyed sitting outside where it was hot and a constant stream of homeless people harassed them, but because they wanted to be seen by as many anonymous passersby as possible. Because of the rain, the crowd had moved inside, and we could barely fit through the vestibule.

"I feel like I'm on the subway," I said.

"Stop complaining," Julie said. "There they are – at the bar."

As we weaved through the crowd, I noticed how everyone seemed to be exactly the same – twenty-two years old, Jewish or Italian, born and raised in the suburbs, went to a State University of New York school, wearing conservative, fashionable clothing. The guys and girls were wearing backwards baseball caps, and every woman wore the same shade of chocolate brown lipstick. The lipstick must be in *Vogue* this month, I thought. I remembered what Lisa had said about how all the guys on the Upper East Side were alike and I realized how true this was – I honestly couldn't tell any two people apart.

Julie kissed Sharon and David hello. I kissed Sharon lightly on the cheek, then shook hands with David. Even his handshake annoyed me. It was ultra firm, as if he was doing a grip-strengthening exercise, and while he did it he put on a fake smile that reminded me of a campaigning politician. Wearing a backwards Florida Marlins cap, he looked like any of the other guys in the bar, except that he was about nine years older than most of them. He was the type of guy who insisted on living and acting like he had just graduated from college even though he was thirty-one years old.

Sharon had short black hair, parted down the middle. She had an MBA from Columbia and she worked as a Senior Analyst for a Wall Street securities firm. I used to wonder how she wound up marrying a loser like David. Then Julie told me a story about how David and Sharon had broken up after graduating from college, and Sharon had immediately gone into a deep depression. She lost about forty pounds and had to be hospitalized for anorexia. When she got out of the hospital, she started going out with David again and a few months later they got engaged. Obviously, Sharon was a very manipulative woman and she liked David because he was easy for her to control. David liked Sharon because, outside of work, he was unable to make a simple decision on his own, and he liked being controlled by a dominant woman. Julie once told me that Sharon sometimes tied David up during sex, and it wasn't hard to imagine David strapped to a bed, and Sharon squatting over him in a Brooks Brothers suit, wielding an enormous leather whip.

I don't remember exactly what David and I started talking about. I think he asked me about my forehead and I told him the story about how I was mugged at Grand Central. He told me that he had stopped taking subways "years ago" and then he told me about his work as a corporate lawyer for Ernst & Young. Besides the fact that I was completely bored by David's conversation, it was very noisy in the restaurant, what with the crowd and the loud music, and I hardly heard a word he said. But then I thought he asked me something about myself.

"What was that?" I said, cupping my ear. "I can't hear you."

"The job hunt," he said, leaning toward my ear. "How's the job hunt going?"

"Fine, fine," I screamed back. "Hanging in there!"

"You're not still telemarketing, are you?"

"What's that?" I said, although I'd heard him loud and clear.

"Telemarketing!" he screamed. "Are you still doing that?!"

"For the time being," I said. "I mean I have to pay the bills somehow, right?"

"I gotta hand it to you. I don't know if I'd be able to do what you're doing – working beneath myself. I think I'd commit suicide first."

"Suicide?"

"What's that?!"

"I said – suicide?"

"Yes. It must get very depressing to be out of work as long as you have. You must start wondering what your purpose in life is."

"What's anybody's purpose in life? I'm just out of work, that's all. I'm not dying."

"But you know what they say, a man's life is his work. A woman can have kids and still be happy, but all a man has is his work."

"So you must be the happiest guy in the world," I said, trying to change the subject. But it didn't matter because the hostess came over and said our table was ready. We sat at a table in the back of the restaurant –

Julie and I on one side, David and Sharon on the other. After the waiter took our drink orders, Sharon said to me:

"So Julie told me how you got mugged. That's terrible. Did you call the police?"

"The police don't care about this sort of thing," I said.

"It's so terrible. There're so many animals out there, it's terrible – just terrible."

"What can you do?" Julie said. "It's the whole world these days."

"It's not the world, it's the city. That's why David and I are looking for a house in Scarsdale."

"Really?" Julie said. I knew she was jealous. "I didn't know that."

"We've had it with the city," David said. "We're sick of the dirt and the drugs and the homeless. You can't go anywhere these days without seeing those people somewhere. And now that my salary's up in the six figures and Sharon's making over eighty, we don't see why we have to torture ourselves anymore."

"You two should move to Scarsdale too," Sharon said to me and Julie. "That would be so cool if we all lived up there together."

"I don't think that's possible," Julie said uncomfortably.

"Why not?" Sharon said. "I'm telling you, the city's not all it's made up to be. And it's only a half hour commute on Metro North."

"It's very expensive to live up there," David said.

"Oh, I know," Sharon said. "I didn't mean now. I meant after Bill gets a job. I just think it would be nice if eventually we all lived up there together. I know they can't afford it now."

Sharon started telling a story about a wedding she'd

recently gone to and I opened my menu, trying to pay as little attention to the conversation as possible. My beer arrived and I started drinking it. A few times they tried to get me involved in the conversation, but each time I'd either smile tensely or give an obligatory one word reply. I grew increasingly restless. I was thinking about what David had said before and I decided it was true – a man's life *is* his work, which meant that I had not had a life for two years. Our meals arrived, but I didn't eat anything. I just sat there, poking my enchilada with my fork, trying to keep my anger inside, but knowing that it was impossible – too much had been building up inside me for too long.

That's when I did something that nearly ended my relationship with Julie. David was in the middle of telling a story about a ski trip he'd taken the year before when I interrupted and said:

"The hell with skiing, let's talk about something more interesting, like bondage. Tell me David, when was the last time Sharon tied you up and whipped you?"

Sharon and Julie's cheeks turned bright pink. My face was hot too – I couldn't believe that I had actually said what I was thinking. It was as if I had crossed a forbidden line – the line that separates thoughts and action.

David tried to play it cool, as if he thought I'd been trying to make a joke.

"She hasn't tied me up in years," he said sarcastically. "Not since our first date anyway."

"That's not what I hear," I said. "I hear she ties you up a lot, and you ask for it too. I bet it's the only way you can get it up."

Sharon glared at Julie, but Julie was glaring at me. Her eyes were so wide and motionless I could see the whites above and below the pupils.

"Hey, what the hell's wrong with you?" David said. "Why are you trying to start something?"

"I'm just trying to have some pleasant conversation," I said. "You guys have been talking all night about things you're interested in, well this is something that interests me. I always wanted to get into the head of a real-life sadomasochist, and I just thought I'd get it from the horse's mouth. Pardon the expression."

David grabbed a fistful of my shirt.

"Stop it!" Julie yelled. "Just stop it! We're in a restaurant for Christ's sake!"

"You better apologize right now," David said.

"I can't take this anymore," Sharon said. She stood up and hurried toward the bathroom. A few people near the bar were looking in our direction, but the place was too loud for anyone to hear what was going on.

"You don't have the balls to hit me," I said. "As soon as we start fighting, the bouncer's gonna come over and then the police might come and who knows? Word of the fight might somehow reach your office. And you know that if you get the reputation as a drinker or a brawler it might affect your next raise or even your job. Your life's too meaningful to risk your hundred-and-five a year salary."

David held my shirt for a few more seconds, then he let go, realizing that what I'd said was probably true. I didn't know what else to do so I left the table and pushed through the crowd. It seemed like a second later I was outside, walking up First Avenue. I heard Julie's voice behind me.

"Where the hell do you think you're going?"

"Home," I said.

She was walking next to me now, swinging her arms furiously back and forth.

"I can't believe what you just did to me in there. Those are my friends and you embarrassed me so much in front of them. You better go back in there and apologize right now."

"I'm going home," I said.

"I'm not going to forget about this, Bill. This is too much. This time you went too far."

I kept walking at the same steady pace. After I crossed the next street I looked behind me and saw Julie standing on the sidewalk, her hands on her hips. I was starting to feel guilty, but not guilty enough to go back and apologize to Sharon and David. I was proud of what I'd done, even if it was irrational and thoughtless.

The storm had cooled things off, but it was still about eighty degrees and muggy. I walked along the dark, wet streets, enjoying my aloneness in the city. When I got home I lay in bed naked with the window open, the damp breeze against my chest, replaying the episode in the restaurant again and again. I still thought I had done the right thing. I'd been home about fifteen minutes when I heard Julie come home and slam the door. A moment later she was in the bedroom.

"I've had it with you, I've absolutely had it. I don't know what's wrong with you or why you somehow have the need to hurt me, but I'm not taking it anymore. This weekend I'm leaving. I mean it too. Unless you explain why you did that to me, I'm leaving."

"I told you, I'm not apologizing," I said.

"You think I'm kidding, don't you? I'll go and I'll never see you again. I don't want to do that, but I'll do it if I have to. You can't believe how upset I am. And Sharon, forget about it. I'm lucky if she ever talks to me again. They left the restaurant without even saying goodbye to me. She was crying hysterically. How could you do something like that to me and my friend?"

"Friends," I said, shaking my head. "How can you call Sharon and David your friends? Did you hear what was going on tonight? Did you hear those comments they made every two seconds? You couldn't hear what David said at the bar, but believe me I had good reason for doing what I did. And what really pisses me off is you barging in here and defending them. What about me? I'm your boyfriend. Don't I count for anything?"

"What comments? What are you talking about?"

"What's the matter, are you deaf? Or maybe you've heard so many comments like that from them over the years you've gotten used to it. He's always talking about his stupid job, dropping comments about how much money he's making, or making digs at me for telemarketing. And then all that bullshit about Scarsdale, Sharon saying, 'I know they can't afford it *now.*' I was sick of just sitting there and letting comments like that pass by. So I stood up for myself and made some comments of my own."

"You don't get it, do you? You didn't just insult them, you insulted me. When I told you that stuff about Sharon and David's sex life, you swore you'd never mention it to anyone. And I can't believe you'd do that to me."

Tears were streaming down her cheeks. I reached up and grabbed her hand. In the dark room, her body appeared gray, framed by the bright light of the living room.

"I admit I might've gone a little too far," I said. "Maybe I shouldn't've said exactly what I said. But at the bar, David made a comment to me about a man's life being meaningless without work. I was thinking about it at the table and I thought – maybe he's right, maybe my life is meaningless. Then the idea came to me to make those comments and instead of just *thinking* about saying them, I decided to actually say them. I don't know why I did it, but I did."

"Let go of me."

"You know this isn't me," I said, pulling her closer. "You've known me long enough. You know the real me isn't like this."

She yanked her arm free.

"I think you're crazy."

"New York's crazy," I said, realizing I wasn't making much sense. "I've been here too long. All I need is to change cities – to go someplace where I can get a job – like Seattle. I've been thinking that might be the best place for me to go – I mean us to go – as far as me getting a job. There're a lot of agencies out there and with my background and contacts I can get a job at one like that. Who knows? Maybe the agency I interned at during college will hire me back? It might not be the highest paying job in the world, but it'll be a job still, and that's the most important thing – that I get back to work again, in my field."

I realized Julie wasn't in the room anymore. I heard the water running in the kitchen.

"What's wrong with you?" I said in the kitchen. "Weren't you paying attention to me?"

She was leaning over the sink, splashing her face with cold water. I went up behind her.

"Stay away from me," she said.

I followed her to the bathroom and held the door open as she tried to close it.

"Weren't you listening to what I said?"

"I don't care what you say until you apologize."

"I'm sorry," I said. "Of course I'm sorry. But I'm

talking about a plan – a real way we can change our lives."

"I like my life."

"I mean our life – together. I know I've been acting weird lately, but once I get a job everything will go back to normal again. And we can be together, you know get married, but not in this hell hole. We'll go to Seattle, live by the water."

"What about me?" Julie said. "What about my job? I can't just quit like that. And what about my family? I don't know anybody in Seattle."

"You'll meet people. I don't know anybody out there anymore. It's just gonna be me and you out there, just like it is now except we'll be happy. It's true what Sharon said – New York's a dying city. How many times do I have to get mugged before we decide it's time to move? And I know you want to have kids eventually and New York's definitely not the place to do it. I sent out those resumes today, but I know I'm just going through the motions. People are gonna wonder what's wrong with this guy, why has he been telemarketing for two years, why can't he find a job? But if I go back to Seattle, it'll be different – I'll say I did some freelancing in New York and they probably won't check my references too carefully. And I'm sure you can find a job out there in a second. There are a lot of publishing companies in Seattle and in a couple of years you probably won't want to work too much anyway, once my salary kicks in and you start pumping out babies."

She had toweled off her face and now she stood in front of the bathroom door, staring at me with a serious, contemplative expression. Without makeup, she looked about thirty-five years old. Lines and areas of darkness were visible under her eyes and her skin was coarse and ruddy. That's when I realized that I had Julie under my thumb, that I could do or say whatever I wanted and there was no way she would ever leave me. She was dying to get married and have kids, and in her mind I was her last chance to do it. Like a lot of single women, she firmly believed that there were no single men left in the world, and that if she didn't marry the man she was with, she'd spend the rest of her life as a lonely old maid. If I walked away, she'd grab on to my ankles and beg me to stay.

"I guess it wouldn't be the worst thing in the world," she finally said. "I mean I guess a change of scenery is good sometimes."

"I love you," I said, hugging her. "I love you so much."

"But we can't leave right away," she said. "I have to give some notice at work and take care of a lot of things."

"The sooner the better," I said. "I'll send out resumes tomorrow and hopefully I can start interviewing next week. Maybe next month sometime we can go out there and start looking for a place to live."

"Next month! What about all our stuff? And what about our lease?"

"We'll sell everything and we'll give the landlord a month's notice. Come on, Julie, it'll be an adventure."

"Yeah, that's what I'm afraid of," she said.

# 5

THE NEXT MORNING I was the only happy person on the number 6 train. People pushed me and shoved me and gave me dirty looks, but I smiled and said "excuse me" or "sorry" or said something to ease their tensions. I even offered to help an elderly woman carry a heavy shopping bag up the steep steps leaving the Times Square subway station. "Get your filthy hands off me," she growled, but I didn't get upset. I merely walked ahead and let her continue on her own, realizing that the entire world wasn't as enlightened as I was.

At work, I was also unusually pleasant. When I got off the elevator, I smiled and wished Eileen, the receptionist, a good morning, even though she was staring at her nails and didn't notice me. At the time clock, I spoke to a few people I had never spoken to before, asking if they had any plans for the weekend and complimenting them on their clothing and hairdos. They looked at me with baffled expressions, as if I was wearing a mask, or had just taken one off. Before the morning meeting, Harry Pearlman asked me if I'd won Lotto last night.

"If I did, would I be here today?" I said.

"Something must've happened to you," he said. "Such a happy face, I didn't even recognize you."

I went into the conference room for the morning meeting, still very relaxed and confident. I even told a joke and had the whole room laughing. Then Ed arrived. He didn't make eye contact with anyone. Instead, he went directly to the front of the room and clapped his hands loudly.

"Come on, let's settle down everybody. We have a lot to discuss this morning."

Everyone recognized the unusual urgency in Ed's voice. They took seats on the floor or in chairs and quieted down.

"First off, I want to say that this is going to be the most difficult day I've had since I've been with the company. I was up most of last night, thinking about how to introduce this subject this morning, so you'll have to forgive me if I lose my train of thought every now and then or repeat something. I'll do my best to be as clear and accurate as possible."

Ed paused to wipe his nose and we all remained silent, wondering what this could possibly be about. Personally, I wasn't worried because I knew that whatever he said wasn't going to affect me.

"As we know, the nature of the telephone industry can be quite tenuous," Ed continued. "Changes are constantly occurring, and that isn't only true for us, but for the major telephone companies as well. That said, I'm afraid I'm going to have to announce that there is going to be some restructuring around here."

A few people spoke at once, complaining, and Ed raised his voice:

"Believe me, nothing you say is going to change anything, and if there was anything I could do, believe me, I would've already done it. Unfortunately, sales for the company have been falling for some time now and the President of the company insists that we trim our staff."

"Bullshit!" someone shouted.

"Yes, it is bullshit," Ed said, "but unfortunately it is a fact and we'll all just have to deal with it. Now before everybody flies into a panic, I want to assure you that not everyone's job will be affected. We are currently employing fifty-two telemarketers, including morning and afternoon shifts, and we are looking to trim that number down to about forty. At that point, as sales start to recover, we'll begin to replenish the staff. The obvious question is who will be kept on and who will be replaced? Yesterday afternoon, Mike, myself, and the other supervisors reviewed all of your records and today you'll be called into my office for individual conferences. The goal will be to only keep the telemarketers we feel will be the most profitable for the company. We'll take into account your sales performance as well as your recent conduct. Everyone will be called in at some point this morning, regardless if we're planning to terminate you, so please don't fly into a panic when your name is called."

As Ed headed out of the room, people shouted questions at him. I heard Greg yell: "What about our commissions? What about our damn commissions?!" but Ed didn't answer anyone.

"See, I know what they're trying to do," Greg said to me. "They're gonna fire all the people they owe money to. Watch – you'll see."

"They better not fire me," a guy next to Greg said. He was tall with a shaggy goatee. I think his name was Roy. "I know I've been late for work a couple of times, but I don't deserve to be fired."

"I know he's gonna try to fire me," Greg said. "After that shit he said to me yesterday, about taking off my Walkman and shit, but to be completely honest I don't care what the fuck he does. I'll tell you one thing, he better give me my fucking commission money he owes me or he better watch his ass."

"I don't buy that stuff about cutbacks either," the guy with the goatee said. "I've worked at a lot of sales jobs and it's always the same, you've got that whole chain of command bullshit. They tell us lies and their bosses tell them lies and their bosses tell their bosses lies and you never know what's the truth."

Mike came into the conference room and told everyone to get back to work, that today was a normal work day. Yeah right, I thought. They announce they're going to be firing twenty percent of their staff and they consider that "normal". But after two years, nothing that happened at A.C.A. surprised me.

I returned to my cubicle, proud of myself for not getting upset or anxious. I knew that after everything that had happened recently, I'd probably be the first person to get fired. But it didn't bother me – I *wanted* to get fired. I was only planning to stay with the company another couple of weeks anyway. As for rent, I had one paycheck due to me, and I could always find a temp job to make some quick cash.

After the ten o'clock break, Ed started calling people into his office. First, Cathy Hendricks went in. She'd been with the company for several months and as far as I knew she was a quiet, dependable, humorless employee – exactly the type of person A.C.A. liked. I watched her sitting in Ed's office, nodding as Ed spoke to her. Her expression was calm, but she was always calm, so it was hard to tell what was going on. Ed looked as serious and inhuman as a Nazi prison guard. After about five minutes, Cathy was through. We all watched her, to see if she was going to leave the office. But she returned to her cubicle and started making calls and I saw her give the "thumbs up" signal to the person next to her.

The next two people who were called into Ed's office also left unscathed. Then Tanya Parks was called in. She was a young black woman, a college student at F.I.T., who'd been with A.C.A. for several months. I always thought she was one of the best telemarketers at the company. On the phone, she was calm, yet aggressive – polite, yet persistent. She won telemarketer-of-the-month her second month with the company, and since then she'd been among the top five telemarketers. Needless to say, I didn't expect her to get fired. But when she ran out of Ed's office crying uncontrollably it was clear that that was exactly what had happened. She gathered some things from her desk, stuffed them into her pocketbook, then left the office without saying goodbye to anyone. People were stunned, shaking their heads and exchanging looks of disbelief.

"All right, let's just forget about it," Mike said. "Let's get back to business as usual. Everybody, back on the phones."

"Now I get what's going on here," Greg said so everyone in the room could hear. "He's gonna keep all the white people, and fire all the black people. I shoulda known that's what his plan was. It figures."

Mike came up behind Greg and put a hand on his shoulder.

"All right, Greg, let's just forget about it, okay?"

"Get your faggot hand off me!"

Mike yanked his hand back, as if it was on fire. He gritted his teeth and became extremely pale.

"Get back to work, Greg. Right now, or else!"

Infuriated, Mike went into his office and slammed the door shut. People laughed, like children making fun of a teacher who has left the room. I felt sorry for Mike, but I was also glad. I felt I had gotten some revenge for the way he and Ed had embarrassed me at the meeting the day before.

Greg continued to complain loudly about Ed and

white people and how the black people in the office shouldn't take this without a fight. A few whites got into a debate with Greg about racism in general, but I didn't say a word. I felt completely removed from the entire situation, as if I was watching it happen on a television or movie screen.

During the next hour or so, six more people were fired. In total, five black people had been let go and two white people. The big surprise came when Harry Pearlman was fired. Of all the workers, I'd thought Harry had the best chance of keeping his job.

"He told me my sales were down," Harry said, trying to stay calm. "So what, I said, they're down a little. You'd think after three-and-a-half years that time would mean something. But not in this place it doesn't. Here, they don't know from loyalty, they don't know from respect."

Although more blacks had been fired than whites, I still wasn't sure Ed was making his decisions based on race. I didn't know what he was doing, but I knew one thing – that it was only a matter of time until I got fired.

Ed came out of his office holding a clipboard.

"Greg Brown."

Greg took his time getting up. He stayed in his chair for several seconds, then he slowly took the Walkman headphones off from around his neck. He waited a while longer, then got up. He walked confidently into Ed's office, eyes focussed straight ahead. Everyone was watching; even Mike was standing outside his office, staring in that direction. It was great drama, as good as any play or movie. For a while, Ed did all the talking. He consulted his notes occasionally, but mostly he spoke to Greg directly, his hands interlocked on the desk. Of course we couldn't hear what he was saying through the glass, but knowing Ed it was probably some discourse on "professionalism" and "responsibility." Greg sat calmly with his arms folded in front of his chest. Then – it happened so fast, I hardly even noticed it – Greg was on his feet, leaning over the desk, punching Ed repeatedly in the face and chest. Everyone was too stunned to react. Through the glass, the fight was noiseless, making it seem unreal. I was the first one to reach the scene. I pulled Greg off the desk and tried to hold him back. He pushed me aside and went after Ed again. I tackled him from behind. By that time, other people had come into the office, and as a group we were able to hold Greg down.

"Racist motherfucker!" Greg was shouting. "Let me go! I want my fucking commission!"

Someone helped Ed up off the floor. He wasn't hurt very badly. His nose was bleeding out of one nostril, but he had no other bruises.

"I'm pressing charges," Ed said, pointing at Greg. "I'll make sure you pay for this."

Greg continued to scream and shout at Ed. Finally, we were able to move him out of Ed's office. Ed was on the phone, calling the police.

"You better get out of here," I said to Greg. "He's serious. He's calling the cops."

"Why'd you pull me back, man? Why'd you do that?"

"Because it's not worth it," I said.

"He owes me money. I'm not leaving here till he pays it to me."

"He won't give you any money now," I said. "Get out of here, before you get in even more trouble."

"I was gonna kill him," Greg said. "You know that, right?"

"I know," I said. "Just get out of here."

Greg took a few things from his desk, then walked slowly toward the front of the office. Ed started shouting maniacally:

"You won't get away with this! I have your home address! I'll press charges! I'll do whatever I have to!"

"Come to my house," Greg said. "Try it. I wanna see you try it."

After Greg left, everyone started talking at once about what had happened. Cursing, yelling – a violent energy was growing in the office. I realized what it must feel like during the moments before a riot – I was waiting for the next person to throw a punch. Mike screamed for everyone to get back to their cubicles, but everyone ignored him. Ed went into the bathroom to clean his face. When he came back, he was pressing a paper towel against his nose.

"All right, we're going to continue with the meetings," he said. "No one can leave the office until his or her name is called."

A few minutes later, the police arrived. The two tired, overworked-looking officers went into Ed's office, took a statement from him, then left. By that time, most of the telemarketers had returned to their seats, but no one was making phone calls. Everyone was still talking about the incident with Greg, about what a crazy company this was to work for, and about what kind of jobs they would look for if they got fired. I listened to the conversation, secretly amused, anxious to be called into Ed's office. I couldn't wait to be fired and then to watch the expression on Ed's face when I told him I didn't care.

"Bill Moss."

As I stood up, a few people wished me luck, but I

wasn't scared. I sat across from Ed and tried to keep a serious expression. It wasn't easy.

"Bill Moss," Ed said, involved in thought, shuffling through some papers. "Bill Moss, Bill Moss, Bill Moss, Bill Moss."

"That's my name," I said.

"I guess I should thank you," he said.

"Thank me?"

"That's right. If you didn't jump in there when you did, that crazy nigger might've really hurt me."

Hearing the word "nigger" angered me, like it always did, and it made me think that Greg was right about Ed all along – he *was* a racist, and the worst kind of racist too, the kind that will only make racist comments when the person he's offending isn't in the room. I'd always disliked Ed, but it wasn't until right then that I started hating him.

"I just didn't want things to get out of control," I said.

"I appreciate that," Ed said. "But it's my fault for hiring niggers in the first place."

I laughed.

"I'm sorry, did I say something funny?"

"Well, yeah," I said. "I mean you were kidding, weren't you?"

"Did I sound like I was kidding?"

"But you can't not hire black people to work for you," I said. "It's against the law."

"I didn't say I wasn't going to hire black people – I said I wasn't going to hire niggers. There's a difference, you know. There're educated black people, and then there're the uneducated, bike messenger type of black people. Those are the niggers. Besides the fact that they're erratic and difficult to get along with, it's too expensive to employ them. I don't care what anybody says, they can't learn as fast as white people can. We've created models to prove it too. We can train white people much faster, and thus they become more cost-effective for the company."

I'd heard enough. I was ready to announce I was quitting when Ed said:

"But enough about Greg Brown. He's created enough of a distraction as it is. Let's talk about you. To be honest, until this incident happened I was thinking about releasing you. But now I'm having second thoughts. I'm thinking maybe there's a place here for you after all."

I couldn't believe what I was hearing – did he really think I needed a job so desperately he could throw any bone my way and I'd jump for it? He picked up a file folder and started turning pages. "I have the resume you gave us when you started here. It says you worked for an ad agency."

"That's right."

"You were a Marketing Vice President?"

"That's right, but –"

"That sounds like a good job – you must've been making some good money. Why the hell did you quit?"

I used the explanation I always gave, that I was taking some time off "to evaluate things."

"Two years is some time all right."

"What can I say? Things didn't work out exactly like I thought they would."

"You went to the University of Washington, studied economics and history, did a semester abroad in London, got an M.B.A. at Washington State..."

"I feel like I'm on *This is Your Life*."

"You seem to have quite a background. Why didn't you ever come in here and ask for a promotion?"

"Actually, I think I left something in your mail box once."

"I don't read half my mail. What about computer skills? It says here you know ACTi for Windows."

"I know a lot of database programs," I said.

"That's perfect," Ed said. "We're going to be looking for somebody with exactly your experience. I want to make a proposal to you, Bill. As I mentioned during the meeting this morning, we're going to be doing a lot of restructuring around here. As we trim the telemarketing staff, we're going to expand the management staff. It's part of a philosophy that the President of the company has that when things are going bad, you expand from within, create a stronger nucleus. So I was planning to hire an assistant, somebody who can help build a database to manage our leads more efficiently. I have an ad set to run in the paper tomorrow, but it would save me time interviewing if you wanted the job."

"You want to hire me to be your assistant?"

"Why not? You have a good background, with management experience, and these past couple of days you've showed your dedication to the company. Besides, you've been here a while, so you know how things are run. It would save us a lot of time and money in training."

"I'm flattered that you want to consider me," I said, "but I think I've been here too long. It's about time I move on to something else."

"Do you have another job lined up?"

"Well, no," I said. "Not exactly anyway. But I was thinking about moving back home to Seattle."

"Seattle?" Ed said like it was the name of a planet. "You're joking, right?"

"Do I look like I'm joking?"

"Why would you want to do a thing like that? You're in New York now, the capital of the world. And you're still fairly young, what thirty, thirty-one years old? Why would you want to take a step backwards now?"

"It's what I've decided."

"But you said you're only *thinking* about going. That means it's not definite yet, right?"

"Well, I –"

"The job pays thirty-six a year. With bonuses and floor incentives, you could make forty a year easy, and that's just for the first year. Management jobs aren't a dead end here. Look at me – I started as a Floor Supervisor here five years ago and now I'm running the department. And you'd have a step up on the Floor Supervisor as far as promotions, since Assistant Manager is technically a higher up position than Floor Supervisor. But it's up to you – I can only offer the job, I can't make you take it."

I paused, thinking about the money. Thirty-six a year wasn't going to make me rich, but it was more than anyone else had offered me recently, and it was definitely a lot more than I'd make at an entry level ad job in Seattle, if such a job even existed. Of course I didn't want to work for Ed or A.C.A., but what was the sense in turning down a job offer? My goal was still to get back into advertising, and working in a management position at a decent salary would certainly improve my resume. Besides, Ed was right – why would I want to move back to Seattle? I remembered how bored I'd been in Seattle before I moved to New York, and how before I left Smythe & O'Greeley I swore I'd never live there again.

"If you want to think about it for a couple of hours, be

my guest," Ed said. "But I'm going to need an answer from you by the end of the day. Things are happening fast around here now. If I don't have this position filled by lunchtime tomorrow, I'd be disappointed."

I was thinking about what David had said last night, that a man's life is his work. And now I have it, I thought – a chance to make a life for myself again.

"Of course I'd be interested," I said.

"Great," Ed said. "Of course you'll have to meet the President of the company Monday morning to make it official, but assuming there aren't any problems, you'll start work next week. Congratulations."

When I left Ed's office, I noticed people staring at me. Ed and I had been talking for some time and I realized that everyone must have been watching us, wondering what was going on. What would they say, I wondered, when they found out what had happened? Would they believe it?

"So," the guy next to me said when I sat down at my cubicle. "Are you staying or going?"

"Staying," I said.

I decided not to get into it any deeper than that. People would be upset or jealous if they found out I'd been promoted. Besides, they'd find out soon enough.

At five to one I went to the time clock to clock out.

"Where are you going?" Mike said. "Your shift's not over for another five minutes."

I didn't answer him. I realized that as Ed's assistant I was going to be Mike's superior, but I decided to wait for a better time to get my revenge.

"We're not going to tolerate this type of behavior from you anymore," Mike said as I was leaving. "I'm going to report you to Ed. You'll be sorry!"

As soon as the elevator doors closed I experienced an

inner peace I hadn't experienced in years. The answer wasn't to leave New York, I suddenly realized, but to embrace it. My only gripe with New York had been that I didn't have a real job. But now that I had a real job all my problems would be solved. I wouldn't be angry and irritable all the time – my life would have meaning again.

Outside, it was cooler and noticeably more comfortable than it had been in weeks. Julie had made an appointment for me to see Dr. Goldman, the plastic surgeon who had trimmed off the tip of her nose. She had given me three hundred dollars, but I cringed at the thought of having to turn the money over to some doctor just to put some stitches in my forehead. You might think I was crazy – and maybe I was – but it just wasn't important for me to get my face fixed. The cut didn't hurt anymore and I didn't really care if it left a scar. I'd be much better off spending the money on something important, like a present for Julie. I felt guilty about how selfish I had been acting recently and I wanted to do something nice for her.

Standing near the corner at Eighth Avenue was a blonde in a short leather skirt and a tight red velvet tank top. I had seen her on the corner a few days before, soliciting men. Hookers were common on the side streets around the office and, although I usually saw them in the evening, they sometimes worked afternoons. As I got closer, I noticed her bright red lipstick and fake gold hoop earrings. Her hair was dyed blond and her features were dark. I couldn't tell what nationality she was, but I guessed she was Italian or Spanish. Our eyes met. Something about her expression – I think it was her bright green eyes – gripped me, and I thought something about me gripped her. She smiled at me and I couldn't stop myself from smiling back. When I got to the corner, I looked back at her over my shoulder. She was still smiling.

# 6

I WENT TO the Jewelry District. When I turned off Sixth Avenue on to Forty-seventh Street I felt like I was on a street in downtown Tel Aviv. The narrow sidewalk was mobbed with Hasidic Jewish men dressed in white short-sleeved dress shirts, tucked into gray or black slacks. All the stores looked the same to me, so I went to a large mall-like store that had about twenty dealers. An old Israeli man with thick black hair that looked too good to be his own spotted me looking at his display case and told me there was a sale today, everything was forty percent off.

"I want to spend three hundred dollars," I said.

He directed me to the end of the display counter where he took out a tray of earrings. I didn't know which were nice and which weren't, but the ones with the tiny diamonds in them looked like something Julie would wear. I bought them and had the salesman wrap the box with shiny gold wrapping paper. Next, I went to a card store on Fifth Avenue and bought a card. It said something like "Thanking you for being a special person in my life," which pretty much described how I felt about Julie.

When I got home, I called Julie to see when she was getting off work. She wasn't in so I left a message on her voice mail. I showered, then cooked some noodles and cheese the way I liked it, with an extra slice of American cheese melted into it. I sat in front of the T.V. and ate the food out of the pot.

I'd spent a lot of afternoons this way over the past two years. When I didn't work extra hours I was home by two o'clock, and I usually did all my resume sending on Mondays. Sometimes I took walks in the park or went to the movies, but on most days I came home, cooked a cheap lunch, and started watching talk shows and soap operas on television.

I hated my routine, but I had no hobbies or anything else to keep me busy. I hadn't worked out or played sports since college and I didn't have the attention span to read books. Some days I thought I was the biggest loser in the world.

But I knew my days of boredom were about to end. Starting Monday I'd be working nine-to-five again, like a real person, and these days of depression and laziness would be a bad memory.

I watched the first half of a soap opera. I knew all the characters, but this didn't make the story lines any more interesting. Finally, I got bored and started flipping channels. Sally Jesse Raphael was doing a show on prostitution. A woman who had her face blocked out was telling about her life as a prostitute in Los Angeles. Then the woman's husband came on stage and explained what it was like to be married to a prostitute. He said that as he made love to her he imagined all the men she'd been with during the day and that this was a great turn on for him. The audience booed. After a commercial, Sally Jesse announced that she had a surprise for the audience. Without the man knowing it, she had invited his ex-wife on to the show, whom the man hadn't seen since he'd left her to marry the prostitute. The woman sat next to the man, but didn't make eye contact with him. She told her story of how the man had left her with months of unpaid bills and how he was months behind on his alimony payments. The audience booed again. Then the woman announced that she was three months pregnant, with a child fathered by the man! The audience booed even louder and people stood up and called the man "a loser," "a scumbag," "a slime bucket," among other names. The man denied that the baby was his which made the woman start screaming at him, calling him names so vulgar that the station had to bleep them out. Sally Jesse herself stood between the embattled couple and finally calmed the woman down. As the credits started to roll, she asked the man why exactly he had left his wife for the prostitute.

"Because she was better in the saddle," the man said. "I'd be lying if I gave any other reason."

I thought the show was boring, but I watched it straight through till the end anyway. It made me think about the prostitute I'd seen outside my office building. I remembered the way she'd smiled at me, running her tongue lightly over her top lip and then puckering her lips seductively. I'd never had sex with a prostitute, but the idea had always appealed to me. When I was sixteen, my friend Johnny Brewer asked me if I wanted to go with him and some other guys to Vancouver for a weekend. He said they were going to pick up some prostitutes and take them back to their hotel room. I was a shy, sexually repressed Catholic kid who had never even kissed a girl yet so of course I refused. I never stopped regretting it.

When I got older, there were other opportunities. At a college frat party, guys were taking turns with a prostitute in one of the bedrooms. I'd lost my virginity by then, but when it was my turn, I said I wasn't into it. It was a lie. I was dying to go in there, yet I didn't know what I would do when I got there, what I would say. Would I kiss her? Would I look at her? I never had any girlfriends in college or graduate school. Every once in a while I'd meet a girl at a party or a bar and we'd have sex, but the girls were inexperienced and the sex wasn't very good. To make things more exciting, I'd imagine the girl was a prostitute that I'd just picked up on a street corner. It was an incredible turn on for me.

After graduate school, when I came to New York, I promised myself I'd finally live out my fantasy. I bought a copy of *New York Magazine* and circled the names of a few women who advertised that they gave "erotic body massages." I knew this was just a catch phrase, that they were really high-class prostitutes.

I called all the numbers and decided to make an appointment with a woman who lived in the West Village. She had a sexy British accent and promised me that her customers always left satisfied. I went to her apartment that night. She was even sexier than I'd imagined. She must've been about forty, but her age didn't hurt her beauty, it enhanced it. She had long golden blond hair and she was wearing a red silk robe that couldn't hide her huge sagging breasts. I could never understand why some guys preferred small, pointy breasts. To me, if breasts weren't big and soft, they didn't serve any purpose.

The woman led me into the spacious apartment which was dimly lit and decorated with antiques. After putting on a Chopin CD, she seated me in a padded arm chair and started rubbing my shoulders and neck. Her touch was gentle, yet firm, and I could feel her breasts rubbing against the back of my head. My whole body was starting to tingle and I didn't want to wait any longer.

"I'm ready," I said.

She was silent for several seconds and I wasn't sure why. Then she said curiously:

"Ready? Ready for what?"

"You know," I said, "what I'm paying you for. Aren't you gonna take me into the bedroom or something?"

She pulled me up by the hair and practically dragged me out of the apartment.

"Pervert!" she screamed. "If you come back here again I'll clip off your balls and flush'em down the toilet!"

As you can imagine, I felt humiliated. I decided to forget all about prostitutes and go on with my pathetic life. A few days later, I met Julie at the laundromat. I thought this would put my desire for a prostitute to rest, but after we'd been going out a few months we started talking about marriage and living together. Before I settled down, I wanted to go to a prostitute one time, just to see what it was like.

But I knew it was impossible. If Julie found out our relationship would be over. I tried to forget about the idea, to convince myself that prostitutes were vulgar and dirty, but this only made things worse. I was attracted to prostitutes *because* they were vulgar and dirty.

Then I had an idea. I started to pretend that Julie was a prostitute. I didn't call her names or ask her to do kinky things. The fantasy was mine, not hers. When we made love, I imagined a scenario where she had solicited me on a street corner and asked me to get into a car with her. After some bargaining I'd convinced her to come up to my apartment with me where she'd taken off her white fake fur coat and her leather skirt and got into bed. She'd pulled down her fishnet stockings, snapped off her black brassiere, and lay on her back with her legs spread and her red pumps high in the air, screaming perversely.

Sometimes Julie asked me why I always kept my eyes

closed during sex and I told her it was because I was concentrating on my orgasm. Of course she believed me. Why wouldn't she? She had no reason to believe that her nice boyfriend from Bainbridge Island, Washington was dreaming up perverted fantasies. The fantasies kept me from thinking about having sex with an actual prostitute for more than a year.

Then the desire came back, stronger than ever. I'd left Smythe & O'Greeley by then, and I was working mornings at A.C.A. With afternoons free I had a lot of time to myself, which meant I had more time to think about prostitutes. I'd walk around the streets of Hell's Kitchen looking at the prostitutes behind the Port Authority, on theater row between Ninth and Tenth Avenues, outside the seedy bars near the West Side Highway. There were more prostitutes out at night, so sometimes I told Julie I was meeting an old friend from Seattle or from an old job when I was really out on the streets, looking at prostitutes. I know it sounds like I had some kind of problem, that I should've gone to see a shrink or something, but there was no harm in what I was doing. I was just fantasizing, like other guys might fantasize by looking at magazines or porno videos. It wasn't like I was having an affair.

My favorite spot was between Eleventh Avenue and the Hudson River on West Twenty-eighth Street. It was a dark, deserted block crammed with factory buildings. The prostitutes roamed the sidewalks in their gaudy outfits and high heel shoes, trying to get guys to pull over in their cars and pick them up. It was the danger factor that really excited me. I imagined how erotically terrifying it must be for the woman to get into a car with a total stranger, a guy who might rape or murder her, and then to pull over to a dark quiet place and do whatever the guy paid her to do! That's what the guy on the *Sally Jesse Raphael Show* had meant when he said the prostitute was better in the saddle than his wife. The sex wasn't better, it was just more dangerous than the sex with his wife. His wife knew he wasn't going to kill her, but the prostitute didn't know for sure. Then there was the possibility of disease, the thought of all those men, those sleazy bodies she'd let inside her.

I needed to experience the perversity once for myself. Turning on the *Sally Jesse Raphael Show* had been an omen. The T.V. was trying to tell me that my time had come, that I needed to have sex with a prostitute now, before I got married and it was too late. I didn't want to cheat on Julie, but if I did it now, before we got married, it wouldn't be cheating. At least it would be a different kind of cheating, definitely not as bad as having an affair. And I knew Julie would want me to get something like that out of my system before I made a commitment to her.

I was sweating. The air conditioner was on full blast and it certainly wasn't hot in the apartment. I took off my shirt and went into the bathroom and splashed cold water on my chest. When I looked in the mirror I didn't recognize the man staring back at me. His face was gaunt and pale, there was a deep two-inch-long gash on his forehead that wasn't healing. But it was his eyes that frightened me most. They were two dark, dull circles that didn't seem to be alive.

I looked away, frightened to see any more.

When Julie came home, at about six o'clock, I was back on the couch watching T.V. But I was so happy to see her that I jumped up and ran to the door and kissed her.

"So?" she said. "What happened?"

"Happened?"

"With the plastic surgeon. You went, didn't you?"

I'd forgotten all about not keeping the appointment with Dr. Goldman.

"Of course I went," I said.

"So? Where are the stitches?"

"He said the same thing the guy at the hospital said – they aren't necessary."

"What do you mean, aren't necessary? You'll have a scar there for the rest of your life. You're already getting a scar."

"What can I do, force him to stitch me up? He gave me a shot of antibiotics and said I should just keep rinsing it out."

"Are you sure you went?"

"I haven't seen you all day and this is the hello I get? You call me a liar?"

She kissed me. I tried to keep kissing her, but she pushed me away.

"What's wrong?"

"My breath," she said. "I had the salad bar for lunch and I taste like onions."

I didn't care. I grabbed her cheeks and squeezed so hard it made her lips pucker. Then I kissed her again, this time swirling my tongue around in her mouth.

"Your breath tastes delicious," I said. "I wish the whole world tasted like your breath."

"Why are you in such a good mood tonight?"

"I missed you, that's why. I've been thinking about you all day."

She blushed.

"I've been thinking about you too."

"I have a surprise for you," I said.

"A surprise?"

"Wait here."

I went into the bedroom and got the earrings and the card. When I came back, I told Julie to close her eyes.

"What is this?"

"Trust me. Close your eyes."

I held the box with the earrings and the card in front of her and said: "Okay."

When she opened her eyes she smiled like I'd never seen her smile before. Her eyes were glassy, her face was trembling.

"I can't believe this," she said, tears dripping slowly down her cheeks. "This is just so...I can't believe this. It's...unbelievable!"

She read the card and started to cry full force. Then she wrapped her arms around me and kissed me with her salty lips.

"Go ahead," I said. "Open the present."

"I will," she said. "I'm just trying to prepare myself."

After a couple of deep breaths, she started to unwrap the box. She paused a couple of times and smiled and told me how much she loved me. I told her that I loved her too, more than anything in the world. She finished taking off the wrapping paper and slowly opened the box. The way her expression suddenly changed I thought the guy in the store forgot to put the earrings inside.

"What's wrong?" I said.

"Nothing," she said softly. "It's...they're wonderful. Thank you. Thank you very much."

She wanted to put the earrings back in the box, but I made her try them on. They looked good on her, at least I thought they looked good. But something was obviously wrong. She wasn't making eye contact with me anymore; she looked like she was about to start crying for real. I thought she didn't like the earrings or that she was upset over something I'd said. Then I suddenly knew what was wrong.

"You were expecting an engagement ring, weren't you?"

"No," she said defensively.

"It's okay," I said. "It's nothing to be embarrassed about. Anybody would've thought that when they saw the box and after the discussion we had last night."

"But I wasn't thinking that at all," she said. "It may've been in the back of my mind, but I wasn't really expecting a ring. I just didn't expect earrings, that's all."

She started toward the bedroom when I came up behind her and grabbed her around the waist.

"I didn't mean to disappoint you," I said, resting my chin on her shoulder. "I just felt like doing something nice for you today, and I was passing through the Jewelry District on my way home from work and I figured, why not get Julie some earrings? But believe me, one day, and probably not too long from now, you'll come home from work and I'll have that ring here waiting for you. And when I get it it's not gonna be some little diamond you need a magnifying glass to see. I'm gonna get you the biggest rock you've ever seen. It's gonna be so big you'll hardly be able to lift your hand."

"It's not the size that counts."

"That's what all women say – until you get into bed with them."

She laughed. I started to tickle her underarms and stomach and she laughed even harder.

"I'm sorry," she said, turning to face me again, laughing. "I was acting like a big baby, wasn't I?"

"It's all right."

"No, it's not all right. You did something really nice for me and I didn't appreciate it. The earrings you got me are so nice. I'm going to wear them to work tomorrow."

"I'm glad you like them," I said. "I spent a long time picking them out."

"How did you pay for them?" she asked, suddenly curious. "I thought you were saving all your money for rent?"

"That's the other surprise I have," I said. "I got an advance at work."

I was waiting for a big smile, but instead she looked confused. Her eyes were shifting back and forth like she was watching a tennis match inside my head.

"I thought you were quitting your job today. I mean isn't that what we –"

"Something happened," I said, smiling. "A really freak thing and it changed everything."

I told her what had happened at work and how Ed had hired me as his assistant.

"What about Seattle?" Julie said. "Last night you –"

"Last night I didn't know I'd be promoted. Now there's no reason to go – not yet anyway. I mean maybe after six months or a year we can think about going to Seattle, but right now –"

"I gave notice today," Julie said. "I told my boss we were moving."

"So tell him your plans changed," I said.

"It doesn't work that way. You can't give notice then say you changed your mind. He'll think I'm some kind of idiot."

"Well, what do you expect me to do?" I said. "You know how long it's taken me to find a decent job? I can't just walk away from this. This is the big break I've been waiting for. This is a chance to get back into the nine-to-five world."

"But it's a telemarketing job. It's not like you're going to be working in advertising again."

"I'll be a supervisor," I said. "That's basically what I was doing at my old job. And besides, at least I won't be hanging around the apartment every afternoon."

"But it's a telemarketing job. A telemarketing job, Bill."

I was getting frustrated. It felt like the argument could go on forever – I could keep saying the same things over and over again and Julie still wouldn't understand what I was saying.

She had backed a few yards away from me and had her arms crossed in front of her chest.

"This really upsets me," she said angrily. "I mean it's really just unbelievable to me that you could do something like this, without even calling me. And for a telemarketing job – a telemarketing job."

"Are you going to keep saying that?"

"You didn't even call me and tell me. What, you think I'll just automatically do whatever you decide to do?"

"I called you at work, you weren't there."

"This is so insensitive of you."

"I don't see what the problem is. I thought you'd want to stay in New York."

"You think your career is more important than mine?"

"Of course I –"

"That's what it seems like. It seems like you'll do whatever the hell you want to and you just expect me to follow along like a dog or something. Why didn't you talk to me first? Why didn't you say you'd let him know?"

"Maybe when you calm down –"

She grabbed my arm. I hated when people grabbed me like that. Julie wasn't just anybody, but still.

"I'm not an idiot, Bill," she said. "I know sometimes you might think I'm an idiot, that you can do whatever the hell you want to –"

I pushed her off me. I cocked my fist back, ready to hit her. I don't know why I stopped because I wanted to do it. Maybe it was fear. I'd never hit anyone before and I'd certainly never hit a woman. After what had happened the other day, when I pushed Julie, I was suddenly afraid that something was happening to me, that I was turning into one of those wife-beaters Sally Jessy always had on her show. I imagined the audience booing me, women saying that they'd kill me if they ever had the chance. I didn't think I really wanted to hurt Julie, but that's what the guys on the show said about their wives and girlfriends. The expert psychologists said they were in denial. Was I in denial too?

"I can't believe you," Julie said. "I can't believe you just did that."

"Did what?" I said defensively.

"You were going to hit me. That's what you wanted to do, right?"

"Of course not," I said. "What do you think I...let's just forget about it, all right?"

"Stay away from me," she said. "I'm so angry right now I could kill you."

"I didn't do anything," I said.

"But you wanted to. It's the same thing. Almost the same thing anyway. I'm not going to take this...this bullshit either. I'm a good woman. I have a lot to offer. I don't understand how you could do this to me after everything I've been through."

Feeling extremely guilty, I walked away to the kitchen. I knew exactly what Julie was talking about – she'd told me all about it on our first date. It had to do with her old boyfriend from college. She'd gone out with him for three years, off and on. He was in a fraternity at Albany and she was in the sister sorority. At first it was a dream relationship. They took classes together, took trips together, they even moved off campus together junior year. Her parents loved him. Why wouldn't they? He was Jewish, from a good family, and he was planning to go to law school. Then something changed. He started spending more time with his friends, less time with her. She heard rumors about other women, fraternity gang bangs. He went out drinking every night of the week and when he came home he'd yell at her, call her "bitch," and "whore." A couple of times he hit her. She broke up with him twice, but each time he promised he'd change and they got back together. But the violence got worse. One day she had bruises all over her face. She called her parents for help, but they didn't seem to understand. They just couldn't believe a nice Jewish boy would really hit their daughter. Finally, she moved in with a friend. Her parents were furious with her for ending the relationship; her father said she'd destroyed her future. She wouldn't talk to her parents for months. She went into therapy and gained twenty-five pounds. She avoided relationships with other men, fearing the same thing would happen. She once told me I was the only man she had ever really trusted.

"Is that your response?" she said. "You're just turning away from me?"

"I feel so awful I don't know what to say," I said. "I mean I didn't mean to do that. It was just a reflex. It had nothing to do with how I really feel about you."

"It scared the hell out of me."

"I swear I'll never do anything like that again. If I do, that's it, I'll walk out of here. I'll never hurt you."

"I hope you mean that."

"I do. I swear I do."

After a couple of minutes of silence, which is a long time for two people to be silent in the same room together, Julie said:

"So when does the job start?"

"Monday," I said, happy to be on to a new subject. "And I'm really looking forward to it too. I think it's gonna change me, make me like I used to be before I lost my job."

Julie seemed to like this idea.

"What about Seattle? That plan's totally off now?"

"Not totally, just for now. This is very important to me. This could change my life – our lives, I mean. That's the most important thing, that we stay together."

"As long as we're happy," she said. "I guess that's the important thing, right?"

"Of course that's the important thing," I said. "I knew you'd understand."

I wanted her right then – on the kitchen floor. I wanted her like I'd wanted that prostitute.

"What are you doing?" she said. "Wait, I have to get out of my work clothes."

"I'll get you out of them," I said.

My hand was up her skirt, reaching under her panties. Why not? She was just a whore I'd picked up on a street corner. She didn't expect me to kiss her or look at her while I did it. I was paying her for this time, like I'd hire a maid to clean the house or a plumber to fix my pipes.

But I couldn't do it.

"It's okay," Julie whispered into my ear. "We don't have to do it now. We can wait till after dinner."

But I wouldn't give up. I kept trying to get it inside her – bending it, pushing it, massaging it, tickling it, but no amount of stimulation helped. Even fantasizing that Julie was a prostitute hadn't been able to get me hard.

"I'll go down on you if you want me to," Julie said.

But that didn't help either. After about five minutes, it was still like trying to hit a baseball with a piece of rope. Julie snuggled next to me and started to comb my hair with her fingers. I was covered in sweat.

"Are you having some kind of problem?" Julie said. "Because if you are we can discuss it."

"I'm just distracted," I said irritably. "Maybe it has to do with work, everything that's been going on."

"But we haven't had sex in almost two weeks."

"What? Have you been keeping track on a calendar?"

"I'm just scared," she said. "And it's not just tonight. It seems like whenever we do try to do it lately, you either don't want to or you can't or something happens. I was reading in a magazine about male sex problems and how to deal with them and they said it's never because the man isn't attracted to the woman anymore, but I still can't help worrying about it. I mean I know I've put on a few pounds the past few weeks, but I'm trying to lose them and –"

"For God's sake, Julie, I think you're gorgeous. How many times do I have to say it to you before you believe it?"

"I know I'm just being insecure, but you can't blame me. I just want us to have a normal sex life – I want everything to be normal. I called Sharon today to apologize again for last night and I know you don't like them and they can be real pretentious sometimes, but at least they're happy. And that's how I want to be. I mean not that I'm not happy now or anything but, you know. I don't want to have to worry about my life."

"What does this have to do with me?"

"I don't know, nothing I guess. I just wanted you to know how I feel. How do you feel?"

"Tired," I said. "I didn't sleep much last night and then I had that crazy day at work."

"Poor thing," Julie said. "Why didn't you tell me?"

"I didn't think it would matter," I said. "But I just want you to know there's nothing wrong. Everything that's been happening lately is just because of what's been going on at work. None of it is real."

"I have an idea, let's just stay in tonight – relax, order Chinese food, watch T.V. I think I've been putting too much pressure on you lately. Let's just forget about sex tonight."

"That sounds like a great idea," I said.

We got up together from the floor. Julie went into the bedroom to put on sweat pants and a T-shirt while I went into the bathroom. I didn't want to admit it to Julie, but I was terrified. I'd never been impotent before and I feared I'd never be able to have sex again. I sat on the toilet. Because I was very anxious it took a while to get started, but I finally came back, as big and hard as ever. I started breathing normally again. The problem was nothing worse than I'd hoped. The magazine article was wrong – sometimes male impotence *is* caused when men don't find their partners attractive anymore. There wasn't any one reason I could put my finger on, but Julie simply didn't turn me on like she used to. I didn't know how I'd break the news to her, or what would happen the next time we tried to have sex, and it didn't really concern me at that moment. I was too busy thinking about gaudy dresses, fishnet stockings and pumps.

## 7

THE WEEKEND PASSED by quickly. We stayed in the rest of Friday night and we were in bed asleep by eleven o'clock. On Saturday, we took a walk in Central Park and picnicked on the hills behind Bethesda Fountain. It was a gorgeous summer day, not too hot and brilliantly sunny. As we ate our goat cheese and sun dried tomato on baguette sandwiches, we watched the couples, families and tourists strolling by. I was in a good mood and joked about the outfits people were wearing and I tried to guess where people were from and what they did for a living based on how they were dressed. Afterwards, we went to the Central Park Zoo and then we ate ice cream sandwiches and walked aimlessly through the park. We held hands and occasionally stopped and kissed, like any other couple in love.

That night, we took the D train from Columbus Circle to Yankee Stadium to watch the Yankees play the Indians. My favorite team was still the Seattle Mariners, but baseball was my favorite sport so it didn't really matter to me which teams were playing. I loved being inside a baseball stadium, and I don't care what you say about Camden Yards and Fenway Park, Yankee Stadium is the most beautiful stadium in the country. We arrived in time for the first pitch and we had good seats, in the mezzanine section behind home plate. Julie wasn't crazy about baseball, but she drank beer and ate a greasy hot dog and she enjoyed making fun of how tight the players' uniforms were. She said she had a great time.

On Sunday, I got up early and snuck out of bed

without waking Julie up. I bought hazelnut coffees and bagels and cream cheese and lox – even though I hated lox – and a copy of the Sunday *Times*. I prepared the food carefully on a tray, then snuck back into the bedroom and whispered "surprise" into her ear. When she woke up, she was very excited.

"Lox!" she said. "I can't believe you bought me lox!"

We had a leisurely morning, eating and drinking and trading back and forth different sections of the *Times*. For the first time in weeks, I was able to leave the Help Wanted section untouched. In the afternoon, while Julie was getting her nails done, I went to Barnes & Noble and read through a few management and sales books, trying to get myself prepared for Monday morning. The books said nothing I didn't already know and I left confident I was going to do well at my new job. When I came home, Julie had a surprise for me – she'd gone shopping and bought me a shirt and tie to wear to my first day of work. I told her how much I loved the gift even though the shirt was a little too small and the tie had an annoying floral design. At night, we went out to a quiet Italian restaurant on Second Avenue. Afterwards, we had iced cappuccinos at a small cafe and then we walked arm-in-arm back to our apartment.

During the entire weekend, Julie didn't ask me how I had afforded to pay for the earrings. She was a smart woman and she must have realized that it was ridiculous that a company would give a Telemarketing Supervisor an advance. She also must have realized that I'd really bought them with the money I was supposed to give to the plastic surgeon. But she didn't say a word about it, probably because she was sick of arguing. We didn't try to have sex all weekend and neither of us seemed to mind. I liked to spend time with Julie and make her laugh and I even liked to kiss her, but I simply didn't want to make love to her. Of course I was hoping that that problem was temporary, that eventually we could have a normal, healthy relationship again. But I didn't know how a relationship could possibly be more normal and healthy than ours was that weekend.

Sunday night I had trouble sleeping. I set the alarm for six o'clock and I woke up every half hour or so and checked the clock, paranoid that I'd oversleep. When the alarm finally rang, I had already showered and dressed.

By seven forty-five, I was at work. I didn't know exactly where to go so I sat across from the elevators, in the reception area, waiting for Ed to arrive. I was wearing my favorite navy suit, the one I usually wore to job interviews, and the maroon shirt and floral tie that Julie had bought me. The shirt was still a little uncomfortable and I didn't like the tie's design any more than I had yesterday and I was kicking myself for not wearing something else. I wished I'd worn one of my comfortable shirts and simple striped ties I usually wore with my navy suit. I looked too snazzy this way, as if I was trying to impress people.

When Ed arrived at about eight-thirty, the first thing he did was comment on my clothes.

"Bill Moss in a suit," he said. "I never thought I'd see the day."

I laughed politely, although secretly I was angry. The outfit was too loud, people were going to be commenting on it all day. It was my fault – I didn't want to hurt Julie's feelings, but I should have told her I didn't like the shirt and tie, I should have been honest. But then I started feeling anger toward Ed. Who was he to make a comment about me wearing a suit? I used to wear suits five days a week when I worked at Smythe & O'Greeley. Who was he to condescend to me like I was some kid just out of college? Especially when his suit was wrinkled and the sleeves were shabby at the ends. It looked like he'd bought it at a thrift shop and never took it in for dry cleaning.

Ed and I had a typical office conversation. I asked him how his weekend was and he said he played tennis on Saturday. I told him that I played on my college tennis team (which was true, but I was on the non-active roster and never played an actual match). It didn't matter anyway because he wasn't paying attention to me.

I followed him into his office. I asked him what had happened with Greg.

"I had him arrested."

"Arrested?" I said. I wasn't sure if he was joking. "When?"

"Last night. I don't know if I'm going to go through with it yet, but I filed assault charges against him. Since the judge couldn't see him right away, they kept him overnight in jail."

It was apparent now that Ed wasn't putting me on.

"I didn't think you were serious."

"Why wouldn't I be serious?" Ed said defensively. "You saw what happened here Friday – the dirty nigger tried to murder me. I'm lucky you're not at my funeral right now."

I didn't want to seem combative with Ed, like I was siding with Greg, so I said:

"I meant I didn't know you were serious about Greg spending a night in jail. Of course I understand why you'd want to have him arrested. Anybody would've done the same thing."

This seemed to relax Ed.

"I have to talk to my lawyer today," he said, "but I'm thinking about going all the way with this, taking him to court. I mean the guy's a walking time bomb. If I don't do something he might go ahead and kill his boss at his next job. The guy's out of control, like a wild animal."

Ed went into a monologue about how black people's brains are physically smaller than white people's brains and how black people should all be put onto ships and sent back to Africa because they'll never make it in the "technological world." The argument was as ridiculous and ignorant as any of the arguments Greg had made against white people, but somehow Ed's comments didn't come across as funny. He sounded like the typical redneck calling in on a right-wing radio show.

But I pretended to be interested, smiling and nodding in agreement with his various points. Finally, he finished. He told me to wait in his office while he went to the bathroom. When he came back, about ten minutes later, he told me that Nelson – Nelson Simmons, the President of the company – wasn't in the office yet, and that as soon as he came in he wanted me to meet with him. I was suddenly very anxious. I'd assumed all weekend long that the job was a given, that I'd just show up and start working, and I'd almost forgotten that Ed had said I'd have to meet with Mr. Simmons first. I wondered if I'd neglected to remember that on purpose, because I didn't want to confront the possibility of not getting the job, or if it was because Ed had presented the situation differently to me last week. On Friday he'd made it out like meeting with Mr. Simmons was a technicality, but now he made it seem like a major obstacle.

I imagined what would happen if I somehow didn't

get the job. How would I break the news to Julie? What would I say, start packing, we're moving to Seattle after all? After what happened Friday, I didn't know if our relationship could withstand another big argument. She'd finally realize that I was nuts and go move in with her parents in Great Neck. And then what would happen to me? Even if I convinced Julie to go to Seattle with me again, I'd be starting at square one again – searching the Help Wanted sections, writing resumes and cover letters, meeting with head hunters. I couldn't stand to go through that nightmare again! Of course I didn't plan to work at A.C.A. forever, but I needed a break from the grind of searching for a job. And I certainly didn't want to leave New York anymore. After the great weekend I'd had, I was falling in love with the city all over again. I didn't want to leave Central Park and Yankee Stadium and bagels and cream cheese for a city whose main attraction was a giant replica of a hypodermic needle. I was prepared to do anything not to let this opportunity slip away. If it meant literally getting down on my hands and knees, stripping off Mr. Simmons' pants, and kissing his butt cheeks, I was ready to do it. In fact, I probably would have done a lot more than that to not leave that office unemployed.

At a few minutes before nine o'clock, Ed said that Mr. Simmons could meet with me, but only for about five minutes because he had to attend a meeting at nine-fifteen. I knew this was bad. When I was working at Smythe & O'Greeley I'd often given my secretary similar instructions when I had to meet with someone I didn't really want to meet with. His nine-fifteen meeting was probably a fabrication, a built-in excuse to keep our meeting short.

Ed led me into Mr. Simmons' swank, corner office

that had a view of the Hudson River. Although I had passed Mr. Simmons in the hallways, urinated next to him in the bathroom, rode in the same elevator with him, and stood behind him on line in the deli on Ninth Avenue, I had never said a word to him. It wasn't proper office etiquette for telemarketers to make small talk with the President of the company. In fact, it was against A.C.A. rules. On the first day of training, we were told that there was a strict chain of command at the company, and if any telemarketer was seen conversing with a superior who was not in the Telemarketing Department, that telemarketer would be terminated immediately. When Ed introduced us, Mr. Simmons didn't appear to recognize me. I panicked. He had to have at least *seen* me before. Did he have any respect at all for his telemarketers?

I shook his hand firmly, but not so hard that I made him feel intimidated. I'd been to enough job interviews in my life, and I'd interviewed enough people myself, to know exactly how to impress an interviewer. And I was going to do everything possible to make a favorable impression on Mr. Simmons.

Ed excused himself. I sat in the swivel chair opposite Mr. Simmons, and crossed my right leg over my left, and rested my embraced fists on my thigh. I knew this casual position would make me appear non-threatening, and yet at the same time confident. But Mr. Simmons wasn't even looking at me. He was looking through his reading glasses at my resume, which apparently Ed had given him. He was reading it slowly, following the words with his index finger. I didn't know how old Mr. Simmons was, but he couldn't have been any younger than fifty. He had a ruddy face, silver hair and very large ears.

"How long have you been with A.C.A.?" he asked, still looking at the resume.

"Two years," I said. "You have an old resume there. I'll give you a new one."

I handed him a copy of my updated resume. He read for about another two minutes and I wondered what could possibly be taking him so long. I'd only listed three jobs and given a brief description of my education. Even if he read the whole resume twice it should have only taken him several seconds.

Finally, he rested the resume on the desk and smiled at me politely. I knew, for whatever reason, my background hadn't impressed him. That isn't to say that he didn't think I was qualified for the job, but if one of my qualifications had really piqued his interest, I knew he would have made some sort of comment about it. By saying nothing he was basically saying "So, why do you think I should hire you?" I knew it was up to me to impress him now with my personality. But I didn't want to seem over-eager. I had to find the right balance.

"So why did you leave your job in advertising?" he asked.

I had prepared for this question. I told him it was because I'd been thinking about going into the creative end of advertising and I wanted to take some time off before I made the career change. He seemed to buy the explanation, if he was listening at all. I knew the point was just to hear me speak and that it didn't really matter what I said.

"So Ed tells me you have some computer experience?"

From the way he phrased the question, I guessed that he was uncomfortable with computers, and that he might be impressed with a younger person who wasn't.

So I talked extensively about computers and databases, using as much lingo as possible, hoping that it might impress him. Although I saw his eyes widen with interest once or twice, he didn't seem to care one way or another about my computer experience. Suddenly, I realized that I might be overdoing it – making myself sound dull and pompous – so at the end of my speech I down played my computer skills, going for the modest approach, saying that although I *knew* a lot about computers, I didn't consider myself an *expert* by any means, and that it probably sounded like I knew a lot more than I actually did. It was too late. He was already looking away and I sensed that he was about to remind me about his non-existent meeting. I feared that the interview was going nowhere.

He asked me a few more questions about my background – what I majored in at college (marketing), what my salary was at Smythe & O'Greeley (seventy a year, but I didn't want to make myself sound over-qualified, so I said fifty) – then he started telling me about the job I'd be doing at A.C.A. In a dull, method-ical tone, he explained how A.C.A. was going to be restructuring, but how he envisioned the company becoming the number one reseller of telephone services by the year 2000. He said that the key was to stay two steps, not one step, ahead of the competition, and that meant taking full advantage of the new marketing technologies. He gave me xeroxes of articles from various marketing magazines which all explained how companies needed detailed databases of potential clients in order to market new products to their customers more efficiently. The idea was not new, but Mr. Simmons seemed very excited when he spoke about it. This confirmed my suspicion that Mr.

Simmons knew little or nothing about computers and databases. I wondered if I'd sounded intimidating before. Then he started talking about how A.C.A. needed to focus on MCI and Sprint customers, but how the company had no way of focussing specifically on these markets. He asked me if I could implement a program where telemarketers could input such information into a database and I said that many such database programs already existed and how I was confident the company could build a huge database of information. He nodded politely, exhibiting no particular positive or negative emotions, then he asked me if I had any questions for him. I didn't, but I knew it was bad to say nothing, so I asked him about the company's sales volume and what their projections were for the future. I didn't listen to the answer. I was angry at myself for asking such a banal question. Finally, he said that he'd love to meet with me longer, but he had that meeting to run off too. Yeah right, I thought. Then he said that he was going to be interviewing for the job all week and that I could expect to hear from him by Friday. My heart started racing. Friday? That was as good as telling me that the position had already been filled. He didn't even tell me to call him later in the week or that it had been a pleasure meeting with me. I was about to lose my chance to enter the working world again and it felt like a large hollow hole had reopened in my stomach. I knew what I had to do. I had to make an impression on him. He had to take a personal interest in me or I didn't have a chance. I'd noticed two pictures of sailboats. In one of the pictures he was standing on a dock in front of a yacht, his hand resting on the hull.

"Your boat?" I asked.

"Yes," he said in a suddenly interested, less professional tone. "Why? You sail?"

"You can say that," I said, intentionally modest. "I'm from Bainbridge Island, Washington. I practically grew up on a sail boat."

"No kidding," he said. "What did you have? A ten, twenty-footer?"

"Not me, my dad, God rest his soul. The last boat he had was a sixty-five-footer."

"Sixty-five feet!" he said. "Jesus, that's quite a ship."

"It *was* nice," I said modestly. "I was practically his first mate. 'The Jib Man' he called me. When I was a teenager I started taking it out on my own. It was great. Then in college I was in the sailing club."

"You competed?"

"A couple of races here and there. It wasn't like our yacht was going to compete for the America's Cup or anything, but we had a lot of fun. I really miss the water and fresh air. I was thinking about joining the New York Yacht Club at some point."

"This is fantastic," he said. "There's finally somebody in the office who knows something about sailing."

I'd definitely struck the right chord in him. He started going on and on about the different boats he'd owned over the years and the trips he'd taken to the Caribbean and Central America. From his desk drawer, he took out a stack of pictures showing him and his wife on the deck of a boat. In all the pictures he was bare-chested, wearing dark sunglasses, and the wind was rustling his thin hair. I listened closely, adding an anecdote whenever I thought it was necessary, but the truth was I knew very little about sailing. Yes, my father had owned a sailboat when I was growing up, but it was a fifteen-footer and I don't think I went on it more than one or two times. And I was never in a sailing club in college, nor did I know whether such a sailing club existed at the University of Washington. In actuality, I was afraid of water and I never even went swimming at the beach. But a roommate of mine in college had been into sailing and I'd picked up a lot of the lingo from him. I told Mr. Simmons specifics about the different sail boats my father had owned and details about month long trips I used to take with him during summers. I'd recently read one of Julie's *National Geographics* in the bathroom, so I gave details about trips we took along the coast of Alaska and Canada, dropping the names of specific ports we'd visited. I could tell that Mr. Simmons was hanging on every word I said and that, unlike my experience with computers, my experiences on the high seas of the Pacific were impressing him greatly.

"I can't believe we've had this big secret at the company for two years and we never took advantage of it," Mr. Simmons said. "Imagine, a sailor who knows databases. This really is a lucky break for us. Why didn't you ever put in a request for a promotion sooner?"

"Actually, I did but –"

"That's not important now. What's important is we've discovered you now and we can't let you go. Let me let you in on a little secret," he said whispering, as if we were suddenly members of the same old boys' club. "Ed may be a nice guy, but he's not the brightest guy in the world. We need somebody like you in the depart- ment, somebody young, somebody with a vision. There's going to be a lot of rough water ahead in this business, and I'm not convinced that Ed can handle it – not alone anyway. And now that I'm starting to know you a little better, I think you're going to be the perfect man for the job. Welcome aboard, Bill."

"Thank you, captain," I said.

Mr. Simmons laughed, harder than would be expected for such a silly joke.

"You don't have to call me captain," he said. "Nelson is fine."

"I won't let you down," I said.

"I'm sure you won't. And you'll have to come out to Sag Harbor some time and see my yacht. Maybe we can go for a little spin together."

"I'd enjoy that a great deal," I said. "I haven't done any sailing all summer. I'm itching to get back on the water again."

Nelson patted me on the back and walked me back to Ed's office. The morning telemarketers had begun their shift, and I noticed people eyeing me strangely as Nelson and I walked across the telemarketing floor. I realized that they must not have known about my possible promotion and that they must have found it strange to see me in a business suit, side-by-side with the President of the company.

"We can stop our search," Nelson said to Ed. "I think Bill here is going to be perfect for the job."

For a moment Ed appeared surprised, perhaps that I had become so chummy with Nelson so quickly, but he erased the expression from his face quickly.

"That's great news, great news," Ed said. "I had a feeling you'd be impressed with him."

"I just wonder why you didn't bring Bill to my attention sooner. We had this budding talent here and we were wasting it on the telemarketing floor."

Ed seemed to be trying to think of a response, when Nelson said:

"Just make sure you get all of Bill's paperwork in order today so we can get him set up as soon as possible." Then he turned to me. "If you have any questions or problems I have a light schedule today, so just come by my office any time and I'd be happy to talk. I'm sure we'll be talking to each other again soon."

Nelson shook my hand firmly. I smiled, realizing that there was suddenly no talk of Nelson having to attend an urgent meeting.

"Is something funny?" Ed asked.

"No," I said.

I knew Ed must have resented the apparent special treatment I was getting from Nelson and that he might have thought I'd been laughing at some inside joke Nelson had made against him.

"Come on," Ed said unamused. "Let's get you set up."

We went to the vacant office next to Mike's office. Like Mike's office, this office had glass windows facing the telemarketing floor, but – I was happy to notice – it was larger than Mike's office and it had a bigger desk and more filing cabinets. Ed explained that my formal training was going to begin tomorrow. In the meantime, he was going to bring me some material to read about the company and the telecommunications industry.

"I'll formally announce your promotion at a meeting this afternoon," he said. "I'll also bring you the appropriate paperwork to sign. Oh, and I just want to remind you that we take our chain of command very seriously at A.C.A. Mike, as Floor Manager, will bring all his grievances to you. You bring your grievances to me, and I bring my grievances to Nelson. Under no circumstances should you approach Nelson directly about anything."

"But Nelson told me before that I should come to him if I have any questions."

Ed inhaled and then exhaled a long stream of air.

"Today only. After today, you come to me. Understood?"

I nodded.

"Thank you."

Ed left me in the office alone. I sat at my new desk and adjusted my swivel chair to an appropriate height. The office was stuffy and I wished there was a window facing outside. The drab pale-green paint on the walls gave the office a stale, bureaucratic feel, but I knew after I added a personal touch – put up a few paintings, maybe a small rug for the floor – the place would begin to liven up. The important thing was that the office was my own. Whenever I wanted to, I could close the door and be by myself. I could stay there until ten o'clock at night if I wanted to, catching up on work or just relaxing. It might not sound like such a big deal, but having my own office was very important to me. It made me feel powerful. I was no longer a "telemarketer", a faceless employee sitting in a cubicle, like an anonymous egg in a carton of eggs. Suddenly, I was alive again. This is what had been missing from my life for the past two years, I realized. I used to be a workaholic, working twelve-hour days sometimes. I was the type of guy who brought his work home with him, who couldn't have a conversation if it didn't in some way relate to work. It didn't make me the most interesting guy in the world, but it made me feel comfortable. Without a job I had nothing to do with my life, and too much idle time is dangerous for a man.

Someone knocked on the door. Come in, I said, and Mike entered the office. He was smiling cautiously, almost embarrassed to be intruding. He looked nothing like the stoic man who had sent me home from work four days ago. I realized that Ed must have told him that I'd been promoted. He must have also learned that I was now his supervisor.

"Hope I'm not interrupting anything," Mike said.

"Of course not," I said in an overly pleasant tone that must have been unsettling to him. "Come in, come in."

Mike closed the door, but remained in the same place, nervously fiddling with change or keys in his pockets.

"Just wanted to congratulate you," he said. "Ed told me the good news."

"Thank you," I said. "That's very kind of you."

"You must've been surprised, huh?"

"It's true," I said, "four days ago I didn't think I'd still be at the company, no less be promoted. But I guess the world works in mysterious ways."

"Yeah, mysterious ways," he said, obviously out of things to say. "Well, I guess I'll be seeing you later."

"Oh, Mike," I said, "can you do me a little favor?"

"Sure, what is it?"

"Can you run down to the deli and get me a cup of coffee?"

He paused, waiting to see if I was serious.

"Coffee?"

"Yes, with one milk and two sugars. Actually, better make that skim milk and Sweet'N Low. Two Sweet'N Lows, unless they have Equal. Then make it Equal. But just one Equal."

I saw his teeth grinding together.

"Sure," he said. "No problem."

"Let me give you some money," I said. "Here's five bucks. Also, get me a muffin. Chocolate chip if they look fresh. Otherwise banana walnut or blueberry, you decide which."

He took the money and started out of the office.

"One more thing, Mike." He stopped. I heard him breathe heavily. "I want to schedule a meeting with you, let's say three o'clock this afternoon, if that's all right with you of course?"

"What are we going to meet about?"

"It's just going to be a bit of an orientation. I'm going to tell you what I expect from you, what your new responsibilities will be, that sort of thing. I'd advise you to bring a pen."

Although his face remained expressionless, Mike's eyes looked like spears that were about to fly out of their sockets and stab me.

"Three o'clock," he said. "I'm looking forward to it."

I was looking forward to it too. This job was going to be a lot of fun.

# 8

IBECAME ABSORBED in my work. Most nights I didn't go home until eight o'clock, and sometimes I stayed as late as nine or ten. Mornings, I was in my office by eight, eight-fifteen the latest. Although I didn't have to work these long hours, I enjoyed it, and I would have felt that I was cheating myself if I worked any less hard.

In addition to learning everything there was to learn about the telephone industry, I was also working on updating the company's database program, trying to work out every possible kink. Every day it seemed I had meetings or phone conversations with technical support people and computer programmers. I knew that the first job a new employee does is usually the one he is most remembered for, and I wanted to make the best first impression possible.

During this period, Julie was very understanding. She knew how much working at a full-time job meant to me and she never complained about my long hours. I think she actually preferred that I was working more. When I'd had afternoons off I was often tense and irritable when Julie came home from work, and this always led to arguments between us. But now that I was expending so much energy at work, when I came home I was much more relaxed and easy to get along with, and our relationship benefited from this.

On most days, I walked home from work, taking new routes each time. Sometimes I walked straight up Broadway to Eighty-sixth Street, then crossed through Central Park. Other times I'd weave through the midtown side streets until I reached Second Avenue and then I walked straight home. But my favorite walk was along the perimeter of Central Park. I'd either take Broadway and cut over on a street in the Fifties, or go straight up Eighth Avenue to Columbus Circle. I found it very relaxing to be in midtown in the early evening. It was after rush hour so the streets were quieter and the sidewalks were emptier and there was still a simmering energy in the city, a pulse that reminded me I was alive. It was especially pleasant to be near the park. The joggers and dog walkers and roller bladers and bicyclists gave the city a festive, invigorating atmosphere. I'd walk alongside Central Park until I reached Fifth Avenue and then I'd head north with the park still on my left. The walk always seemed shorter when I was next to the park. I'd be watching the designs of orange and yellow light in the trees that the setting sun made and before I knew it I'd be crossing Seventy-ninth Street. When I got to the Metropolitan Museum of Art, I always felt that I was home, even though I still had almost a mile left to walk.

Later, I'd feel energized from my walks, never fatigued. I'd talk to Julie for a while, ask her about her day, then – if I hadn't picked up something on the way home – I'd fix myself something to eat. If Julie wasn't watching T.V., I'd watch the last couple of innings of the Yankee games, or if the Yankees weren't playing I'd watch the Mets. Then, at about eleven o'clock I'd join Julie in bed. Usually, she'd already be sleeping. I'd read some work I'd brought home with me, then I'd fall asleep. In the morning, I was usually gone before Julie woke up.

At work, the telemarketers treated me differently than before my promotion. Now that I was technically their boss, some people resented me and rarely said hello to me or spoke to me about the latest office gossip.

But others – a few of whom had never spoken to me before – tried to become very friendly with me. They started conversations with me all the time, offered to work extra hours. One woman – an N.Y.U. creative writing student named Mary Weiss – even bought me a present, a book of poetry by Galway Kinnell. I thanked her graciously for the book and I acted pleasantly toward all the people who were trying to be friendly with me, but I secretly resented all of them. I'd always hated people who kissed their teachers' and bosses' asses, and I'm proud to say that I've never reduced myself to that level. Even if it meant that I got a lower grade or that I was passed over for a promotion; if I wasn't being rewarded for the work I'd done, the reward meant nothing to me. I also hated the people who were brooding over my promotion, because these people were obviously selfish and there is no place for selfishness in the business world. The only people I had respect for were the few people whose opinions of me hadn't changed at all. These people either continued to ignore me or to be halfway friendly toward me as if nothing had changed and I was still a telemarketer. I mentioned these people to Ed and I made sure they received their commissions faster than other people, and I made sure their phones and computers worked better. I also mentioned the names of the people who were trying to kiss up to me and the people who were angry at me, telling Ed that I questioned "their attitudes." Ed appreciated the information and he subsequently fired two people, including Mary who had bought me the book of poems.

For the first few days, I continued to take revenge on Mike. I made him do mundane errands, reprimanded him in front of the telemarketers, and was overall rude and condescending toward him. Then I decided enough was enough. I'd never liked Mike and I didn't start to like him any better, but I also realized that there was nothing really bad about him. I was still angry that he had sent me home early that day without pay, but now that I was a member of management I realized the bind he'd been in. If he didn't send me home that day and Ed found out that I had been late three times in July, Ed may have fired him for not doing his job properly. Of course the odds of Ed figuring that out were almost nil, but nevertheless I understood Mike's position. As the Floor Supervisor, he had the toughest job at the company. He had to enforce all of Ed's policies and then Ed could sit in the background like Mr. Nice Guy while Mike took all the abuse. I really felt sorry for Mike.

Ed and I got along well. At least that's how it must have *seemed*. I was always with him and I never disagreed with anything he said, unless I felt very strongly about something, and then I always tempered my comments and was sure never to raise my voice or to be at all disrespectful. Sometimes it was hard to stay calm, especially when he made his daily snide racist remarks about blacks. I would nod in agreement, as if what he was saying was very enlightening, and I doubt he ever had any idea how much I hated him. As far as he was concerned I was just another white guy who was sick and tired of hearing black people complaining that they couldn't get a fair shake in America. Ed was so obsessed with hating black people that I sometimes wondered if something had happened to him as a child. Had a black bully beaten him up in junior high school? Did a black person rob or hurt someone in his family? He would get so angry during his tirades that his face would turn red and perspiration stains would appear on his shirts.

But Ed never had a clue how I felt about him. He was very impressed with my computer knowledge and my apparent loyalty toward him as an assistant. After two weeks, I had revamped the entire computer system, including upgrading the network and installing new software programs, and I handled all the purchase orders. I overheard Ed telling Nelson that I was "indispensable to the company" and that because of me the company had saved "thousands of dollars." I knew that by being overly resourceful I was impressing Nelson, and that I was also making Ed look good to Nelson. Since Ed had technically "discovered me", whatever I did indirectly reflected on him, and I knew that as long as I did my job well, he would brag about me to Nelson.

On the first day that the new computer network was up and running, Nelson called me into his office to personally congratulate me. He told me how impressed he and Ed were with me and that if I kept up the good work I would definitely be rewarded for it. Then he invited me to Sag Harbor the following Saturday for lunch and a spin on his yacht. I made up an excuse that I had a wedding to go to that day. Then he suggested a date in August. Hesitantly, I agreed. There was no way I was going to actually get on a boat with him, but I knew I could always make up an excuse once I got out there. Perhaps I would wrap my ankle with an Ace bandage and make up a story about how I had fallen getting out of the shower. Or I could show up coughing and say that I had a terrible case of the flu. Then there was the possibility that he had only suggested the other date as a formality, and that by August he would forget all about it. I hoped this was the case. I felt bad about lying to Nelson and I wanted to avoid having to lie to him anymore. However, I couldn't help rejoicing over the irony of it all. Here I was, worrying about how to politely turn down a sailing invitation from the President of the company, when only a couple of weeks earlier I had been forced to humiliate myself by apologizing to the entire telemarketing staff. And it had all happened because of a single lie!

As Ed's assistant, I learned a few shocking things about A.C.A. For example, I found out that A.C.A. intentionally withheld commission money from telemarketers, and that the commissions of black telemarketers were held more frequently than the commissions of whites. Since most telemarketers only lasted with the company for about a month, the idea was to avoid having to pay out commissions to employees who were no longer with the company. Ed had made up some crazy statistic that black workers were fifty percent less likely to keep a job for a month than white workers, so he withheld the commission revenue of black employees until they had been with the company for two months. Then, since Ed's statistics said that a black employee had a less than ten percent chance of remaining with a company for more than six months, their commission was released gradually, while the white employees received almost all of their commissions after six months. The real reason Ed had fired those telemarketers – and why he had intended to fire me – wasn't because the company was in financial trouble like he had claimed, but because the company owed those telemarketers hundreds of dollars in commissions and they wanted to avoid paying the money. Although you may not believe that a modern business could be run in such a backwards, counter-productive way, I assure you that I'm not making any of this up. To Ed, it didn't matter that he was firing telemarketers who had been productive for the company and who would have continued to be productive. He felt that he could hire new telemarketers to do the same work and at the same time "save" thousands of dollars in commissions.

I had a lot of ideas about how to run the Telemarketing Department more efficiently – and more rationally – but I kept them to myself. I wanted to focus on doing my job and impressing Nelson and the last thing I wanted to do was to create any rifts with Ed.

The workaholic side of my personality had returned. When I was in my office, the world consisted of me and my work and nothing else. Sometimes I'd be staring at my computer, trying to crack some difficult problem, when I'd become aware of someone standing behind me. I'd turn around and the person would say he'd been there, trying to get my attention for several minutes, and I wouldn't know whether or not he was lying. It was as if working at a serious job again had given me the power to make the world disappear, whenever I wanted it to. It may have made me seem annoying and irritable to other people, but I was happy.

When I'd leave the office, I'd still feel dazed and a little disoriented and a few times I stepped outside without remembering leaving the office or taking the elevator down to the street. I saw the prostitute with the phoney blond hair on the corner near Eighth Avenue a couple of times. I'd almost walk past her when I'd realize she was standing there, smiling at me. Caught off guard, I'd react awkwardly, either smiling back or rushing ahead, stone-faced, pretending that I hadn't noticed her. My heart would start pounding, as furiously as it does when I wake up from a nightmare. I'd tell myself that I was being ridiculous, that I had no rational reason for feeling so much anxiety. After all, she was just a woman, no different from millions of other women in New York. And wasn't it true that I never felt so excited, even when I was surrounded by women on a crowded subway car? But of course I was only kidding myself. I knew exactly why the prostitute made me feel so nervous, but I didn't want to admit it. Because I knew if I admitted it, I'd want to confront it, and I didn't want anything to come between me and my work.

Julie and I still weren't having sex. When I came home from work or on weekends when we were lounging in bed, Julie would sometimes start to come on to me. She'd touch my hand or move to kiss me and I'd move away and suggest that we go somewhere or say that I was hungry and needed something to eat. One time Julie got frustrated and suggested that we go to a relationship counselor. The idea wasn't new. She'd suggested it once before, after I'd lost my job at Smythe & O'Greeley and fell into a depression. I'd been avidly against it then and I told her that my position hadn't changed. She told me that she didn't understand, that I didn't seem to care one way or another about our relationship. She knew couples, she said, who had gone for counseling, and it had done wonders for their relationships, and she begged me to try it, just once. I wouldn't budge. I told her the truth, that I didn't think there was anything wrong with our relationship, that in fact I thought our relationship was better now than it ever had been. Yes, we weren't having sex, I said, but how many couples have sex all the time and still wind up breaking up? Don't women always complain that men only want sexual relationships? Well, we were having a non-sexual relationship, and it wasn't as if it was going to be that way forever. I was just going through a transition now because of my new job, and I assured her that as soon as I got comfortable in my routine, our sex life would pick up again.

Then one day – I think it was a Wednesday or Thursday – I was sitting in my office, looking over some telemarketing statistics, when something strange happened. On my computer screen, I saw myself naked on a bed in a hotel room. I thought I must have overworked myself, so I closed my eyes tightly and took several deep breaths, but when I opened my eyes the image was still there. I stared at the screen, my eyes not blinking at all, and I wondered if I was going crazy, or if I was asleep dreaming and that in a few seconds I would be awake. The prostitute from the corner appeared next to me in bed. She was smiling, the same way she always smiled at me on the street, with her tongue running gently over her top lip. She was naked too and her body was perfect; she didn't have a blemish or a scar anywhere. She started to run her hand gently up my leg, and I felt the sensation of my leg hairs sticking up. Her tongue was inside my mouth, and then her other hand pinched my nipple. The pain was so sudden and real that I actually screamed. I stood up and walked quickly to the vending machines. I bought a can of soda and drank it in one gulp, unaware of the carbonation. Ed came into the room and asked me if I was all right.

"Fine," I said. "A little thirsty, that's all."

I returned to my office. The statistics had reappeared on the computer screen, but it didn't matter; I still couldn't get the vision of myself and the prostitute out of my head. Finally, I decided that I had to confront the fantasy, once and for all. I'd cashed my first paycheck at my new salary so I had enough money. I had about two hundred dollars on me and I doubted the prostitute's fee would be any higher. After work I'd pick her up and we'd go off to an apartment or hotel room somewhere and have sex. It seemed so simple to think about, but somehow I knew it wouldn't be so easy to actually go through with it.

I was fine until about four-thirty. Then I started worrying about every detail – how I should look, how I should act, what I should say. I thought about movies I had seen where guys picked up prostitutes, but nothing ever worked out like it did in the movies. Would she ask me if I had any diseases? Should I ask her if she had any diseases? What about condoms? Was I supposed to bring one or would she have one? And what about my appearance? I was wearing a business suit, so I looked presentable, but I hadn't showered since early this morning. I sniffed my underarms and realized the problem was as severe as I'd feared. How could I have sex with a woman when I smelled like I'd just worked out in a gym?

I went into the bathroom and scrubbed my underarms with moist paper towels. After several minutes, I convinced myself that I didn't smell anymore, or that at least I didn't smell as bad as I had before. But what about my breath? I'd eaten tuna fish on an onion bagel for lunch and I didn't have a toothbrush at work to brush my teeth. From the vending machine, I bought a packet of mints. I ate every last one of them, but when I blew air against my hand it smelled like a fish market. What if she kissed me when we were having sex? Or what if she smelled my breath on the street and refused to even have sex with me? What could be more humiliating than being turned down by a prostitute?

I waited in my office till about six o'clock. I had to just do it, I told myself, not even think about it. In an hour I'd be laughing and realizing how ridiculous I was for being so nervous. I was probably going to be the cleanest, best-smelling guy she'd been with in months. Then, going down in the elevator, I had a thought that terrified me. What if she wasn't there? She wasn't there every day and there was a very good chance that she wouldn't be there today. But she had to be there. I'd built up the courage to approach her, and I didn't know if I could do it again.

When I reached the street, my pulse was raging. She was there all right, in the same place I had seen her all the other times. Today she was wearing dark sunglasses and she had her hair up in a bun. But she was wearing the same outfit as usual – the red velvet and the leather skirt and the gold hoop earrings. She had her hands on her hips, balancing herself somehow on three- or four-inch red pumps. Then time skipped ahead, the way it sometimes does in dreams. Suddenly, I was in front of her, tapping her on the shoulder to get her attention. She turned around angrily, as if she thought I was a cop or a bum harassing her. I couldn't think of anything to say and I wanted to walk away and pretend none of this had ever happened.

"Looking for a date?" she said, with a strong Bronx or Brooklyn accent. Up close, I noticed the layers of makeup she was wearing and a large gap between her front teeth.

"I can't talk here," I said, fearing someone from work might see us. "Meet me around the corner on Forty-fourth Street off Eighth Avenue."

"Are you bullshitting me?"

"No," I said. "Just meet me."

I went around the corner, hoping no one had seen us talking. I realized I had taken a stupid risk. What if Ed or Nelson had seen us? Or what if Mike saw? He'd think it was his duty to tell Ed how I spent my time after work. But almost everyone had left the office at five o'clock and I knew it was unlikely that I'd been seen. I had waited in the middle of the block for about five minutes when I felt someone tap my shoulder from behind.

"So, you want a date, honey, or what?"

She was next to me, so close I could smell the grape bubble gum on her breath. I realized she must have come around the corner the other way, from Ninth Avenue instead of Eighth.

"You scared me," I said. "I was just...Never mind."

"You're not a cop or something, are you?" she asked suspiciously.

"A cop? Of course I'm not a cop. Why? Do I look like a cop?"

"You could be undercover, though it would be a hell of a disguise."

"I swear I'm not a cop. Is there somewhere we can go? Somewhere you usually take your...your clients?"

"It's a hundred bucks, money up front. Plus thirty for the room. No hundreds neither, and no fifties."

"I have to give you the money here?"

"Money up front. If we don't do it my way, we don't do it no way."

We went near the doorway of an apartment building and I gave her a hundred dollars in tens and twenties. She counted the money three times before she stuck the wad in her pants somewhere.

"So what do we do now?" I said. "I mean is there some apartment you take people to?"

"Yeah, with a doorman and a health club and a fucking swimming pool." She rolled her eyes. "There's a hotel on Forty-third between Ninth and Tenth – The Royal. Don't say nothing to Bobby. Just give him the thirty bucks and he'll give you a key. You get a half hour with me. More time, more money, honey."

"Do we have to go there together?"

"Whatever you say. Wanna meet me in the lobby, meet me in the lobby. I got no problems."

We agreed to meet in the lobby in five minutes. I knew it was stupid of me to give her the money, that she could run off and I'd never see her again. On the other hand she was a prostitute, not a hustler, and my hundred dollars wasn't going to buy her a ticket to a new life.

There was nothing royal about The Royal. It was an old, narrow dump with chewed up wooden floors and peeling paint on the walls. I waited inside, near the door. There were a couple of junkie types on the bench in the lobby and in my business suit I didn't exactly blend into the wallpaper. A few minutes later, the prostitute arrived. She waved for me to follow her inside and I did as I was told. Bobby, the desk man, must have been ninety years old. I gave him thirty dollars and he slid a room key over to me like it took all the strength he had. I wondered how many times he'd been through this routine. A guy that old probably didn't know who he was anymore.

I followed the prostitute up the creaky stairs. It was impossible not to notice her big butt shaking back and forth in front of me. I wondered if she was trying to make it shake or if she'd been doing it for so long that it had become natural.

I wondered if her tits were real.

On the first floor landing, a water bug skidded past my shoes and I noticed mouse or rat droppings near the walls. I didn't even want to have sex with the prostitute anymore. I just wanted to be home, having a quiet night with Julie. I made a pact with myself that after this was over, I'd never do anything like this again. I'd be faithful to Julie for the rest of my life.

We went into a small, musty room at the end of the hallway. The room wasn't much bigger than the bed and there was no bathroom, and only a small, antique-looking sink in the corner. There was no cover or blanket on the bed and the sheet was marred with yellow stains and cigarette holes. She let me in ahead of her, then as soon as she closed the door she started taking off her clothes. I don't know how she did it, but in about ten seconds she was completely naked.

"What are you waiting for?" she said.

I couldn't move. I was staring at her body, not able to decide whether I hated it or loved it. She was heavier out of the clothes than in them and the weight wasn't very well distributed. Most of it was in the form of fat and it was mostly on her thighs and stomach. Her tits were silicon double Ds. She didn't have the perfect skin I imagined she'd have either. There were several large pimples on her breasts, and her left leg was noticeably lighter than her right leg, probably because it had been burned in a fire. I guess you're getting the picture now that there was nothing terribly attractive about this woman, and yet to me...to me she was one of the most beautiful women I'd ever seen. Maybe it was because it had been so long since I'd been alone in a room with a naked woman who wasn't Julie. Or maybe it was because she was a prostitute and the thought of the hundreds or thousands of guys she'd serviced in her

JASON STARR

lifetime gave her a kind of beauty that some people can't recognize. Whatever the reason, my impotence had become a thing of the past.

"Come on," she said impatiently, sitting on the bed. "I'm not gonna take your clothes off like your mommy. I ain't gonna talk to you like a little girl neither. I do straight fucks, that's all. You want me to suck your dick that's fifty bucks. You wanna come that way it's another fifty, but you're gonna have to wear a rubber. And the clock started ticking when we met outside. You'll have to give me another thirty bucks if you want that time back."

"I don't think I'll need any extra time," I said.

I started taking off my clothes clumsily and I couldn't do it nearly as fast as she could. Finally, I had all my clothes off. I was going to ask her about condoms when I realized she was holding one in her hand. I realized how dumb it was of me to think she wouldn't have one.

She spread her legs and stuffed some lubricant or jelly into her vagina. Suddenly, it occurred to me that she didn't tell me her name. It seemed strange to have sex with a woman, even a prostitute, without knowing her name.

"Why do you care?" she asked.

"Just in case I want to call you something, you know, while we're doing it."

She paused. "Call me Spanky. And that doesn't mean I'm into any kinky stuff. It's just a nickname I have."

"What's your real name?" I said.

"I don't give out my real name."

"You don't have to tell me the last name. Just the first name."

"I'm telling you, I don't give out no names. You don't tell me your name, I don't tell you my name."

"My name's Bill. Come on, I promise I won't tell anybody."

She stared at me.

"Denise, all right?"

"Denise?" I said. "That's funny."

"What's so funny about it?"

"It's just all those times I saw you I thought you'd have some exotic name, something Spanish or Italian."

She looked at me blankly, as if she had no idea, and didn't care to have any idea, what I was talking about. I realized right then that in her mind she had never seen me before today.

"You don't recognize me, do you?" I said.

"What's this with the questions? Are you here to fuck me or interview me?"

"You're not joking. You really don't know who I am."

"Why?" she said. "You famous?"

"No, but I've seen you so many times, for weeks now. You always smile at me and I smile back. That's why I came to you today, because of your smile."

She had the same blank look.

"Sorry, honey," she said. "I never saw you before today."

By her voice, I knew she wasn't lying. I couldn't help feeling offended. I knew she probably had to smile at a hundred men to get one of them to pick her up, yet I still felt I should have stood out. Even if it was just the color of my eyes or my hair or my teeth. *Something* about me should have been familiar to her.

She fitted the condom on me and made sure it was secure. I thrusted in and out in a slow, rhythmic motion. Although I was looking directly at her, her gaze was focussed at my left ear or some point beyond it. It was nothing like how I'd fantasized it would be. There was no screaming or moaning or cursing. She didn't kiss me passionately, or kiss me at all for that matter. She might as well have been dead because she was as rigid as a piece of wood.

It only took me about a minute to finish. Right afterwards, I thought about Julie waiting for me at home. Then the guilt set in. Suddenly, I felt like a disgusting person, someone I didn't even want to know. I couldn't believe I'd had sex with another woman. Not even with another woman – with a whore. A whore who didn't even have the decency to recognize me!

"Hey, what's the matter?!" she screamed. "You crazy or something?"

I hit her again, not because I was mad at her, but because I was mad at myself. The trouble was at the time I couldn't tell the difference.

I stood out of bed and left her there holding her cheeks. She was screaming and cursing at me, calling me all kinds of names. I barely heard any of it. It was just noise to me, no louder or more sensible than the noise inside my head.

I ran down the steps, out to the street. Then I started walking, unaware of what direction I was heading. I felt totally alone. It was the lowest point in my life, and I've had a lot of low points. Like a kid who discovers there's no Santa Claus, my biggest fantasy had come crashing down to reality. I'd had sex with a whore and I had nothing left to live for.

## 9

"I WANT TO become a Jew," I said.

Julie stared at me incredulously for a few seconds, then started to laugh.

"Right," she said. "Like you really expect me to believe that."

"I'm serious," I said. "I thought about it a lot when I was walking home tonight. I mean, as you know, I'm not very religious, but I know religion is important to you, so I don't see any reason why I can't be Jewish. And it's not something I plan to take lightly. I'll study and I'll go to temple with you, or shule, or whatever it's called. Who knows? Maybe I'll like it. And if I don't like it, I guess I'll just be a non-believing Jew which I guess won't be much different from being a non-believing Catholic."

"What happened to you today?" she asked suspiciously.

"Nothing," I said, afraid she might somehow suspect I'd gone to the prostitute. I wondered if I had lipstick on me or smelled like perfume. I said, "I just suddenly realized how stubborn I've been about this, and for no reason at all."

Now Julie made a sad face.

"You don't have to convert for me," she said.

"But I want to," I said. "I've given it a lot of thought and I really want to do it."

"But people only convert for each other when they're getting married. We're just living together."

"But I want to marry you," I said. "I mean if you want to marry me."

She continued to look sad.

"Of course I want to get married," she said. "You know that."

"Then let's do it. Let's get married."

"You don't mean it."

"Do I look like I'm joking? I'm proposing to you, Julie. I want to marry you."

She stayed sad awhile, then her face slowly brightened as she started to believe me. Then it hit her. She wrapped her arms around me and kissed me again and again and kept telling me how happy she was and how much she loved me.

Then I said, "Well, you didn't give me an answer."

"Yes! Yes! Of course I'll marry you! What did you think? Of course! Of course!"

I apologized for not having a ring and I explained that the idea to propose had come to me suddenly and that I'd get her a ring as soon as I could afford one.

"Oh, I don't care about a stupid ring," she said as if I was being ridiculous. "It's the emotion that counts. Besides, it'll give me something to look forward to."

The rest of the night, Julie made phone calls, alerting what seemed like every friend and relative she had about our engagement. Although I preferred to have a simple wedding, perhaps even at City Hall, I knew better than to suggest this to Julie. When she called her parents, I overheard her telling her mother that she wanted to start calling wedding halls and caterers as soon as possible, and that she didn't want to go overboard, she definitely wanted to keep the wedding under three hundred people.

By the time she made her last call it was after midnight. I put on a CD of old Billy Joel songs she liked and lighted two candles. We danced close together and, I have to admit, my eyes started to tear during *Scenes from an Italian Restaurant.* I don't think I realized until that moment how badly I wanted to get married myself. Rather than confining me as I'd always thought it would, marriage would free me, allow me to concentrate fully on other parts of my life.

Gradually, Julie and I moved into the bedroom and started making love. I felt like I had become a different person again, completely different from the one who'd stormed out of the room with the prostitute just a couple of hours before. That wasn't me, I was convinced. That was someone else, and I wanted to forget that that other person had ever existed.

For the next several days, Julie and I started living a normal life again. My impotence disappeared completely and we had sex regularly, sometimes two or three times a night. Although I'd thought that Julie and I had been getting along well, I realized how much intimacy had been lacking in our relationship. Now when I came home from work, instead of parking myself on the couch and watching Yankee games, Julie and I talked, exchanging stories about our days, offering advice and support to each other. In the mornings, we took showers together and then Julie would leave the apartment at the same time I did, so we took the same subway to work. We talked about life after marriage – moving to the suburbs, perhaps to northern New Jersey or Rockland County. I had new fantasies, fantasies that had nothing to do with prostitutes. I dreamed about continuing to do well at my job and then getting another job at an ad agency. Eventually I'd be a Senior Executive, making twice what I'd made at Smythe & O'Greeley. Then Julie and I would have children, maybe two or three. I imagined how satisfying it would be to come home after a long day at the office to my family, knowing that I was living a successful life. Going to the prostitute had been a real blessing in disguise. It made me realize how much I had in my life, and how much I had to lose.

Then things started to happen. Ed stopped by my office after lunch one day and told me that he needed to speak with me right away, that it was "urgent." It was the middle of August and less than a week had gone by since I'd gone to the prostitute. Things had been going well at work. The new computer network was still up-and-running and the Telemarketing Department had been running much more efficiently because of it. Appointments and sales were up and there was talk of expanding the department, perhaps even moving to a new location. I'd thought that Ed wanted to speak to me for some routine reason, perhaps to review the call report of a telemarketer or to discuss a change in scheduling. But when I arrived in his office and saw his grave, serious expression, I knew there was something more important on his mind.

"Is your computer on the blink again?" I said, hoping I was still wrong and he had called me for some minor problem.

"Sit down," he said coldly. "Make yourself comfortable."

I sat down, starting to feel nervous. Had I done something wrong? As hard as I tried, I couldn't think of one possible reason why Ed would want to reprimand me.

"We have to have a talk, Bill. Now. Before this gets out of hand."

"Before what gets out of hand?"

Ed paused, as if he had so many things to say, he didn't know what order to put them in.

"Something has been brought to my attention, something that disturbs me a great deal, and I'm not exactly sure how I want to deal with it. So I want to talk with you and get your side of the story. I think that would be the best thing to do."

"Sorry," I said. "Did I do something wrong?"

"You tell me," Ed said. "I had lunch with Nelson Simmons today. He had a lot of interesting things to say. Things that you and he had discussed."

"Okay," I said, and my confusion was genuine. "Was it wrong of me to speak with Nelson?"

"I told you very clearly when you started working for me what the chain of command is here. I told you that you bring all your grievances to me, not to Nelson."

"First of all –"

"I'm not finished. You're my assistant, not my boss, and any policy changes that you think should be implemented must be delivered to me first, in writing, and if I think the points raised are valid, then, and only then, will I bring them to the attention of Nelson. If you ever go to Nelson without going to me first you'll be terminated immediately, is that understood?"

"I don't –"

"Is that understood?"

"No," I said calmly. "I mean I understand what you're saying, but I don't understand why you're saying it."

"I thought it was all very clear."

"It's true I spoke to Mr. Simmons yesterday, but I didn't go into his office to talk to him – he called me in there. You see, we both like sailing and he wanted to tell me about this trip he's planning and –"

"I don't care why you spoke to him. The fact is you spoke to him."

"He asked me how things were going at the job. I told him they were going well. Then he asked me whether or not I thought the company should hire more telemarketers. I thought it would be rude if I didn't answer him so I told him how I felt."

"You told him how you felt all right. You told him that you thought it was 'a mistake' to fire all those telemarketers, that you felt the department was mismanaged."

"I didn't say that. There must have been a misunderstanding."

"Are you trying to suggest that Nelson was lying to me?"

"Of course not," I said, fighting to stay calm. "What I said was that if we had the computer network up a few weeks ago, we might not have had to fire all those people. But since we didn't have the new network, of course we had to fire them. At the time, it wasn't cost-effective."

"You told him that you questioned the policies of the department and that you thought morale was down."

"He asked for my opinion, and I didn't say it like *that*. He asked me what I thought about the morale of the telemarketers and I was honest – I told him that it's not as high as I thought it could be. He asked me why and I told him I thought people were still upset about the firings and that a lot of people felt the rules in the department were too strict. I also said that people wanted more information about their commission money and they wanted to be paid more promptly. But I never questioned the leadership of the department or said any of those other things. That was taken out of context."

Ed stared at me, holding my gaze until I became uncomfortable. But I didn't look away. I knew that looking away would make me seem less believable, so I kept staring at him, trying not to blink.

"This time I'll give you the benefit of the doubt," Ed said. "But you understand why this concerns me, don't you?"

I didn't answer.

"It concerns me," he continued, "because I'm afraid you might be trying to show me up to Nelson. You've done some good work here with the computer network and, overall, I'm happy with you as my assistant. Yet that's exactly what you are – *my assistant*. You don't run this department and no one makes suggestions about the policies of this department except for me. I don't care what the circumstances are, if you act as if you're running this department, you're going to be terminated, understood?"

I nodded.

"Good. And remember – this conversation, and all of our conversations, are between you and me and you and me only. Under absolutely no circumstances are you to tell Nelson that I spoke to you, and I don't care who initiates the conversation. If you want to keep your job here, you'll play by my rules. If you don't have any questions, you can go back to work now."

Feeling completely humiliated, I returned to my office. In some ways it was worse than when he'd made me apologize to the company in front of the other telemarketers. Then I was a ten-dollar-an-hour employee and I didn't have any emotional investment in my job. But now I took my job seriously. I was planning to use it as a stepping stone to rejuvenate my career and I felt that by attacking my work Ed was purposefully trying to attack me. I hated Ed, more than I ever had before. What difference did it make that many of the things he had accused me of were true?

Nelson hadn't asked me about office morale and the management of the department, I'd volunteered all of that information. Why shouldn't I have? It wasn't as if I'd lied to him. It was true that despite the increased sales numbers, morale in the department was incredibly low, and it was all Ed's fault. Everyone hated Ed. Black people hated him because he was racist, and everyone hated him because of the idiotic backwards way he ran the department. As an employee in a management position, why shouldn't I alert the President of the company to a potential problem before the problem explodes? If I were President, I'd want someone to alert me.

That night I told Julie what had happened.

"Ed's just a jerk," Julie said. "He probably just feels threatened by you."

"Threatened?" I said, wondering if that could be true. "You really think so?"

"Of course. You're young and educated and ambitious, and what does he have going for him? He sounds like a fat ex-alcoholic from Long Island who probably hasn't gotten any sex recently. Why do you think he always makes those racist comments? There has to be a lot of anger in there someplace."

"I think he's afraid I'm trying to take his job away from him, that's what I think."

"Are you?"

"Am I what?"

"Trying to take away his job."

"Of course not. I mean I'm trying to do as good a job as possible and I'm trying to be friendly with Nelson, but I'm not trying to get Ed fired. But I think that's what he thinks."

"He probably didn't mean anything he said to you.

140

He was probably angry at something completely different. My boss gets like that all the time. He has fights with his wife and then comes to the office and starts making life hell for everybody else. Believe me, tomorrow Ed'll probably forget all about it."

I decided Julie was right, I'd probably blown the whole thing out of proportion. Ed was probably in a bad mood and not nearly as angry at me as he'd seemed. So I probably shouldn't have gone around his back to talk to Nelson. It wasn't as if I'd said anything *that* awful. By tomorrow, Ed would probably forget that the incident had ever taken place. There was no harm done and in the future I'd be more careful about the things I said to Nelson. There were ways of impressing him without criticizing Ed and I knew it wouldn't work in my favor if I got on Ed's bad side.

The next day everything at work appeared to be back to normal. I spent the morning talking to software vendors and in the afternoon I met with Mike to discuss the telemarketers' performance reports. Although Ed was in meetings all day, I passed him once in the hallway near the bathroom before lunch and he smiled at me as if all was forgotten and forgiven. I was relieved. I decided I'd go back to how I was before I'd gone to the prostitute – absorb myself in my work and avoid any confrontations.

Pouring over statistics and sales trends, I sat at my computer until about seven o'clock. I thought everyone had gone home for the night so I was naturally surprised when Ed appeared in my office.

"Jesus, you scared me," I said, turning around suddenly. "I thought I was all alone here."

"I have some unfortunate news for you, Bill," Ed said in a serious tone, as if he was unaware that I'd spoken.

141

"We're letting you go. You can clean out your office and take everything home with you tonight."

It sounded unbelievable – it *still* sounds unbelievable. I'd been doing great work for the company and I was being fired? Why? What had I done?

"If you're still upset about the things I said to Nelson, I'm really sorry about that. You were right – I should've gone to you first."

"It has nothing to do with that. Just get out of here. I don't want to see your face in this office anymore."

"What did I do?" I said. "You can't just fire me without a reason."

"I have a reason all right, a very good reason. I know something about you, something that you've been trying to hide from all of us."

Immediately, I thought of the prostitute. Could someone have seen us talking on the street that night and told Ed about it? It seemed unlikely, yet what else was I trying to hide?

"I can explain," I said. "I mean it's not like I do things like that all the time."

"Things like what?"

"Whatever you're talking about."

"I'm talking about the resume you gave us. I decided to look into a few things, out of curiosity, on the chance that we might have overlooked something. Well, my detective work paid off. I found out something about you, Bill – something that you were obviously trying very hard to hide."

"I have no idea what you're talking about."

"Maybe I should refresh your memory. On your job application you said that you resigned from your old job at that ad agency. But it turns out you were fired."

"I wasn't fired, I –"

"There's no use denying it. I called up the Personnel Department over there and they gave me the whole story."

"So what difference does it make? That was two years ago. That has nothing to do with my performance here."

"They also gave me the reason why you were fired. Apparently there was an incident between you and your secretary and she filed a sexual harassment suit against you."

"It was all blown way out of proportion," I said. "And it wasn't the reason I left there anyway."

"According to the woman I spoke to in the Personnel Department today it was. I believe her name was Ms. Daniels. She remembers you well and she gave me a full account of the whole incident. She said you were having an argument with your secretary and you called her 'a whore.' There were witnesses there and everything, and apparently it wasn't the first time you'd used that kind of language with her. You called her degrading names all the time."

"The comments were taken out of context," I said. "My secretary had a long psychiatric history. If you don't believe me you can do some more research. She started arguments with everyone in the office and a few times I just got carried away."

"It's not my job to try you," Ed said. "To be honest, I couldn't care less whether you harassed her or not. The problem is you lied to us on your job application and you signed a statement swearing that all the information you had given us was truthful. I have no choice but to terminate you."

"This isn't fair," I said. "You just want me out of here. You think I'm after your job."

"I want you out of here because you violated

company rules, not to mention the law."

Ed started to leave. I stood up.

"You can't fire me, only Nelson can."

"Wrong. I'm your boss, not Nelson. Besides, I'm sure Nelson will want you out of here too once he finds out what you did."

"Why are you doing this to me?" I said, almost crying. "What did I ever do to you?"

"It doesn't matter what you did to me. The fact is you don't deserve to work at this company."

That's when it hit me what was really happening. I was about to be unemployed again, back in the same place I was two years ago.

I could forget about my dreams of finding another job in advertising, of starting a family and moving to the suburbs. I was going to be a loser again.

Then I stopped thinking. I tackled him from behind and went right for his throat. I squeezed hard, watching his face turn pink, then red, then blue. It happened that quickly. At first I was thrilled to see Ed's limp body collapsed on the floor because I felt like I had won something. Then I realized exactly what had happened. I had ruined the rest of my life.

# 10

I SHUT THE lights in my office and closed the door. Part of Ed's body was blocking the entrance so I had to force back his head and one of his arms with my foot. One of his fingers got caught in the crack and I heard it snap when the weight of the door closed against it.

I walked around the office to make sure no one was around. It was empty, even at the other end of the hallway where the executives worked. And I knew there were no security cameras in the office because I'd heard Ed and Nelson discussing the possibility of installing them a couple of weeks ago. I decided that I had to get Ed out of my office as fast as possible, the question was where would I take him? Should I put him in his office or should I carry him to the street and try to get rid of him somewhere? I still didn't see or hear anyone around, but that didn't mean that someone couldn't appear at any moment. Sometimes the executives went out for dinner, then returned to the office to work late. A building custodian could also show up, since the custodians seemed to have no set schedules and they often cleaned in the early evening.

Trying to move as quickly and quietly as possible, I dragged Ed's two hundred-plus-pound body to the office men's room. It wasn't easy for me, a guy who weighed about one-seventy. I don't know exactly why I decided to take his body to the men's room, but perhaps I wanted a place where the body would have the least chance of being discovered quickly. As I've mentioned, Ed's office had glass walls facing the telemarketing floor so the body would have been discovered there by anyone who happened to pass by. There were more secluded places in the office than the men's room, like the storage closets or a space in the back of the mailroom, yet it's easy to talk now about the things I could have done differently to cover my tracks. Believe me, there were plenty of things I could have done. But at the time I was nervous and I probably wasn't thinking as clearly as I was capable of and I just wanted to get out of the office as fast as I could.

I reached the bathroom safely, unseen and unheard by anyone as far as I could tell. Dragging the body behind me, I backed into a stall. I managed to maneuver Ed onto the toilet bowl. It wasn't exactly like putting a baby on his potty. I had to grab him below his knees and use all my might to get him up there. I was out of breath and sweat covered my face and neck when I was done. Then I thought I heard someone in the hallway. I closed the stall door and went outside to check. No one was there, but I stayed for a couple of minutes listening just in case. Then I heard the noise again; it was someone walking along the hallway in the office upstairs. I took a deep breath and prayed to God that everything would turn out all right. But this only frightened me even more. I didn't believe in God, I realized, and even if I did believe in God, He probably wouldn't want to help me. He was probably mad at me for deciding to become a Jew. Perhaps this was proof that God *did* exist, I thought – as punishment for deserting Catholicism, He had turned me into a murderer. It made perfect sense to me at the time, but now I realize how obviously ridiculous and irrational I was being.

I went back to Ed's body and loosened the belt of his pants and unzipped the fly. I hoped that the police would think that Ed was about to go to the bathroom when he was attacked by someone who wanted to rob him. To make this look more legitimate, I took his wallet out of his back pocket and put it in my own pocket. Then I beat him in the face with the back of my fist. This was a mistake. I didn't realize how easy it is to hurt your knuckles by punching someone bare-handed. I didn't think I'd broken anything, but the pain was excruciating. I took off the shoe I was wearing which had a metal heel. I swung the shoe, heel first, against Ed's nose, as hard as I could until I was certain I had broken the bone. I wasn't very worried about fingerprints. Since I worked in the office, my fingerprints were as likely to be found in the bathroom as any other guy's in the office. Just to be safe, however, I scrubbed the part of the stall door I thought I had touched and the back of the toilet with a piece of toilet paper and threw it out before I left the bathroom.

Back in my office, I took a couple of seconds to look around and make sure nothing looked unusual or out of place. Except for a chair which I had turned over while I was attacking Ed, there was no indication that a struggle had ever taken place in my office. I put the chair in place, logged out of my computer, then left my office, like I'd do on any normal evening.

Fortunately, as a routine, I clocked out on the time clock at five o'clock no matter how late I stayed, so the police would have no way of determining the actual time I had left.

But my trouble was far from over. I knew I couldn't be seen leaving the premises or the person who saw me could easily remember it. Since the elevators were often crowded with people from other offices, and I wasn't sure whether the elevators had security cameras or not, I decided it would be much safer to take the stairs.

I walked along the back of the telemarketing floor,

past the time clock and bulletin boards. About to turn left in to the corridor that led to the stairwell, I heard someone walking toward me. A thousand thoughts must have gone through my mind at once. The person was very close, only a few feet away, so it was too late to turn back and hide. I had to stand there and confront the person face to face and then the police would show up at my apartment as soon as the body was discovered. Although this all happened in only a few seconds, they were the longest, most terrifying seconds of my life.

I squeezed my eyes shut, praying that God existed and that a miracle would happen. It did. The noise of the footsteps had suddenly stopped. At first I thought that the person was playing a cruel joke on me and was hiding around the corner, waiting for me to appear. Staying as close to the wall as I could, I peaked around the corner and saw that no one was standing there. There was only a vacuum cleaner next to a door that led to a storage room. I didn't waste a second. I backtracked across the telemarketing floor and took the back hallway to approach the stairwell from another direction. This time there were no mishaps. I sprinted down the stairs as fast as I could – there were no security cameras on the stairwell – and a few seconds later I was outside, heading toward Eighth Avenue. I felt like how a prisoner on death row must feel when he's pardoned by the governor. My life was over and now, suddenly, I was alive. It made me think that maybe there *was* a God after all.

Walking east through midtown, I was so excited about escaping the office without being seen, it didn't even occur to me what potential danger lay ahead for me. I had forgotten that I had murdered my boss and that his body was waiting to be discovered, perhaps by that same janitor who had gone into the storage room. I also forgot that this janitor may have seen me, perhaps when I was leaving the bathroom or when I was straightening up inside my office. Then, as I was heading up Lexington Avenue in the East Fifties, a heavy weight dropped in my stomach and I felt like I was going to faint. It all suddenly hit me. I stopped for a moment, catching my breath. There was going to be an investigation tomorrow morning, or perhaps sooner, and the police would certainly make me a prime suspect. So what if that janitor didn't notice me? Everyone from the office was going to be questioned and when the police found out I didn't have an alibi for that time, well, they weren't going to forget about it. They'd take me to the station house, grill me over and over again, and eventually they'd find a hole in my story. Maybe I wasn't as careful as I'd thought. Maybe I'd left something in the office, some kind of evidence that could prove that I committed the murder. If I wanted to murder Ed, why the hell didn't I plan it more carefully? I could have killed him on Long Island, in a dark parking lot at a train station or a shopping center. I could have made sure there was no evidence linking me to the crime. Instead I –

Enough, I thought. There was no use thinking about should'ves, could'ves and would'ves. If I didn't kill Ed I'd be unemployed, back sending out resumes and going to job interviews. No ad agency would hire me after being out of work for so long, and what if someone called up Smythe & O'Greeley and found out the real reason why I'd left like Ed had done? But by working at A.C.A., maybe even running the whole Telemarketing Department some day, my references would be updated and new employers would be less likely to find out about the harassment incident. The way I saw things, it was the difference between the end of my career and a new beginning. Killing Ed was definitely the right thing to do – it was the *only* thing to do under the circumstances – and now I had to live with it.

At a deli, I bought a bottle of water and saved the paper bag. I went down a side street to an alley between two buildings. I took out Ed's wallet and opened it. There was about forty dollars – a twenty and a bunch of small bills. I put the money in my pocket and wrapped the wallet up in the paper bag. In a garbage can near Hunter College, I dropped the wallet in the garbage and continued uptown. I was about forty blocks away from my office and I doubted that the police would look farther than the immediate area for the wallet. Of course someone could find the wallet and bring it to the police, but even if this *did* happen, it would fit well with the theory that someone had robbed Ed and dumped the wallet in a city garbage can. Crooks did that all the time.

When I got home, I had a lucky break. Julie wasn't home from work yet and there was a message on the tape from her saying that she wouldn't be home until about eight o'clock. It was ten after already so I didn't have much time. I hurried out of my work clothes into sweat pants and a T-shirt. Then I went into the bathroom and wet my hair enough to make it look like I had taken a shower within the past hour. Finally, I lay on the couch and flicked on the Yankee game. I couldn't concentrate on the game much and I never found out the score. However, I remember sensing a general feeling of gloom coming from the T.V. set so I assumed the Yankees were losing.

The sound of a key wiggling the lock in the front door jolted me off the couch. Julie came in, looking as exhausted as she always did. I flicked off the T.V. and went to kiss her.

"I had the biggest fight with my boss today," she said. "I don't even want to talk about it."

"I missed you too, sweetheart."

"Where were you before?"

"Before?" I said innocently.

"I called at about seven. Were you working late tonight?"

"No," I said, "I've been home since about six-thirty. I must've been in the shower when you called."

"Oh," she said, obviously believing me. "I called you at your office too. I was afraid you'd be worried if you called home and I wasn't here."

"Did you leave a message for me at work?"

"I think so. Why?"

"No reason. I had some problem with my phone and I wasn't sure I got all my messages."

"Actually, I *did* leave a message at about seven o'clock. I have to get out of my work clothes. I'm sweating like a pig."

I'd had my second lucky break. The voice mail system at work recorded the day and time of all incoming calls. If the police were curious enough to check, they'd discover that the message from Julie was left at a time close enough to the time that Ed was murdered to suggest that I hadn't been involved. In reality, I was probably in the bathroom bruising Ed's body when Julie had called, but unless that janitor had seen me – and I was feeling more and more sure that he hadn't – the police wouldn't be able to prove that I was in the office at that time. After all, why would I have left the office without playing my phone messages?

Even if I was in denial, I didn't care. For the rest of the

night, I forgot all about the murder and had a normal night at home with Julie. I didn't have to act normal, I *was* normal, and for this reason Julie had no idea that anything was wrong.

As we cooked spaghetti and tomato sauce for dinner, Julie told me about the fight she'd had with her boss. Her boss had yelled at her for misplacing a file and she didn't yell back at him. I consoled her, convincing her that she did the right thing. I told her that fighting with a boss is no way to advance at the company and that sometimes you just have to swallow your pride and roll with the punches. At the time, I didn't see the irony in any of this.

Later, she asked me how things were going at my job.

"Great," I said. "Ed was in meetings all day, but when I passed him in the hallway he smiled at me so I assume everything's back to normal again. I realized there are more important things in life than a stupid job."

"Really? Like what?"

"Like you," I said.

It was the right thing to say. Smiling, she turned off the light on the spaghetti, got on her knees, and unzipped my fly. As I ran my fingers through her hair, I let my hands slide gently down to her neck. It was strange to think that just a couple of hours earlier, the same hands were strangling a man. It was so easy to kill, much easier than I'd ever thought. All I had to do was squeeze.

"Hey!" Julie screeched.

"Sorry," I said.

I'd accidentally pulled on a few strands of her hair and I apologized a couple of more times.

"It's okay," she said. "Just enjoy yourself."

Afterwards, I felt very relaxed. I was also starving.

The spaghetti came out over-cooked, but I ate three or four bowls of it anyway. Afterwards, I watched the ten o'clock news, flipping between channels five and eleven. Neither station mentioned anything about a body being discovered in an office building in Hell's Kitchen. At eleven o'clock, I watched the other news programs and there was still no mention of it. So I decided to forget about it. Whether the body was discovered or not didn't really affect me, I thought. I still had to go to work tomorrow and act as surprised and upset as everyone else in the office. Not knowing anything might make my reaction seem more legitimate.

When I got into bed, Julie was already sleeping, a bridal magazine spread over her chest. I didn't want to wake her, so I shut off the light and got into bed quietly. I slept well most of the night, but toward morning I started having nightmares. Although they were about a lot of different things, the only one I remembered clearly in the morning was a recurring dream I'd been having since I moved to New York. In it, I was preparing for high school graduation when I suddenly remembered that I'd forgotten to attend a chemistry class the entire year. I couldn't graduate without passing the class and I'd have to spend another year in high school. It was a typical anxiety dream, I guess, like everyone has from time to time. When I woke up, I was certain that the dream was real, that I was seventeen years old. Then reality set in when I saw Julie sleeping soundly next to me. I thanked God that it was all a nightmare and that everything was fine. It didn't even occur to me that the dream might have had something to do with the murder and that things were far from fine.

I fell back asleep and slept soundly until the alarm

clock rang at seven o'clock. While Julie was showering, my curiosity peaked again. I turned on the radio to see if there were any reports of the murder on the news yet. There weren't. I decided that it was silly of me to have thought that the body might have been discovered overnight. Since Ed wasn't married and he didn't have a steady girlfriend, there was no one to report him as missing, and the body probably wouldn't be discovered until this morning.

As I got ready for work, I was still very relaxed. In retrospect, it was a good thing I was so calm because it gave Julie no indication that I knew anything about Ed's murder.

Like any normal morning, we took the subway downtown together. She got off at Fifty-first Street and I continued to Grand Central where I transferred for the shuttle to Times Square. It wasn't until I got out at Forty-second Street that the real panic set in. Suddenly, I realized that I had forgotten to hide one important piece of evidence, and that it could nullify my alibi and make me a prime suspect for Ed's murder. I was ready to kill myself for being so stupid.

## 11

WHEN I'D LOGGED out of my computer last night the log-out time was recorded on the file I'd been working on. If the police thought that the murder was committed by someone who worked at the office, they might check the hard drives of all the employees and the company's network files, and then they'd discover that my log-out time was *after* Ed was murdered.

I started walking faster until I was practically jogging up West Forty-third Street. I was afraid I'd been wrong and someone had discovered Ed's body last night. The police could have been investigating the crime scene for hours by now and they may have already checked the computer files. They could be waiting to arrest me at the office, or at least waiting to question me.

There were no police cars in front of the building which brought me some relief, yet I was still nervous. Before the elevator doors slid open on the seventh floor, I took a deep breath, expecting to see detectives waiting for me in the reception area. Instead, Eileen the receptionist was the only one there. She was sitting at her desk, looking bored, tired and unhappy to be there. In other words, everything was normal.

"Good morning, Bill," she said.

Even this was normal. Ever since I'd been promoted, Eileen had included me in her list of upper-level employees whom she said good morning to every day. But today her words took on a more than obligatory meaning. It *was* a good morning, at least it was so far. The police weren't in the office yet which meant that the body hadn't been discovered. Relieved, I went into my office and brought up the file I'd been working on. The log-out time – 7:07 – was in clear view on the main directory. I couldn't believe I had left such an obvious piece of evidence. I recalled the file and saved it again, replacing the old log-out time with the current time. Then I copied the file on to my two back-up disks and the evidence was gone. For a few minutes, I was able to relax.

Then other problems occurred to me. They came so fast, one after the other, that I hardly started worrying about one before I started worrying about another. The thing I feared most was that Ed had spoken to someone else in the office before he spoke to me. If he told someone that he'd investigated my background and that he planned to fire me, it wouldn't take Sherlock Holmes to figure out that I had a motive for the murder. I also worried that Clara Daniels from the Personnel Department at Smythe & O'Greeley would hear about the murder and realize that she'd spoken to Ed just hours before he was killed. When the police found out what they'd spoken about, the trail would lead directly to me. I also worried if there was other evidence I might not have concealed, people who might have seen me, conversations that might have been overheard. I couldn't believe that last night I'd thought my trouble was over. My trouble was far from over.

At about eight-thirty, Mike came into my office. When he said hello to me, I watched his reaction closely. I knew if Ed had told him about his intention to fire me, Mike would have loved to rub it in, get even with me. Mike didn't have any unusual reaction, but just because Ed didn't tell Mike didn't mean he didn't tell someone else.

I was hoping that Mike would go into the bathroom and discover the body. The faster things got started, the faster they would end. But Mike went into his office and started reading a newspaper and sipping a cup of coffee.

I don't know how I stayed calm. Toward nine o'clock, other people arrived. There was another bathroom on the other side of the office so the only people who were likely to discover Ed's body were telemarketers and people who worked in the Telemarketing Department. Simon Peters, a young British guy with a punk haircut who'd been with the company for about a month, walked past my office toward the bathroom. I braced myself for the scream, the panic. It didn't happen. A few minutes passed, then Simon returned and sat down at his cubicle as if nothing was wrong.

Several other telemarketers arrived and went to the bathroom without discovering the body. It occurred to me that this could go on indefinitely. Someone would have to want to use the stall Ed was in or be curious enough to open the stall door if they were going to find him. It was very possible no one would find the body all day, maybe not until the janitor came to clean again tonight. I didn't know if I could wait that long. I kept thinking about Ed with his pulled down pants and smashed-in nose sitting on the toilet seat. It was starting to get me nauseous.

Mike came into my office and asked me whether Ed had called in sick.

"Nope," I said. "Why? He's not in yet?"

"No, and it's past nine o'clock. I've never seen Ed late for work as long as I've worked here."

"Me neither," I said. "If it happens two more times I guess we'll have to send him home without pay."

Mike smiled, leaving the office.

We held the morning meeting without Ed. Afterwards, I was so worried that the body wouldn't be discovered all day that I thought about going into the bathroom and discovering it myself. I would have, except I decided it was too risky. I had no way of knowing what my actual reaction would be when I came out of the bathroom, how convincing I would seem, and I didn't want to say or do anything that could give me away. Some acting ability would have helped. I'd only acted one time in my life, in a play in high school. It was a Shakespeare play, I think *The Merchant of Venice*. I played a messenger. I only had one line, but when I came out on stage I was so nervous, thinking about all the people staring at me, that I messed it up. I felt the same way now. I felt like everyone in the office was staring at me, waiting for me to mess up my line. Just like in high school, I swore that after this was over I'd never put myself in this situation again.

I booted up on my computer and tried to get involved in my work. I just sat there, staring at the screen. Mike came into my office again. He looked a little more worried than before, a little more serious.

"I think I'm going to try Ed at home," he said.

"Good idea," I said. "Let me know if you find out anything."

I hoped I was acting worried enough. On the other hand, I didn't want to act *too* worried or that might give me away too. I had to deliver my lines carefully.

Mike returned.

"No answer. It's really weird, isn't it?"

"Let's not get carried away," I said. "Ed lives on Long Island, right? The Long Island Railroad has delays all the time. I bet that's what happened."

"You think so?"

"I'm sure. Anyway, there's nothing we can do about it."

"I guess you're right. I just think it's really weird though, Ed O'Brien late for work. I never thought I'd see the day."

Mike left. I was proud of my performance. I'd mixed the right amount of concern with the right amount of nonchalance. Now if I could only keep it up.

During the ten o'clock break, a few people went into the bathroom. Again, the body wasn't discovered. I started getting paranoid, thinking maybe something happened to it. Maybe the police found it and moved it, hoping it would make me crack up, confess. Or maybe Ed wasn't dead. Maybe I only knocked him out and then he woke up and now he was playing a sick game with me, getting his revenge.

I had to go to the bathroom anyway so I decided to check. While I was using the urinal, I looked back over my shoulder at the reflection of the stalls in the mirror above the sinks. I couldn't see the bottom of the stall I'd put Ed in, but the door was slightly open just like I'd left it. After I washed my hands, I casually kneeled down to tie my shoes and glanced under the stall. I saw Ed's rolled down pants and underwear hanging off his legs. I tasted the stomach acid in my throat and I left the bathroom before my nausea got any worse.

The morning dragged on. People went to the bathroom, came back, discovering nothing. After the eleven o'clock break, Mike came back into my office.

"Still no word, huh?"

"You?" I said.

"Not a thing. You really think he's stuck on a train?"

"What else could it be?"

"Who knows? Car trouble? He drives to the train

station in Long Island, doesn't he?"

"It could be a lot of things, I guess."

"But why wouldn't he call?"

"Got me. Maybe he can't get to a phone."

"Are you sure he didn't have some sort of appointment or something today?"

"He didn't tell me anything," I said. "Maybe Nelson knows. Want to ask him?"

"Sure. Why not?"

I went with Mike to Nelson's office. He had someone in with him, so he didn't talk long with us. He said he hadn't heard from Ed, but to let him know when Ed arrived, that he wanted to speak to him about something important. I hoped the important thing he wanted to speak to him about wasn't me. If Ed had told Nelson that he was planning to fire me then...well, I didn't want to think about that.

"I guess there's nothing we can do but wait," Mike said to me in the hallway. "I'm sure he'll show up eventually."

"I agree," I said. "Let's just forget about it."

That's when the screaming started. It was a male voice first and then there were other voices and soon the whole Telemarketing Department was in chaos. Marie Stipaldi came running down the hallway.

"Get an ambulance! Call the police! Quick!"

"What?!" I screamed back, convincingly alarmed.

"It's Ed," she said. "He's in the men's bathroom. They say he's dead! He's dead!"

Mike and I ran toward the Telemarketing Department. There was a crowd in the hallway leading to the bathroom. People were screaming and crying. Mike and I pushed our way through. The stall door was in the same partially closed position.

"Where is he?!" I yelled.

"In the stall," a guy behind me said. "The first one over there."

Mike went to the stall door. When he looked inside he lost his balance and stumbled backwards. He started shaking. A few seconds later he was crying. I went to open the door to see for myself. I knew my reaction was important. If I didn't seem genuinely shocked and disturbed, someone could remember it later and tell the police. As it turned out, I reacted perfectly. After I swung open the door and saw Ed's body with his eyes staring right at me, I felt the urge to vomit again. This time I didn't hold back. I let it go, uncontrollably. Mike came over and put an arm around me, then someone helped both of us out of the bathroom.

The next hour or so was very frantic and confusing. Everyone was shouting at once, giving different theories about who could have killed Ed. Most people were saying that Greg had done it. It had occurred to me that Greg would be the most likely suspect, if he didn't have an alibi for the time of the murder. After all, everyone had seen Greg attack Ed in his office, and it figured that he might have been mad enough at Ed for pressing charges that he came back and finished the job. What I hadn't known was that Greg had been at the office yesterday afternoon. Eileen told the whole story. Greg had come to the office, wanting to see Ed. Eileen told him that Ed was away in a meeting and Greg made a scene, yelling and threatening her, demanding his commission money, and promising to come back again. It was enough to convince the crowd. I honestly believe that if Greg had been in the office, everyone would have torn him to pieces.

At some point, the police arrived. I don't know

exactly how many officers were there, but there were probably about ten or twelve. I recognized two of the officers who had come when Greg had attacked Ed. There were paramedics too. The police sealed off the entire telemarketing area and instructed everyone to remain on the other side of the office. There was an officer near the elevator and another near the stairwell, I guess making sure that no one left the office. People were still extremely upset. I remember seeing Nelson, red-faced, tears streaming down his face, as a few people tried to console him. I thought it might look strange if I didn't say anything so I went over and rested a hand on his shoulder.

"Bill, who could have done this?" he said. "Why? Why did they do it?"

I don't remember what I said, if I said anything at all. I was still wondering whether Nelson would suspect me or not. So far he didn't, but he might have been too upset to think about it clearly.

A gray-haired detective in a suit and tie announced that he and his staff were going to speak with people individually. He also said that if anyone felt they needed medical attention for trauma, they should go with him.

The people who were crying the most, including Nelson, went with the detective.

More police and medical personnel arrived, including a man I assumed was a medical examiner. I knew they were going to try to figure out what time Ed died by testing his body temperature or however they did it. About an hour went by when a police officer came from the Telemarketing Department and asked if there was a Bill Moss here. My heart skipped a few beats, although I wasn't nearly as worried as I might have been earlier. Now that Ed's body had been discovered and the police had arrived, I was confident that everything would turn out all right.

"I'm Bill Moss," I said.

"I understand you installed the computer network here," the officer said. "Is that correct?"

"I didn't install it personally," I said, "but yes, I coordinated the project for the computers in the Telemarketing Department."

"If you'd come with me for a few moments I'd appreciate it."

Following the officer, I asked him what was going on.

"Detective Figula wants us to check all the employee files," he said, "to see what time people left here last night."

"Is that important?" I asked. "I mean doesn't he have the time cards?"

"If Detective Figula wants it done it's important."

"But people were using their computers today," I said. "The times from last night might be erased."

"We understand that, but Detective Figula wants the information anyway."

I had a list of everyone's password in my office. The officer and I went through all the available files and made an approximate timetable of when people had exited their computers last night. According to our information, Mike was the last one to leave at 5:16. I'd left a file I'd been working on earlier yesterday afternoon in the computer system so my log-out time was 4:42.

The officer told me to wait in my office while he brought the information to Detective Figula. Through the glass window, I watched two detectives searching Ed's office. They were both wearing long rubber gloves and looked like they were collecting fingerprints and searching for other evidence. It was amusing, watching them work so hard, knowing they wouldn't find anything. In the hallway, a couple of young police officers were talking to each other, laughing. It was obvious that they had no idea I had anything to do with the murder. The computer files were the only way I could have been caught. Now I was home free.

The gray-haired detective who had addressed everyone before came into my office.

"Detective Sal Figula," he said, shaking my hand. "You must be Bob Moss."

"Bill," I said.

"Sorry," he said, smiling without looking at me. "It's been a long day. Mind if I sit down?"

I told him to make himself comfortable. He was short, probably no taller than five-six, but sitting down he looked taller. His chest and back were wide, as if he worked out, and he had a very large head. His sideburns went below his ears. After he unbuttoned the bottom button on his jacket, he started flipping pages in a note pad. Attached to the clipboard on his lap I noticed the list of times the officer and I had compiled.

"I know everyone's very upset around here today and for good reason," he said, "but I hope you understand why we have to go through all of this."

"Do you know how he died yet?" I asked.

"Strangulation," he said.

I grimaced, feeling nauseous again. My reaction must have seemed very convincing.

"He was also beaten badly in the face," the detective said. "We don't know if this had anything to do with his death."

"I get the picture," I said, looking at my lap.

"Do you have any idea who could have done this to him?" the detective asked.

"No," I said. "I mean I don't know who did it to him."

"I didn't ask you if you *knew*, I asked you if you had any idea."

"I guess everyone in the office has the same hunch."

"Greg Brown?"

I nodded.

"I hope it wasn't Greg," I said. "I mean I always liked him a lot and I never thought he was a really bad guy. But I guess sometimes you don't really know people."

Detective Figula flipped to another page on the clipboard.

"I have the report here from the incident that occurred on July twenty-seventh. It says that you came to Ed O'Brien's defense when Mr. Brown attacked him."

"That's right," I said.

"Do you recall what the fight was about?"

"Well, I don't know exactly, but I think Ed was going to fire him. They were doing some restructuring at the company and Ed had to let some people go. When he broke the news to Greg, I guess Greg flipped."

"I was told that as he was leaving he threatened to come back and kill Mr. O'Brien."

"He was very angry," I said. "And he never liked Ed very much anyway."

"Tell me more about this," the detective said. "Did Mr. Brown say things to you about Mr. O'Brien?"

I paused, like I needed to think about it.

"Let's put it this way," I finally said. "Greg is black and Ed is white and they both weren't exactly the most racially tolerant people in the world. Greg made some comments about white people sometimes, Ed included, but I never really thought Greg *meant* any of it. I just thought he was joking around."

Detective Figula had a sarcastic expression, as if he'd already made up his mind that Greg was the killer and there was nothing I could do to change it.

"I spoke to Ms. Marie Stipaldi a few minutes ago," he said. "She told me that a couple of days before Mr. Brown attacked Mr. O'Brien, she, Mr. Brown, and yourself had a conversation and that Mr. Brown said, and I quote, that 'if Ed was in a fire, I'd let his ass burn.' Do you recall this?"

I looked at my lap again.

"This is really difficult for me, detective," I said. "I mean Greg and I weren't friends or anything and I don't want to make things worse for him than they already are, but it's true – he did say that. At the time I didn't take him seriously, and I don't think Marie did either. Oh, God. I wonder if I could have done something to stop him."

"Don't be ridiculous," the detective said. "You did everything you could do to help your boss."

I nodded. Detective Figula started looking at the list of log-out times on his clipboard.

"This list isn't complete, I take it."

"It's as complete as possible," I said. "If someone logged on to a file they were working on today and saved over it, the new time would be saved over it. But if you're trying to figure out when people left the office last night, I don't think that'll be very accurate. Someone could have logged out at five o'clock and stayed at the office much longer."

"I understand that," the detective said. "But unfortunately there are no security cameras in this building so we can't play back a videotape and watch people enter and leave the building."

"That *is* unfortunate," I said.

"For the record, when did you leave work last night?

"Last night?" I said, thinking. "About five o'clock. No, closer to five-thirty because I didn't get home till around six-thirty."

"And you stayed home all night?"

"Yes," I said, "actually we did – my fiancée and I. We ate dinner at home."

"Well, I think I've gotten all the information from you that I need," Detective Figula said. He stood up, putting the clipboard under his arm. "Because of the investigation we're asking everyone to take the rest of the day off today. Is that a problem for you?"

"No," I said. "I understand."

"Also, we're asking everyone to give Officer Donnels, the blond gentleman outside, their phone number and address before they leave, just in case there's anything else that comes up. In any event, tomorrow you can come back to work as usual. That is as usual as work can be under the circumstances."

When Detective Figula was gone, the ambulance workers passed my office, carrying Ed's body on a stretcher. It was covered with a white sheet, but I remembered what his body looked like, how it had felt when I'd carried it into the bathroom.

I gave the officer my home address and phone number then headed down the hallway toward the elevators. There seemed to be more police officers than before and now the reception area was also filled with television and radio news crews. As I waited for the elevator, several reporters asked me questions at once and a cop tried to keep them away from me. I couldn't hear all of the questions, but most of the reporters wanted to know what my name was and whether I knew anything about the murder. A few feet away a reporter who I recognized from the Channel Four News was doing a live broadcast. Behind the camera, men were pointing bright spotlights at the reporter.

I heard the reporter saying, "...and the police have a suspect in the case. He's a former employee at the company who attacked the victim once before. Apparently this suspect, Gregory Brown, tried to get into the office yesterday afternoon to see Mr. O'Brien and left acting irritated and disturbed. Police aren't releasing any more details in the case as of this moment, but they are saying the motive for the killing could have been racial. Gregory Brown is black and the victim, Edward O'Brien, was white."

The elevator doors opened. I got on.

# 12

I WATCHED THE story unfold on television. The media was billing the murder as the latest racial murder in New York, and the police and other city officials feared that the incident might lead to city-wide race riots.

A few weeks earlier, some white kids on Staten Island had beaten to death a black kid who was riding through their neighborhood on a dirt bike. I hadn't paid much attention to the story, but I knew that black leaders had held demonstrations in front of City Hall, and I remembered Greg once saying something about it, that he thought the white kids were going to get off because black people never get any justice in this country, or something like that. He must have said the same thing to other people and someone must have told the police about it because the media was making it out like Greg had killed Ed as revenge for the Staten Island murder. Now whites in Staten Island and in Ed's town in Hicksville, Long Island, were protesting, demanding justice. Meanwhile, extremist black leaders were defending Greg's actions, including one man representing the Nation of Islam who said that "Greg had revenged white America's latest act in the attempted genocide of the black race." He called Greg a "hero" and asked that all Americans, black and white, pray for his soul.

There had already been one retaliation for the murder – an old black man was attacked and beaten by two white teenagers on a subway in Sheepshead Bay less than an hour after Ed's murder was first reported. The Mayor came on the television afterwards and gave a long speech, warning people to stay calm and not to take justice into their own hands. Although the Mayor spoke in a slow, calm voice, I could tell that he was extremely nervous. The weathermen were predicting another heat wave and the police feared that the hot weather would shorten people's tempers, make them even more likely to riot. The Police Commissioner had ordered the police to work overtime all over the city, and some people were planning to leave town for a week, hoping things settled down.

Greg was arrested at about five o'clock. According to the reports, the police had found a witness, someone who worked in another office in the building, who had seen Greg getting out of the elevator at the A.C.A. office at about six o'clock last night. The police had been unable to determine an exact time of death, but were speculating that Ed was killed some time between six and six-thirty. They were about a half hour off, I realized, because I had actually killed Ed at about seven. I wondered if Greg had actually been seen by the witness or whether the person had made a mistake. It didn't make any sense that the police would make an arrest if they didn't have any real evidence to go on. The police may have been under pressure to arrest someone, anyone, for the murder, or they may have taken Greg into custody because they feared for his safety.

I watched Greg being taken into the precinct. He was bending over, covering his face so he couldn't be recognized. In a way, I felt like I had murdered him too.

At first it frightened me how much publicity the murder was getting. I supposed that if the police had thought that a white man had committed the crime instead of a black man, the case might have gotten a small mention in the local newscasts, if it was mentioned at all. Instead, the case was being treated as if it was the biggest news story of the year. Afraid to consider the negative consequences, I convinced myself that maybe all the attention was a *good* thing. The police and media seemed so convinced that the murder was racially motivated that Ms. Daniels, the Personnel Director at Smythe & O'Greeley, probably wouldn't come forward to report her conversation with Ed. Also, if the janitor had seen me, he might not mention it to the police because he'd think that it was an inconsequential detail.

On the six o'clock news, more details of the case were revealed. The most shocking information as far as I was concerned was that the witness who claimed she had seen Greg exit the elevator had picked him out of a police line-up. I wondered whether the woman had been coerced into picking out Greg or whether she honestly believed that Greg had been the person she saw. Was it possible that Greg had actually been at the office at six last night? Eileen claimed that he had been at the office earlier and that he said he planned to come to the office again, so maybe it *was* him who had gotten off the elevator. Since Eileen goes home at five o'clock and the office doors are locked, then Greg would have had to ring the bell for someone to let him in. Then I remembered that there *had* been someone ringing the doorbell yesterday evening at about six-fifteen. I'd assumed it was a delivery person and I hadn't felt like getting up to answer it, but it could very well have been Greg. If it was Greg, I knew that the police would be able to put together a very convincing case against him.

The newscast gave more information on the case. The police had already concluded that the bruises on Ed's face and a broken finger on his left hand were injuries suffered after he was dead, and they were investigating the possibility that Greg had beaten Ed after the murder to make it look like there had been an attempted robbery. This explained why Ed's wallet was missing, since the police believed that Greg had stolen the wallet to make his story seem more legitimate. The wallet hadn't been recovered yet. The police also believed that Ed wasn't killed in the bathroom, but somewhere else, perhaps in his own office. Although there was nothing disturbed in his office to indicate that a struggle might have taken place there, police were investigating the possibility that Greg had cleaned up afterwards. Special police teams were searching the entire A.C.A. office for hair and blood samples.

"I'm so glad you weren't there last night," Julie said to me when the report was over. She was sitting next to me on the couch, hugging me close. "That crazy son of a bitch might have tried to kill you too."

"Why would he kill me?" I said. "He had nothing against me."

"But to strangle somebody like that. He must've been out of his mind."

I wanted to say something in Greg's defense, but I didn't want to make it sound like I was on his side. So I said:

"I just can't believe any of this happened. It feels so surreal now, watching it all on T.V."

Julie leaned her head on my shoulder. It felt good, having her so close to me. Her body was warm and soft.

"Are you going to the funeral?" she asked.

I shrugged. "If people from work are invited. Sure."

"I'm so sorry you have to go through this. It must be so hard for you. Maybe you should take some time off from work, try to forget about it."

"You kidding? I've only been working at my job a

couple of weeks and things are just getting rolling. Besides, with Ed gone, there's going to be twice as much work for me to do."

"Are you going to be in charge of the department now?"

"To be honest, I haven't even thought about it. I just know that things won't be the same around the office, that's for sure."

I was quiet for a while. Julie probably thought I was feeling sad, mourning Ed's death, but I was really imagining how great things were going to be without him. The truth was I'd been thinking all day about being promoted. Nelson had told me himself that he thought I was doing a great job and that I had better ideas than Ed. It made sense that he would promote me, rather than go outside the company to bring a new person in. Everything was going to turn out like I'd hoped it would turn out before the murder, except that things were going to happen ahead of schedule. After six months of running the department, I could start interviewing for ad jobs again, and by next year I'd be back at a high-level marketing job. And this time I'd be careful. I wouldn't say or do anything that could possibly lead to any misunderstandings, and before long I'd be living my dream life again.

It must have been about five minutes later – although I'd been so deep in my fantasy that I'd lost track of the exact time – when Julie said, "Come on, let's get up and go somewhere. Lying around here feeling sorry for Ed isn't going to make you feel any better about things."

"Where do you want to go?"

"How about a movie? We haven't seen a movie in a long time."

"I don't know," I said. "I've had such a hard day."

"Come on, it'll do you good. You have to escape from all of this craziness."

Not wanting to disappoint her, I agreed to go. We went to the multiplex on Eighty-sixth Street. I found the movie, a love story, boring, so I daydreamed, thinking mostly about the future and how great everything was going to turn out. I imagined myself working on a big account for a top agency and travelling around the world with a staff and a big expense budget. Julie seemed to like the movie. She was crying a lot, especially when the couple got back together in the end.

When we got home I was so tired I fell right asleep. In the morning, I woke up worrying. I remembered that the news had said that the police were searching for hair and blood samples and I feared they'd find something they could trace back to me. It wasn't my office I was worried about. I knew that the janitor had vacuumed there the night of the murder and even if the police found a piece of hair there, I didn't see how that in itself could be used as evidence against me. But I was worried about the bathroom. What if I'd left a hair sample on Ed's body? In the shower, these fears intensified when I noticed a clump of my hair in the drain. My hair was falling out constantly and it seemed likely that a single piece of hair could have fallen out when I'd lifted Ed onto the toilet.

On the way to work, I passed a newsstand. All the local papers had front page headlines about the case. One of them read, "RACE WAR"; another, "RACE RIOT"; another, "RIOT". I bought a copy of one of the papers. An article gave a biography of Greg. It told about his mother who died when he was a baby and how his father had raised him and his sister. There was a picture of Greg to the right of the story that looked like it was taken in high school. It was a dark, grainy photo that made Greg look much angrier and unkempt than he really was.

I skimmed the other articles. Another witness had come forward who claimed he had seen Greg getting off the elevator on the seventh floor around six o'clock. Also, the police had found a pair of leather gloves in Greg's apartment that they thought he may have worn at the murder scene. Members of Ed's family were furious with the judge who had released Greg after he'd assaulted Ed. Black groups were planning more marches and demonstrations at different sites around the city. Black parents and white parents were afraid to send their children to school, and some parents were thinking about sending their children to private schools. And there was a small article where Greg's court-appointed lawyer claimed that his client was innocent and that Greg was willing to take a lie detector test.

I arrived at work at the usual time, about eight-fifteen. There was a note on my desk from Nelson that he wanted to see me as soon as I came in. When I got there, he was sitting still, staring vacantly at the papers on his desk.

"Oh, Bill, good, I'm glad you're here. Please, take a seat, sit down, sit down."

I sat across from him, crossing my legs.

"How are you?" I said. "Holding up all right?"

"The best I can under the circumstances," he said. "I was going to play hooky today, but I knew Ed wouldn't want us to sit around here feeling sorry for him. You know Ed and his works ethics. He'd have to die to miss a day of work."

I laughed, holding back a little, the way people do

when they don't want to disrespect the dead.

"How about you?" Nelson asked. "Are you okay?"

"Guess so," I said. "Still a little shocked by the whole thing. I keep forgetting that Ed's gone, that I'm never going to see him again, then when the truth hits me it feels like I'm hearing it for the first time. It seems so unbelievable to me."

Nelson was nodding his head.

"I know what you mean, I know exactly what you mean. But at least the police caught the son of a bitch and he'll never kill anybody again. Did you hear the latest?"

"The latest?"

"The police found Ed's wallet."

"No kidding?"

"I heard about it on the radio this morning. They found it all the way on the East Side. Greg was trying to make it look like a robbery attempt and he went really out of his way to do it. Either that or they think someone found the wallet and dumped it on the East Side. It's crazy, isn't it?"

"Crazy?"

"That he thought he'd get away with something like that. I mean to expect that the police would actually think that Ed was killed during a robbery attempt while he was going to the bathroom! It's just ludicrous."

"Yeah," I said. "I see what you mean."

"But I guess it just shows his state of mind at the time. But I'll tell you one thing, he can forget about an insanity defense. I'm no lawyer, but the way he planned this thing, trying to cover his tracks, I think it shows that he was clearly aware of what he was doing."

I nodded silently, thinking about a lot of things at once.

"Anyway, the reason I wanted to speak to you," Nelson said, "is now that Ed's gone we're going to need someone to run the Telemarketing Department and personally I think you're the best man for the job. Do you think you're up for it?"

"I'd be honored," I said.

"Good. We'll discuss the specifics tomorrow or the next day when things start to settle down. But today just try to run things the best you can. We'll talk about your new salary tomorrow too."

"I don't know what to say," I said. "It's hard to get happy on such a sad day."

"You're a good man," Nelson said. "You deserve it." As I was getting up, he said, "By the way, did you know this Greg Brown at all?"

"I worked with him," I said, "but we weren't friends or anything like that."

"You know how I'm not really in touch with what goes on in the Telemarketing Department. I was wondering, before that incident when he went after Ed, did he ever give you any indication that he was, well, unstable?"

"Like I told the police yesterday, he made comments from time to time, but I never took any of it very seriously. I feel awful about it now, but I always thought he was just joking."

"When you say comments, you mean racial comments?"

"Sometimes."

Nelson suddenly looked angrier. His face was pinker.

"You know me, Bill, I'm an equal opportunity employer. I don't have any black friends to speak of, but in or out of the office I certainly don't consider myself to be a racist. But putting all that aside, if he really did this,

I hope to God that there's a hell, so Greg Brown can burn in it."

I nodded in agreement, then went back to my office. I wished I could enjoy my promotion, but I was still thinking about what Nelson had said about the police finding the wallet. It was stupid of me to have dumped the wallet so close to my apartment. If the police ever had any reason to suspect me for the murder, they'd also realize why the wallet was found on the Upper East Side. I wished I'd dumped it in an out-of-the-way neighborhood or in another borough. But, I remembered, I hadn't had time to do that. To make my alibi stand up I needed to get home as fast as possible and dumping the wallet where I dumped it may have been my best and only option.

By nine o'clock, most of the telemarketers who worked the morning shift had arrived at the office. The atmosphere was glum, subdued, and it surprised me how hard some people were taking Ed's death. I mean I could understand how it could be traumatic to find out that your boss has been murdered, but he wasn't exactly the most lovable guy in the world. A few people were crying and hugging and I went out of my way to thank everyone for coming in today. I'd been playing the role of griever for so long and I was getting so good at it that I was starting to believe in my grief myself. To me, the wetness in my eyes and the sincerity in my voice wasn't fake, it was real, which made my performance all the more convincing.

Near the time clock I said hello to Mike. His eyes were red, as if he'd been crying.

"I don't know if I can handle being here today," he said.

"If you can't, go home," I said. "I'll understand."

"You?" He looked puzzled. "You mean –"

"Nelson told me this morning. I'm going to be running the department from now on."

Although he tried to hide it, Mike's jealousy was obvious. For the first time since I'd left Smythe & O'Greeley, I experienced how it felt to be in power, to control, and I remembered how much I liked it.

"Well, I guess I should congratulate you," Mike said. "This was a lucky break for you, huh?"

"Fate," I said. "Luck had nothing to do with it."

I conducted the morning meeting. With an appropriately grim expression, I announced that I was taking over Ed's position, but not to worry, I wasn't planning any dramatic overhauls of the department. After a couple of weeks, I said, when things started to return to normal, I'd outline some changes I wanted to make. Until then, everything would be run the same as usual, or as usual as could be under the circumstances. I concluded that in light of yesterday's tragedy, I didn't expect people to make an incredible amount of appointments today, and that anyone who felt like it could go home early.

Afterwards, although no one was smiling, I could tell that everyone was happy I was going to be running the department. I was a well-liked guy – a lot better liked than Ed ever was – and I think people were glad that finally things were going to be conducted at the company in a sensible manner.

Marie Stipaldi came into my office. Since that day we had spoken with Greg in the room with the concession machines, I'd only spoken to her once. It was a day last week when we'd met to discuss her recent performance on the phones. She'd been doing well, averaging nearly fifteen appointments per week.

During the meeting, I'd noticed there was something different about Marie. Usually, I found her attractive, in an ethnic Italian kind of way. She had a thin, well-proportioned body and she always dressed well. But today her face looked paler, more drawn than usual, as if she hadn't gotten much sleep last night. When she came into my office the first thing I noticed was the darkness under her eyes.

"You have a minute?" she said.

"Sure," I said. "Come in."

I didn't know why, but I had an eerie feeling about things. She sat down and started crying.

"I'm sorry," she said. "I don't mean to cry."

"It's all right," I said. "Can I get you a tissue?"

"No, no, I have one. Just give me a sec, okay?" She took a tissue from a package of tissues she had and wiped her nose and eyes. "There, I'm better now, it's just so fucking hard."

I was getting impatient, wondering why she had come in here to talk with me. Did she just want someone to cry with or did she have some other agenda? Rather than pushing her, I decided to wait, say nothing. Eventually, she'd get to it.

She was staring at me. I wondered if she was trying to see something.

"So, Bill," she said, "what do you think?"

"Think?" I said. "Think about what?"

"Did Greg do it?"

"Got me," I said. "I hope not."

"Me too. It looks pretty bad though, huh?"

"Sure does," I said sadly.

"I just can't believe he'd actually murder someone," she said. "I mean he could talk a good game, but I thought that's all he was – all talk, no action."

"Me too," I said. "But I guess you just never know with some people."

She stared at me again, the same way as before.

"You Catholic?" she asked.

Caught off-guard, I laughed.

"Why do you ask?"

"No reason," she said. "Just curious."

"For the time being," I said. "But I'm planning to convert to Judaism. I'm getting married."

She didn't seem to be listening to me.

"You know, I keep hoping the police will find some other suspect," she said. "But the way they're talking about it on the news it sounds like they're sure Greg did it."

"I heard he wants to take a lie detector test."

"Yeah?" she said curiously. "I don't know about you, but I'm positive, deep down in my heart, that Greg didn't do it. And I feel awful about the things I told the police. They wanted to know whether Greg ever said anything bad to me about Ed and I had no choice but to tell them what he said to us that day when we were by the soda machines. You remember, about Ed burning in a fire?"

"I know how you feel," I said. "I had to tell them the same thing."

"I tried to tell the detective that I thought he was just joking, but I don't think he believed me. I think they want to believe Greg did it."

For a few more seconds, Marie just sat there, staring at me. I was getting uncomfortable so I told her that we really ought to get to work now. I watched her go to her cubicle, waiting to see if she'd look back at me. She didn't, but this didn't make me feel any better. I was still afraid that she suspected me of the murder. Why else had she come to speak to me? If she just wanted to share her grief with me, she could have approached me in the conference room, after the meeting. But instead she waited until she could see me alone. Maybe she was hoping I'd slip up, give some indication of my guilt. Why else did she stare at me that way and ask me whether or not I was Catholic?

I had to keep an eye on her, I thought. Just in case.

Surprisingly, I didn't think about the murder much the rest of the day. I got involved in my work and thinking about what changes I would make in the department. My goal was to double sales at the company in six months. If I could do that, it would give me something to brag about when I started interviewing again for jobs in advertising. I imagined the first agency I interviewed at falling in love with me, asking me whether I could start immediately. Of course I wouldn't accept the first job that was offered to me. I'd go on other interviews and soon a bidding war would develop over me. Finally, I'd accept a job for six figures a year and then Julie and I could move out of our dump studio apartment into a doorman duplex with two bedrooms and two baths. On weekends, I imagined myself sitting in my health club by the pool, a cellular phone next to me. It would ring and I'd answer it, tell whoever was calling that I was busy right now, could they please call back later.

Passing Ed's office, I paused, imagining how I'd decorate it. The paint on the walls was peeling so I'd have to order a paint job, and I had to buy some room freshener to get rid of the nauseating odor of Ed's cologne. I remembered how less than a month ago I had been seated across from Ed in this very same office, listening to him pompously explain how he had no choice but to back up Mike's decision to send me home early. I'd thought that would be the last day I'd set foot in this office, and I realized how strange it was how well everything had worked out for me. It was almost as if I'd written the script of my life myself, planned out in advance exactly how I wanted things to happen.

The only down part of the day was when Nelson stopped by my office late in the afternoon and told me that Greg had failed the lie detector test.

"So I guess that settles it," he said. "And I'll tell you one thing, there are going to be some hot coals waiting for that young man, if you know what I'm saying."

Although I was happy that the police weren't trying to search for any new leads, I was upset that Greg was still being blamed for the murder. That was the only part of the script I would change, I decided. Instead of Greg, the police would have arrested Mike or Nelson or *anyone* else. Like I've said, of all the people I'd worked with at A.C.A., Greg was the only person I ever considered a friend. I imagined Greg sitting in his prison cell on Riker's Island, scared and confused, without any idea of how he'd wound up there. I wished there was a way I could help him, but my feelings of guilt weren't strong enough that I was about to go to the police and turn myself in. If Greg spending the rest of his life in jail was the price I had to pay for my success, then so be it.

I left the office at about five-thirty. There had been a thunderstorm earlier in the afternoon, but now the sun was shining brightly. It was still very hot, but it felt more comfortable than before because the humidity had dropped considerably. I crossed Eighth Avenue at Forty-fourth Street and walked east. There were several theaters on this block and I was looking up at a marquis when I felt someone grab me from behind. My first instinct was that I was being mugged and I was prepared to give the person or persons whatever they wanted. I may have even said, "Take my wallet," although I already had a hunch that it wasn't my money they were after. I was forced into a black van where a man with a mustache and slicked back hair was smiling at me. A voice behind me said, "Go," and the van angled off the curb and drove away. I knew my script was about to take a turn for the worse.

# 13

THE MAN WITH the mustache had a gun. He had it in his left hand, out on his lap for me to see. The guy behind me, the one who'd grabbed me on the street, was putting handcuffs around my wrists. His hands were hot and sweaty. The whole van smelled like marijuana. It was very dark too. Black curtains covered the windows and the only light came from the small orange bulb on the ceiling.

"What you want me to do, Johnny?" the guy behind me said with a Puerto Rican accent. "You want me to fuck him up?"

Johnny, the man with the mustache, said something in Spanish, then he said, "We'll see what my man has to say for himself first," and then he said something else in Spanish. By his tone, I knew he wasn't complimenting me.

He pressed the gun against my cheek. I tried to move away, but the other guy behind was holding my shoulders now. Up front the driver was laughing. I heard someone else laughing behind me so there were at least four people in the van.

"You know why you're here, my man, so I don't gotta waste no time explaining it to you," Johnny said.

"I think you're making a mistake," I said. "I'm not who you think I am."

Everybody in the van laughed. It seemed like the laughing went on for a minute, but it was probably only for a few seconds. Things were very distorted, like in a dream.

"You a funny guy, my man," Johnny said, suddenly serious. "But I think you should know that me and my friends, we don't make no mistakes. You the one made the mistake. That's why you here."

I thought about the murder, wondering if this was somehow related to it. Could these guys be cops? But why would undercover cops grab me off the street and take me away in a van? It didn't make sense.

"Who are you?" I said. "What do you want from me?"

Again they laughed, talking in Spanish. Johnny said, "I got a bad feeling about you, my man. I usually don't get like that. Ask anybody. I'm usually everybody's best friend." He said something in Spanish, then he said, "People come to me when they need help and I always help 'em out. Ain't that right, Carlos?"

"Word," the guy holding my arms said.

"But you, I don't like you from the minute I seen you," Johnny said. "You got this look like you think you're better than everybody else, but meanwhile you're just a piece of shit. I see shit like you every day on the streets. You act like you king of the world and shit, 'cause you got money and suits and ties and all that shit. But I can see through all that bullshit. I'm like the Puerto Rican Superman, but right now I'm dressed up like fuckin' Clark Kent. I may not look so bad, but what you see ain't what you get."

The van made a sharp right turn, pulling me to the left, pushing the gun harder against my cheek. The curtains on the window moved for a second, letting more light into the van, but I couldn't see where we were going. It got dark again quickly.

"I still don't know what you want from me, man," I said, trying to talk like I was street-wise. "But whatever it is, you can have it. I won't fight with you for it. You want my wallet? If you want it, it's in my right front pocket. You can have it if you want it."

"I don't want your fuckin' wallet," Johnny said. "I show you what I want."

He swung his hand with the gun into my face like a backhand stroke in tennis. The butt of the gun hit my nose and I felt like I couldn't breathe. Then the pain came. I screamed, begging him to stop.

"What's that?" he said. "You want some more?"

He hit me again, harder than the first time if that was possible. I felt the blood pouring over my lips like water from a faucet. I tried to scream again, but the pain was too severe.

"You hit my girl, you hit me, understand, my man? We the same person. Different body, same person."

"I think he said he wants you to hit him again," the voice in the back said.

The driver laughed.

"That what you want?" Johnny said to me. "You want the rest of your nose broke?"

"I didn't do it," I gasped. "You have the wrong guy."

"See, now that's what I hate," Johnny said. "If you just a rich, white, suit-and-tie, king-of-the-world motherfucker, I can deal with that shit. But I hate liars. We all hate liars, right?"

Everyone spoke at once in Spanish.

Then Johnny said, "Carlos, show my man how much I hate liars."

The guy who put me in the handcuffs pulled back the pinky on my right hand until it snapped. They put something in my mouth to keep me from screaming.

"I got a feeling my man still don't understand," Johnny said. "Show him again."

The guy behind me broke my ring finger, then my middle finger, then my index finger. Every time a finger broke they laughed harder.

Johnny said, "Save him his thumb, so he can hitch his faggot-ass a ride home. But understand, my man, and understand me good, you ever touch one of my girls again, I'll find you again, and next time I won't be so nice. I'll break your thumb, and I'll break all your other fingers. Then I'll break your hands and your arms and your legs and your feet and every bone in your goddamn stupid-ass body. Now get the fuck out my van!"

They took off my handcuffs and pushed me out the door. I landed on my back on top of something hard. The van sped away. I stayed on the ground a long time, my face in something mushy and fishy. I was in too much pain to move. I squeezed my eyes closed hoping this was all a bad dream. Finally, I rolled on to my side and saw I was in some abandoned lot. There was garbage everywhere. I pulled the old rag out of my mouth and coughed, trying to catch my breath. I couldn't decide which hurt more, my nose or my hand. I tried not to think about either.

I started walking. I felt disoriented and dizzy, my mouth tasted like shoe polish. Although I didn't know exactly where I was, I guessed I was on the West Side, near the Hudson River. There weren't many other abandoned areas in midtown and I knew we hadn't travelled in the van very far.

I walked straight ahead to Eleventh Avenue. The cross street was Forty-sixth. I was proud of myself for figuring out where I was, but I wasn't about to start celebrating. My pains were getting worse by the second and I knew that this time I couldn't be stubborn – I had to get to an emergency room.

I was happy to discover that I still had my wallet and

all my money was still inside it. I tried desperately, but I couldn't get a cab to stop for me. At first I was baffled, then I realized how awful I must look with my face all covered with blood and dirt. I waved a fifty-dollar bill at a cab that had stopped at a traffic light. I had to bang on the back door before he let me inside.

"New York Hospital," I said. "Fast."

The ride crosstown seemed endless. When we finally got there, a half hour later, I dropped the fifty onto the driver's side of the car, not bothering to wait for change. At the emergency room reception desk, a nurse tried to calm me down, kept telling me that everything was going to be all right. I screamed at her, demanding to see a doctor. The nurse explained that since my injuries weren't life threatening I had to wait my turn like everyone else. She also said that since my left hand wasn't injured and because I was left-handed, I had to fill out some admission and insurance forms before the doctor could see me.

I started filling out the forms, but I couldn't concentrate. I begged the nurse to let a doctor see me. It must have worked because a doctor came a couple of minutes later. I followed him into a small office where he told me to sit on the examination table.

"Jesus," he said. "How did this happen?"

"A car door closed on it," I said.

He looked at me like he thought I was lying.

"And your nose?"

"That happened afterwards. I was running down the street, trying to get a cab, and I fell face first on the street. Isn't there something you can do? The pain is killing me."

He injected an anesthetic into my hand and gave me a cold pack to hold on my nose. Then he told me to

JASON STARR

follow him into an x-ray room at the end of the corridor. I had to wait about ten minutes, then a pretty, red-haired woman arrived and x-rayed my nose and hand. While we were waiting for the results, I went to a phone booth and called Julie. She'd been expecting me to be home from work by six-thirty and it was already past eight.

"Where are you?" she asked anxiously.

I retold the story about the car door closing on my hand and falling on the sidewalk. To make it more convincing, I added more details. An old woman had asked me to help her put some bags into her car. After I put the last bag inside, the little boy who was with her had slammed the car door on my fingers. Then I slipped on some wet newspaper and fell on my face.

"Poor thing," Julie said. "You must be so scared."

I tried to talk her out of it, but she insisted on coming to the hospital to meet me.

The x-ray technician returned and said that my nose was only badly bruised, but that my four fingers had been fractured near the bottom knuckles and that my entire right hand would need to be set in a cast. She wrapped my hand in a bandage and told me to wait in the waiting room until another doctor could see me.

A little while later, Julie arrived. She made me explain what had happened again. I told the same story I'd told her over the phone, but somehow in person she didn't seem quite so convinced by it. I would have told her the truth, but that would have meant telling her about the prostitute and I didn't want to get into that.

"Wet newspaper?" she said.

"Crazy, huh?" I said. "It rained before and there was some soaking newspaper on the sidewalk. It was in front of an abandoned building otherwise I'd think about a law suit."

"But the newspaper was on the street," she said. "Isn't that what you told me over the phone?"

"It was on the street and the sidewalk, like on the curb I think," I said. "Anyway, I was in a lot of pain so I took a cab to the hospital."

"You did the right thing," she said, still sounding skeptical.

I told her about the x-ray results and that they would have to put my hand in a cast. I still had a feeling that something was wrong, that Julie was angry at me.

"I'm really glad you came here," I said.

"You are?" she said flatly. "You didn't sound like you wanted me here on the phone."

"I just didn't want to scare you," I said. "Besides, I was a little embarrassed about the whole thing. I mean slipping on a piece of newspaper isn't exactly like getting a war injury."

Looking angry, she crossed her arms in front of her chest.

"I thought you were lying to me."

"Lying? What do you mean? Why would I ever lie to you?"

"I don't know."

"I can't believe you'd think that. I'd never lie to you. I'm very glad you came. It was scary being in the emergency room alone. Just being here made me think about how much I missed you."

"I don't believe you."

"About what?"

"Never mind."

"Tell me."

"I can't."

"Come on, Julie. If you have something to say I want to hear it."

"Look. I don't know if this is the right time to bring this up or anything, but I found out something today, something that you did, and it's very upsetting."

My pulse quickened. All I could think about was Ed's murder.

"It's hard for me to talk about," she said. "I mean I just can't believe you'd do something like this. I just can't."

"Whatever it is, I'm sure there's some misunderstanding," I said anxiously. "Just don't jump to any conclusions, okay?"

"I'm not jumping to any conclusions," she said. "I'm positive about this. I know what I heard." She paused, collecting herself. "It happened this afternoon. I took part of the day off work to go shopping for a wedding dress. I went to a couple of places in midtown, then I wound up at this cute little boutique in the East Eighties. Anyway, I tried a couple of dresses on and I was getting ready to leave when who walks in but Claire Goldman and her husband Harold."

Julie saw my confused expression and pounced on me.

"See, I was right. You have no idea what I'm talking about, do you?"

"I'm sorry," I said. "Are they relatives of yours or something?"

"I can't believe this. Harold Goldman. Dr. Harold Goldman, Bill. Now do you remember?"

Suddenly, it hit me. He was the plastic surgeon who I was supposed to go to for the cut on my forehead.

"Is that what this is all about?" I said, relieved it had

nothing to do with the murder. "I thought it was something important."

"It *is* important. You lied to me, Bill. I don't understand how you could lie to me."

Julie was speaking loudly. A few people in the room were looking over.

"I can explain everything," I said quietly. "Just give me a chance."

"Is that how you could afford to buy me those earrings?"

"Of course not."

"I knew it was weird that they would suddenly give you an advance at work. I can't believe you'd treat me this way. And now you call me with this ridiculous story of how a car door closed on your hand and you slipped on newspaper? What's going on with you, Bill? Why are you keeping these secrets from me?"

"What are you talking about? What secrets?"

"I don't know. I just know you're up to something, you're living some kind of secret life. I guess I didn't notice it the past couple of weeks because I was so busy thinking about the wedding. But you've been acting strange for a long time now and I'm afraid something's going on, something that you're not telling me."

"Will you stop it? I'm not keeping any big secrets from you. About the plastic surgeon, I admit that was my fault. I should've gone to him, but I was such a jerk I didn't think it was necessary. But I learned my lesson. I'm here now, aren't I? And I have your three hundred dollars too. I was planning to give it to you last week and tell you I didn't keep the appointment, but I got so busy with my job."

Julie looked distracted, as if she hadn't been listening to me.

"There's something else, Bill. I found this in the top drawer of your dresser today."

From her purse, she took out the napkin on which I had written Lisa's phone number.

"Let me guess," I said. "You think I'm cheating on you, right?"

"Well?"

"Julie," I said irritably. "That's Lisa Collins. She's a Sales Representative at a software company I deal with. Ed mentioned her name to me at lunch one day and I wrote her number down on that napkin. If you don't believe me, you can call the number."

From her expression, I could tell that she hadn't called the number yet and had no intention of calling it.

"What did you expect me to think, Bill? The way you've been acting lately, with all this craziness, I just got afraid. I thought everything was going to change between us."

"I understand," I said, touching her hand. "We've both been under a lot of stress lately. Getting engaged is stressful, plus with me changing jobs and now with what happened to Ed. Any two people would be likely to get paranoid and nervous in our situation. But you don't have to worry, nothing is going to change between us."

Starting to cry, Julie said, "So this Lisa is really someone from a software company?"

I nodded slowly.

"I feel like such an idiot, Bill. I'm so sorry. I saw the napkin and I just freaked. I knew I was being ridiculous. I realize it now."

After that, she changed the subject and we started talking about my injuries. It was as if our other conversation had never happened. I had no way of knowing whether she'd call the number and find out that Lisa Collins didn't exist, but at the time I was certain that I could get away with anything.

The doctor bandaged my nose and put my hand in a cast. He said I'd have to keep the cast on for a few weeks, maybe longer. Afterwards, Julie and I took a cab home. I showered and then we ordered Chinese food. I was still in a great deal of pain, but I felt that I had weathered the storm. I had made a few mistakes, paid for them, and now everything was going to be all right.

At eleven o'clock, we watched the news. Racial tensions around the city had eased. Black leaders were still protesting, demanding Greg's release, but there had been no new bias attacks. The mayor commended "the maturity of New Yorkers for maintaining their emotions during a time of intense crisis." There was no mention that any other clues had developed in the case, or that any other witnesses or evidence had been discovered. The footage of Greg being arrested, holding his head down so the cameras couldn't show his face, was shown again. I found this very disturbing. I kept thinking about the jokes he'd always made in the office, how he'd always made me laugh. Finally, I couldn't stand it anymore. I flicked the remote to another station.

"Poor thing," Julie said. "This must be so difficult for you."

I mumbled something incoherent.

"I feel so guilty," Julie said. "You've been going through this terrible time, with your boss dying and then breaking your fingers trying to help somebody and all I do is get jealous and start accusing you of things. You must think I'm so insensitive."

I said I didn't blame her for anything. We went into the bedroom and made love.

The next day at work it seemed like I had to tell the story about the old woman and the wet newspaper a hundred times. I told it so frequently, in such detail, that I was starting to believe it had actually happened.

After the morning meeting, Marie Stipaldi approached me. She seemed very concerned, asking me all sorts of questions about my injuries. I decided that yesterday I had been all wrong – she didn't suspect me at all for Ed's murder.

Later, I met with Nelson. He gave me more information about my promotion, including that my salary would be sixty thousand a year, plus two percent of all sales generated from the telemarketers' appointments. My old salary had been thirty-five thousand a year plus one percent of sales. In a matter of a few days, my pay had almost doubled.

I started moving things into Ed's old office right away. I got a couple of telemarketers to help me put his files and the contents from his drawers into boxes and we moved them into the storage room. When I was fully moved in, I sat in the padded reclining chair and leaned back with my feet resting on the desk, thinking about how fortunate I was. I was so happy I didn't do any work all day.

That night, I told Julie about my new salary. She was thrilled. We agreed to start looking for an apartment in a doorman building as soon as possible, and rather than going to Cape Cod on our honeymoon as we'd planned, we decided that we could now afford to go to the Bahamas or Hawaii. Julie was also ecstatic when I told her we could afford to chip in with her parents and invite more guests to the wedding and have a more expensive caterer. Again, she apologized for the way she'd acted last night, and I could tell that any doubts she may have still had about me had now officially disappeared.

The next day, Nelson hired a van to take several people from the office to Long Island for Ed's funeral. First we went to a church service, then we went to the cemetery. I volunteered to be a pall bearer. Ed's relatives and friends were crying uncontrollably throughout the service. At the cemetery, when they were lowering Ed's coffin into the ground, Nelson put his arm around me for support. I put my arm around him, trying to look upset, but the truth was I didn't feel any guilt or remorse for causing Ed's death. That had happened in the past, and I knew that even if I wanted to, I couldn't do anything to change it. If I felt guilt for anything, it was for what had happened to Greg. He wasn't convicted yet so there was still a chance I could save his life, if I could only figure out a way how.

For the next couple of days, my dream life continued. The telemarketers treated me with fear and respect, making it incredibly satisfying to come into work every day. I decided that to be happy I needed to control people, and that I couldn't live my life any other way. Julie and I booked a date for the wedding – April fourteenth. I had started to save for a ring.

Then bad things started to happen. That night on the news we heard that the two witnesses who had claimed they'd seen Greg on the elevator the evening of the murder had mysteriously changed their stories. On the morning news, the police announced that they were searching for new evidence in the case and that it was possible that they would have to drop their charges against Greg. Later in the day, Clara Daniels from

Smythe & O'Greeley came forward and told the police about the conversation she'd had with Ed before he was murdered. That afternoon the police returned to the office to ask me a few more questions.

## 14

W HEN DETECTIVE FIGULA arrived at about two o'clock, I was eating lunch. I was surprised to see him, but I wasn't worried. I assumed he'd returned to ask some routine questions, probably to firm up his case against Greg. The last thing I expected was that he had come to interrogate me.

When he came into my office, he stared at me strangely.

"Did you have some sort of accident?" he asked.

I had taken the bandage off my nose but it still looked purple and swollen.

"Yes, a few days ago," I said. "Let's just say it wasn't one of my better days."

"Hope it's not too serious."

"I'll be all right," I said. "How can I help you?"

That's when he told me the latest news in the case. I still didn't know whether I had anything to worry about. After all, what could Ms. Daniels say that could really incriminate me? I had my alibi and I knew that as long as I stuck to it I'd be safe.

"Excuse me, Detective," I said, "but I don't really see what this has to do with me. So Ms. Daniels talked to Ed that day. There were probably a lot of people Ed spoke to that day."

"But they were talking about you," the detective said. "I think that could be a significant development."

"You're not saying you think I had anything to do with the murder, are you?"

"Right now we're exploring all possibilities. If you'd just bear with me, I'd appreciate it."

I shook my head cynically, to show him that I

thought he was wasting his time.

"Did Mr. O'Brien tell you about this conversation he had with Ms. Daniels?" he asked.

"Yes," I said. "As a matter of fact he did."

"And why didn't you tell me about this the last time I was here?"

"Because I didn't think it was important. He told me he spoke to someone in the Personnel Department at my old job, just doing some routine check. He said he found out that I was fired from my old job and I explained to him why I didn't put it on my application. He didn't have a problem with my explanation and that was the end of it."

"What time did he talk to you?"

"I don't know. Fiveish?"

"According to Ms. Daniels, Mr. O'Brien was extremely upset when he learned that you were fired from your old job. She said he told her that he planned to fire you."

"Well, he didn't fire me," I said. "Like I said, we talked and worked everything out."

He stared at me with his big dark eyes, as if trying to figure out whether I was telling the truth.

"I understand you didn't have the best relationship with Mr. O'Brien."

"Who told you that?"

"Various sources. I understand you had an argument with him in July and stormed out of the office extremely upset. Then when you returned Mr. O'Brien made you apologize to the entire department."

"That was ages ago," I said. "Ed and I got along great after that. I mean he wouldn't have made me his assistant if he hated me, would he?"

"That's true," the detective said, and I could tell that this point puzzled him.

"Are there any more questions?" I asked.

"There's just one last piece of business, Mr. Moss, then I'll let you get back to your lunch. You said you were home by six-thirty the evening of the murder. Do you have any proof of that?"

"No, actually I don't," I said. "I took the subway home that night."

"You didn't stop anywhere to buy anything?"

I shook my head.

"Didn't get off the subway?"

I shook my head again.

"What about when you got home? Was there anybody there?"

"My girlfriend, I mean my fiancée. She didn't get home until a little after eight."

"And you took the 6 train home?"

"I took the shuttle to Times Square then switched for the 6 at Grand Central."

"The reason I ask is Mr. O'Brien's wallet was found in a public garbage can near Hunter College. I realized that Hunter College is on your route home."

"But I don't get out at Hunter College. I get out at Ninety-sixth Street, so that has nothing to do with me, does it?"

"I suppose not," he said.

His dark eyes gazed at me for a few more seconds, then he stood up.

"I appreciate your taking the time," he said. "If I have any more questions, I'll be in touch."

I watched to see if he would question anyone else before he left the office. He didn't.

I decided that things had gone well, or at least as well as I could have hoped. Although Detective Figula didn't seem entirely convinced of my innocence, his evidence against me was very circumstantial. As long as there were no new developments, I knew I'd be fine.

The detective wasn't gone a minute when Mike came into my office. The way he was smirking, I knew that he had been watching my conversation with the detective.

"So what was that all about?" he asked.

"Nothing," I said. "Nothing at all actually."

Mike hesitated, as if trying to figure out the deeper meaning of my words.

"When you say nothing, do you mean he didn't say anything, or that he didn't say anything important?"

"I really don't feel like discussing it now," I said, holding up my sandwich. "I'm trying to finish my lunch."

"I'm just curious why he came to ask you questions and he didn't question anybody else."

"He wanted to know about the computer system," I said. "Just a couple of questions about the list of log-out times I'd compiled. Now will you get out of here?"

He didn't move.

"He seemed to be asking you more than a couple of questions," he said. "They all had to do with the computer system?"

"This is your final warning. If you don't get out of here right now –"

"Okay, okay," Mike said. "You don't have to get so hot headed. I was just curious."

"I'm sorry," I said. "I've been under a lot of stress lately."

"So have all of us, but you don't have to take it out on me."

"You're right. Forgive me."

"It's okay," Mike said suddenly friendly. "I understand. The only reason I was asking so many questions is I was surprised when I saw a cop here again. I mean I wondered if there were any new suspects in the case."

"Not that I know of," I said.

"I guess they're going to let Greg go now. At least that's the way it sounds on the news."

"Whatever," I said. "As long as justice is served in the end, I don't really care who did it."

"Do you still think Greg did it?"

"I don't think I ever really had an opinion."

"I don't think he did it," Mike said. "I mean the police still haven't explained how he got into the office that day. If he rang the bell, did Ed just let him in? Besides, it just didn't make sense that he would come back to the office with the intention of killing Ed."

"Maybe he didn't intend to kill him," I said. "Maybe they were fighting, like that other time they fought, and it just happened."

"I still don't buy it. I believe he had a motive to get angry at him, I don't believe he had a motive to kill him."

"You never know," I said. "He was pretty upset about his commissions and you know how Ed always made those racist comments."

"But his commissions were only a few hundred dollars and he wouldn't have killed Ed just because he insulted him. Don't get me wrong, I never liked Greg very much myself and I'm not saying I think it's impossible that he killed Ed. I just don't think it's beyond reasonable doubt that someone else did it."

There was suddenly an accusing tone in Mike's voice. I didn't know exactly what he was getting at, but I had a few ideas.

"The New York police are extremely competent," I

said. "If someone else did it I'm sure they'll eventually figure it out."

"It's funny the way it all worked out for you though, isn't it?" he said.

"Funny?"

"Maybe funny's the wrong word. Convenient. That's better. I mean there you were one day about to be fired, and here you are now, running the whole department."

"You're walking on very thin ice, Mike. You better watch out."

"Oh, I'm not accusing you of anything," he said. "I know you didn't kill Ed. All I'm saying is you could make out a pretty good case why you'd want to."

"You could make a case why you'd want to kill Ed too," I said.

"Me? Why would I want to kill him?"

"There're a lot of reasons. You must not have been thrilled when Ed overlooked you and made me his assistant. Maybe you were so enraged that it drove you to murder."

"That's ridiculous. Maybe I was a little angry at him, but I wasn't *enraged*."

"It could be enough to make you into a suspect. To be honest, I wouldn't be surprised if the police came back here and asked you some more questions."

"They'd never do that," Mike said defensively. "Never in a million years."

"I'm not so sure about that. After all, they do have some evidence against you. According to the computer records I compiled, you were the last employee to leave the office the day Ed was killed."

"What are you talking about? I left at five o'clock that day."

"Can you prove it?"

"The time's on my time card."

"The police don't know for sure what time Ed was killed. You could have clocked out on the time clock and logged out of your computer by five o'clock, then stayed around to kill Ed later on. Of course I'm not accusing you of anything, but you never know what the police might think. After all, they arrested Greg on evidence just as circumstantial."

I could tell that I had genuinely frightened Mike. My strategy of putting him on the defensive had worked perfectly. Every good sales person knows that it's impossible to be on the defensive and offensive at the same time. So by accusing Mike, he had been unable to continue his accusations against me!

But I knew this effect would not last forever. Eventually Mike's suspicions would surface again, but for now I was glad that I had avoided an uncomfortable situation.

The rest of the afternoon, I couldn't concentrate on my work. Trying to settle my nerves, I took frequent trips to the concession machines and the bathroom. I felt that everyone I passed in the hallways was looking at me differently from usual. It was as if they all knew that I was guilty and they were just waiting for me to admit it. I couldn't convince myself that it was all in my imagination, that they were looking at me no differently than they always did. I said hello to Maria and, instead of saying hello back, she just smiled politely. Did this mean that she knew something? When I stopped by Nelson's office, he was unusually curt. Did he suspect me too? There wasn't one person I trusted. Everyone was out to get me. I was absolutely certain of it.

Paranoia is very tiring. By five o'clock I was so physically and mentally exhausted that I could barely move.

I didn't know how I'd find the energy to travel home. Nevertheless, I headed toward the Times Square subway station.

On Forty-third Street, near Seventh Avenue, I heard a woman call out my name behind me. I turned around and saw a blond woman wearing a black T-shirt, blue jeans and dark sunglasses. She looked familiar, but I didn't know how I knew her.

"Sorry," I said. "Were you talking to me?"

"You remember me, don't you, Bill?" she said.

Her voice was unmistakable. She was Denise, the prostitute I'd had sex with the other day. In street clothes, without the makeup, she looked like an average, not particularly attractive woman.

I decided to ignore her. I kept walking toward Seventh Avenue, but she started walking next to me.

"I wouldn't leave if I was you," she said. "You may be making a big mistake."

"I don't know who you are."

"Yeah, right. Don't give me none of that shit. You knew me enough to fuck me the other day and you knew me enough to beat me up afterwards."

I kept walking.

"I'm warning you," she said. "I'm not fooling around neither. You better hear what I have to say or you're gonna be in big trouble."

I stopped.

"Look," I said, "I don't want to have anything to do with you, okay? As you can see, your friends already got even with me for what I did to you. Now let's just pretend we never met each other, okay?"

"I don't think I can do that."

"What do you want from me," I said, "an apology?"

"I want ten thousand dollars," she said.

I stared at her incredulously, then I said, "Please. Just do us both a favor and leave me alone."

"I'm not doing anything till you give me the money."

"I'm not giving you any money."

"It's up to you. If you don't give it to me I'll just have to go to the police."

I started away again, then stopped. I looked at her.

"What do you mean, the police?"

"It has to do with that guy you murdered," she said. "If you want to know more about it, meet me in fifteen minutes at the pizza place on Eighth near Forty-fifth. I'll be at the table in the back. And don't follow me there neither. If you follow me, I'm going right to the precinct."

I watched her walk back toward Eighth Avenue. I kept watching until her curvy body turned the corner. I guess you could say I was in a state of shock. I just stood there, stunned, unable to think. Being so tired didn't help. I wondered if it was possible I had imagined the whole conversation. Maybe she had never even been there. After all, the whole thing *was* unreal. How could she possibly know I murdered Ed? There was absolutely no explanation for it. None at all.

I decided that she must have said something else, or maybe I'd misunderstood her. She'd said, "It has to do with that guy you murdered." She didn't say it had to do with Ed's murder. Maybe she thought I'd murdered someone else. That had to be it. There had to be some big mistake.

But I couldn't go home and forget about it. I had to meet her to find out what exactly she knew.

I waited a few more minutes, then headed to the pizzeria. It was a narrow place with a counter to the left and windows to the right. As promised, she was sitting at the table in the very back of the restaurant, her back facing the door. I immediately recognized the strong odor of her perfume. It reminded me of her naked body, the burn scars on her legs.

"I had a feeling you'd show up on time," she said. "Just sit down and don't make a scene."

I sat down across from her and said, "I just came here to tell you that you're making a mistake. I don't know why you think I murdered someone, but I want you to know that you're absolutely wrong."

"If I was wrong you wouldn't be here," she said. "Now I know I was right."

"Right about what? I have no idea what you're talking about."

"Don't give me the stupid routine 'cause it ain't gonna work, honey. I want the money tomorrow night at eight o'clock. I'll be at Seventeenth Street between Fifth and Sixth. There's a parking lot in the middle of the block, the north side. Walk to the back, behind the dumpster, and wait there. I'll show up and you'll give me the money. If you're not there I'll go right to the precinct. If you don't –"

"Hold up," I said. "Just hold up, all right? First of all, I don't have any money. Second of all, why do you think I'd give it to you if I did?"

"Because if you don't you're gonna go to jail."

"For what? I didn't do anything."

"There you go, playing stupid again. I already know what you did, honey. You might as well just admit I got you."

"I only came here because I was confused," I said. "You said something about a murder and I wanted to talk to you before you embarrassed yourself and brought your story to the police. But if that's what you want to do, be my guest."

"You killed your boss," she said. "Now you think I don't got anything on you?"

I stared at her, looking at my reflection in her sunglasses. I was two little heads that looked like they were drifting farther and farther away.

"I still don't know what you're talking about," I said. "I think you're making this up to try to extort money from me."

"The cops came around the other night, the night after your boss was murdered, and they were asking people if they saw anything the night before. Since I was working near your building that night and they know me from around there, they asked me too. I said what time are we talking about and the cop said between six-thirty and seven. And I told him I don't know nothing about any murder, but I remembered seeing you that night, later on, like around seven-fifteen. I knew because I was with my girlfriend that night and when you came out of your building I told her, see that's the guy, that's the guy who slapped me around. But I didn't tell the cops what I knew because I don't like to help out the cops a lot if you know what I mean. Plus, I didn't really think what I saw meant anything. I mean it was later than the cops said and I had no reason to think you killed anybody. Then it hit me later on, when everybody was talking about it in the papers and everything, that maybe it did mean something. I mean you slapped me around so maybe you slapped your boss around too, maybe you got a temper with everybody. I didn't know for sure if you were involved, but I thought it was worth a shot. So I came up with the idea to meet you on the street and see how you acted. I knew if you looked at me like I was crazy and went home that you had nothing to do with it. Then I would've just gone on with my life and forgot all about it. But when you stopped and talked to me I knew I was right. Then when you showed up here I knew it for sure."

"It's a nice story," I said. "Unfortunately it's all bullshit."

"Do what you want to do," she said. "If you don't want to give me the money I'll just go right to the precinct. I'm sure I can make some deal there. Maybe if I give'em the dope on you they won't bust me as much or they'll give me some kind of reward. I just thought I'd give you the chance to save yourself and to make a little money on the side. But if you can't do it, you can't do it."

She started to get up. I grabbed her arm.

"Sit," I said.

She pulled her arm back angrily and sat down.

"I'm not gonna play this shit with you," she said. "Are you gonna give me the money or ain't you?"

"I don't have the money."

"Too bad for you then."

"But we'll make out some other deal," I said. "I mean I'm sure there's something you want that I can give you."

"All I want is cash," she said. "Green and white American dollars. Ten thousand of them."

"I don't have ten thousand dollars!"

I was yelling. A few people on line at the counter looked in our direction. Denise stared at me for a few seconds, then she took off her sunglasses. I was surprised to see that she still had bruises under her eyes. Until then I hadn't realized how hard I'd hit her that day.

210

"How much money do you have?" she asked.

"Nothing," I said. "I'm broke."

"Bullshit. You're wearing a suit. You got cash."

"I started a new job a few weeks ago. I'm telling you, I don't have anything."

"What about your wife or your girlfriend?"

"I'm not married and I'm not seeing anyone," I said.

"You see? What you want is impossible."

"What about your family?"

"My parents are dead. I don't have a family."

She paused, putting her sunglasses back on.

"Then you'll give me payments," she said. "Four payments of twenty-five hundred bucks, one payment every week. If you don't have the money you better find it 'cause I ain't joking around. You saw what my friends did to you before. They'll do the same thing again, maybe worse if you try to fuck around on me."

"Give me a break."

"Eight o'clock," she said, standing up. "If you're a minute late I'm going to the precinct. And you better be there alone or the deal's off."

"Why should I trust you?" I said. "How do I know if I give you the money you won't ask me for more? Or how do I know you won't just take the story to the police anyway?"

"You don't," she said. "But I guess it's the only chance you've got."

She walked away, shaking her butt back and forth. Helplessly, I watched her cross Forty-sixth Street and disappear somewhere on Eighth Avenue.

# 15

WHEN I GOT home things got even bleaker. On the six o'clock news, I found out that the police were dropping the murder charges against Greg and were officially reopening the murder case. Greg's lawyers had produced a witness who claimed that Greg was in a record store in Greenwich Village from five-thirty to six-thirty on the evening of the murder. It was also announced that the two witnesses who had thought they saw Greg on the elevator had mistaken Greg for a delivery man from Federal Express.

Greg and his lawyer were shown at a press conference. Greg said that he was glad that "the truth was finally known" and he hoped that whoever killed Ed O'Brien would "stop being such a coward and turn himself in." Then Detective Figula came on and said that the police were actively pursuing other suspects. He gave out a special police hot line number for anyone who had information about the case.

Before the report ended, I picked up one of my shoes and flung it at the T.V. It hit the channel button, switching the T.V. to a different station. The other station was also covering the story of Greg's release and I had to watch Detective Figula's statement all over again. It seemed like there was no escape from it, that wherever I went the case would follow me. Detective Figula was staring at me through the T.V. set, talking directly to me. "We're actively pursuing you, Bill. You might as well turn yourself in, because you're not going to get away."

I laughed out loud at the television, although I knew there was absolutely nothing to laugh about. My life was slowly falling apart and there was nothing I could do to stop it.

At about seven o'clock Julie came home from work. As soon as I saw her I knew that she was upset about something. The way my day was going, I had a pretty good hunch it had to do with me.

"I'm exhausted, honey," I said. "You think we can order in some food tonight?"

"We have to talk," she said. "Right away."

"Can't it wait?" I said, "I had a very hard day."

"I'm very upset," she said. "I'm so upset I don't even know if I can talk about it."

"All right. Let's sit on the couch and get comfortable. But I'm warning you, I might not be a very good listener."

"Are you lying to me about something?"

"Lying to you –"

"You heard me and I want you to answer me with absolute honesty. Are you lying to me about something?"

"I thought we settled all of this yesterday," I said.

"Answer me, Bill. It's very important."

"I don't know what you're talking about, and to be honest I resent this. I mean I told you I had a very hard day and then you come home and start getting all weird on me."

"The police were at my office today," she said. "They asked me all kinds of questions about you and what you might've had to do with your boss's murder."

"So that's what you're getting all hysterical about," I said casually. "You got me frightened there for a second."

"This isn't something to joke around about," she said. "I asked you a question and I expect an answer."

"What's the question?"

"Are you lying to me about something?"

"I've never lied to you," I said. "You know that."

"I don't know anything. All I know is you've been acting very strange lately, all summer long actually, and you get stranger ever day. First it was showing up with all these mysterious injuries and now the police are involved. They were asking me all these questions about you – where you were that night, if you'd ever threatened your boss, whether I thought you were capable of killing someone."

"What did you tell them?"

"What do you think I told them? If I thought the man I was engaged to was capable of killing someone I obviously wouldn't be engaged to him. After all, I'm not crazy."

"You have to calm down, sweetheart," I said. "Sit on the couch."

"But they made it seem so real, Bill. They said Ed was going to fire you and that's why you got mad and killed him. I said it was impossible, that you'd never do anything like that, then they asked me if I had any proof you didn't do it. They asked me so many questions I couldn't even keep track of them. They wanted to know when I came home that night, when you came home, how you were acting, if I noticed anything strange about you. I had to tell the truth, that I did notice something strange about you, and now it's got me wondering what else I should've noticed."

"They were trying to scare you," I said. "That's what police do. They try to scare people into saying things they don't want to say so if you know any information you'll give it to them. But that's the way they are with everybody, whether they really suspect that person or not."

"But they were so sure about it," she said. "At least they seemed sure about it."

"The police came to my office today too," I said. "They talked to me and they talked to a lot of other people. I don't know if you heard on the news, but they're reopening the investigation."

"But why do they think you did it?"

"They don't," I said. "They're just going through all the motions, checking every possible lead. You've seen how much publicity this case has gotten. They're under a lot of pressure to come up with something."

"I want to believe you," she said. "I really really want to."

"You don't think I'd actually kill someone, do you?" I asked.

"No," she said. "I told you I couldn't."

"Then I don't see what the problem is. The police asked us some questions, we answered them, and now we can go on with our lives. I don't see why you're making such a big deal about this."

"It *is* a big deal," she said. "I'm just not sure I can feel the same anymore."

"What is that supposed to mean?" I asked.

"Nothing," she said. "It's just how I feel."

"Are you saying you want to break up with me?"

"Of course not, I...I don't know what I mean."

"Well, you better think about it," I said, "because to be honest I can't stand not being trusted all the time. If you can't believe me and support me then maybe we shouldn't get married."

For emphasis, I stormed off into the bathroom and slammed the door. My idea was to make her feel guilty so she'd break down and apologize to me. A minute hadn't gone by when she knocked on the door, pleading for me to come out.

"Please forgive me," she said. "I was being ridiculous. I realize that now."

When I came out she apologized to me again and admitted that the whole argument had been her fault. I was happy that my manipulation had worked, but I knew the technique wouldn't work forever. Julie was catching on to me fast. There was a limit to how needy and clingy she could get. Eventually she would realize exactly the type of man she was engaged to and then there would be nothing I could do or say to make her stay with me.

Although she didn't mention the visit from the police again all night, she was much more aloof than usual. When I spoke I felt she wasn't really listening to me and she hardly spoke at all. Most of the time she was looking at her lap or at the T.V., as if she had already divorced me in her mind.

Despite how tired I was, I had trouble falling asleep that night. All I could think about was the twenty-five hundred dollars and how impossible it was going to be for me to come up with it. I wished there was some way I could get out of paying the money, but there didn't seem to be any reasonable solution. Everyone was starting to suspect me now and the prostitute coming forward could be the thing that did me in. It would prove I had lied to the police about my alibi and open the gates for all sorts of questions. Even if the police didn't believe the prostitute, it would focus attention back on me which couldn't lead to anything positive.

There was only one way that I could be sure that the

prostitute would never get to the police. At first the idea seemed insane to me, yet the more I thought about it, the more I believed that it could actually work.

Sitting in the dark living room in the glare of late-night talk shows and infomercials, I thought about murder. The idea of killing another person didn't frighten me, however the idea of getting caught was terrifying.

And it didn't seem like there was any way I could possibly get away with killing the prostitute.

Even if the pimp and her other friends from the black van weren't there like she promised they would be, they would be sure to track me down afterwards. For hitting the prostitute they had broken my fingers; I could only imagine what they would break if I killed her.

Then there would be the police to worry about. If they had really questioned the prostitute about me already, then it wouldn't take a giant leap for them to assume I was involved when she showed up dead. She also said that she'd been with a friend when the police questioned her, and there would always be the danger that her friend could go to the police.

I thought about it for hours, running the same questions through my mind again and again. Finally, when I was almost ready to give up, the solution suddenly came to me. It was so simple and obvious that I was angry at myself for not thinking of it sooner.

I slept for a couple of hours on the couch and woke up feeling surprisingly energized. Julie was still acting strange around me, but I hardly noticed her. In fact, I was so involved in my plan that I hardly remember anything else about that day, until about noon when I left work and went downtown to Canal Street.

I needed some materials to carry out my plan and I wanted to buy them far away from my office and my apartment, in case the police decided to retrace my steps at some point later on. Canal Street wasn't exactly like going to another state, but it would do. First I went to a hardware store and bought a saw. Then I went to a drug store and bought a package of extra-large trash bags. Next I walked up Broadway several blocks and went to a discount clothing store and bought a pair of heavy duty gloves. Most of the workers at the stores were Asian or Mexican immigrants and I doubted that any of them would remember seeing me, an average-looking American.

Finished with my shopping, I took the subway back to the office, glad that I had only been gone an hour. Throughout the afternoon I kept thinking about the plan, rehearsing every last detail. I'd prepared myself for everything that could possibly go wrong and, as far as I could tell, the plan was virtually flawless. The only possible kink was that the pimp could be there with his friends, but last night I had decided that this was highly unlikely and I still thought it was unlikely. The prostitute was expecting to receive ten thousand dollars from me over several weeks and it didn't make sense that she'd be willing to share this "easy money." More likely, she'd only told me her friends would be there as an idle threat, hoping that it would frighten me. That also explained why she picked an out-of-the-way place like Seventeenth Street to meet me, because it was out of her pimp's turf and he'd be unlikely to find out about the transaction.

Of course this was all only a hunch, a reasonable

hunch maybe, but still only a hunch. I had no idea if I was right and I had no back-up plan for what I would do if I was wrong. But I was confident that if the pimp wasn't there the rest of the plan would go through without a hitch.

Although I wasn't supposed to meet the prostitute until eight o'clock, I clocked out and left the office at five o'clock sharp. So this could be confirmed later on, I made sure to board an elevator with Mike and several other people from the office. When we got outside, we split off in different directions. I was carrying the saw, the trash bags and the gloves in my briefcase. At Times Square, I veered north on Broadway. I kept walking at a steady pace until I reached the Zeigfeld Theater on Fifty-fourth Street. A movie was playing there that ran from six to eight forty-five, and a ticket stub from that show would be the perfect alibi for me.

I bought a single ticket then killed time in a nearby cappuccino bar. At a few minutes before six I returned to the theater. Entering, I smiled flirtatiously at the pretty black ticket taker, hoping that I had captured her attention enough so that she would remember me if anyone should ask. Even if she described me as the weird-looking guy with the cast on his hand it would help.

I sat in a seat on the side aisle, about halfway toward the screen. The Zeigfeld is a very large theater and it wasn't even a quarter filled. After about an hour into the movie, I got up and walked along the side aisle toward the front of the theater. It was during a dark, action sequence so I doubted anyone noticed me. I went out a side door and emerged on Fifty-fourth Street.

It was about seven-fifteen, so I still had plenty of time

to get downtown. I didn't want to get into a cab with a cab driver who might remember me, so I took the subway.

Everything was going smoothly until the subway was approaching the Thirty-fourth Street station, when it suddenly stopped. I thought it would just be the one or two minute delay that subways typically encountered, but then the conductor came on the P.A. system and said that due to an emergency situation at Penn Station we would be "delayed indefinitely."

Five minutes passed, then five more minutes, then another five minutes, and another five minutes. I was starting to panic. I convinced myself that there was no possible way I could meet the prostitute on time. It was already twenty to eight and the prostitute's warning that she would go right to the police station if I was even a few minutes late weighed heavily on my mind. If the train didn't start moving soon there was a very good possibility that I would spend the rest of my life in jail. The worst part of it was that I couldn't express any of my anxiety. For fear that someone might remember the frantic-looking passenger who seemed in a big hurry to get somewhere I didn't want to get up and start pacing or complaining out loud. So I had to stay seated, cursing and screaming silently while my life slowly ticked away.

At ten minutes to eight, the train jerked forward and started to creep into the Thirty-fourth Street station. I still didn't think there was any way I could possibly make it on time to meet the prostitute, but at least I had a chance.

Fortunately, there was an express train waiting across the platform. I got on, just beating the closing doors. I prayed there wouldn't be any more delays. The train started slowly, then it picked up speed and in just a few minutes we arrived at Fourteenth Street. Running along the platform, I saw a clock – three minutes to eight.

I don't think I've ever run faster in my life. As I was dodging traffic and pedestrians, sprinting up Seventh Avenue, it occurred to me that I hadn't even been rehearsing my plan. Suddenly, it didn't seem as clear to me as it had earlier. I imagined hundreds of things could go wrong and didn't understand how I ever thought I'd get away with it. But I had no choice, I *had* to go through with the plan whether I wanted to or not. Even if I could think of some way to pay the prostitute the money or talk her out of going to the police, I'd have no assurance that she'd keep quiet forever. She could change her mind at any time and milk me for more money and I'd live my life in constant fear of her returning.

I reached the parking lot where we'd arranged to meet and saw by my watch that it was one minute after eight. The prostitute, wearing jeans and a T-shirt, was already walking toward the street. When she saw me, she turned around and walked toward the back of the lot. It was much brighter than I'd expected. Light from lampposts in the street spread over much of the area and a spotlight attached to a building behind the lot shined light on the lot's back left corner. I realized that I should have come by here earlier to check out the area, but of course there was nothing I could do about that now.

Standing in front of the parked car – the only car in the lot – she was pointing something at me that looked like mace. This didn't surprise me since I knew she wouldn't show up without protection. Seeing the mace actually brought me a sense of relief because I knew it meant that I was right about my assumption that she'd been bluffing about her friends being here to back her up. If her friends were really here, then she obviously wouldn't have a need for the mace.

"That's fine," she said. "You can stop right there."

"What's with the mace?" I said. "You want your money or you want to blind me?"

"Where's the money?"

"I have it – right here in my briefcase."

"Show it to me."

"Let's go back farther first," I said. "I don't want anybody from the street seeing us."

As she considered this and decided it was a good idea, she hesitated a moment, then started backing slowly toward the back fence. I wanted to get her as far back as possible because the back of the parking lot – especially on the right side where we were – was much darker than the front of the lot, and we were much less likely to be seen by any passersby.

She stopped after backing up a few feet.

"That's enough," she said. "Now show me the money."

"All right," I said. "No reason to get excited. Take it easy."

I knew that I was approaching the most dangerous part of my plan, that after this everything would go smoothly.

So I tried not to think about it.

I started to open the briefcase, then I lunged forward, grabbing her right wrist, paralyzing the hand that was holding the mace. Before she could scream, I swung my hand with the cast as hard as I could across her face. The cast was hard so the impact hurt her a lot more than it

222

did me. She fell backwards against the fence, staring at me with wide, confused eyes as blood streamed out of her mouth. I knew that she would start to scream soon and that I had to finish her off fast.

I put my hand and my casted hand against her throat and squeezed as hard as I could. Her neck was much thinner than Ed's and she died even easier. It seemed like I'd only been squeezing for a few seconds when her body fell limply onto the ground.

Quickly, I dragged her body behind the car so we were completely out of view from the street. Facing us were a few windows in an industrial building next to the lot. The building looked dark and vacant, yet I had no way of knowing whether someone was in there watching everything that was going on.

I had to finish what I had started anyway. It was time for phase two of the plan and I had to take several deep breaths to prepare myself for it.

When I thought I was ready, I took out the gloves from my briefcase and put them on. Then I took out the saw. Trying not to think too much about what I was doing, I sawed off the prostitute's head. The blade went through easy at first, then it met some friction near the bone, then it went through easy again. As you can imagine, sawing off someone's head can get you sick to the stomach and I had to fight hard to keep myself from vomiting. I didn't know if the police could trace a person's vomit, but I assumed they could. I kept telling myself that she wasn't a person, she was a piece of wood, and there was nothing sick about what I was doing. Believe me, I was getting no enjoyment out of it and, if I could have thought of any other way of keeping the prostitute from going to the police, I certainly would have done it. But killing her was the only sure way of keeping her quiet forever, and killing her this way was the only way I'd get away with it.

My plan was very simple. I'd heard on the news the other day that someone had killed a prostitute in Queens and chopped off her head and taken it with him. The police were extremely concerned because another prostitute in Newark had been killed a few months earlier and her head had also been missing. The police feared that a serial killer might be responsible for the crimes, so I figured I'd give the police one more victim to think about. If I could make them believe that Denise the prostitute had been killed by the serial killer, then they would never suspect that I had anything to do with it.

I took out a trash bag and tried not to look as I put the head inside it. The head was much lighter than I'd expected. I'd assumed it would weigh about as much as a bowling ball, but instead it felt as though I was carrying a large cantaloupe.

There was blood everywhere, but I luckily managed to keep all of it off my clothing. There was only a little blood on the edge of my cast, but I'd have to worry about that later.

I double-bagged the head and the bloody gloves and put the saw back in the briefcase. I carried the bag and the briefcase out of the parking lot and headed toward the subway.

I wasn't thrilled about carrying the head on the subway, but I had to get rid of it somehow – because that's what the serial killer always did – and I knew that it would be best to take it as far away from the crime scene as possible. I'd decided that the Harlem River would be a good place and I got on the number 1 train going uptown.

The train was pretty much empty and no one seemed to notice me. I tried not to look nervous, although inside I was a wreck. The reality of what I had done and what I was holding on my lap had finally hit me. I feared that I was becoming a lunatic, no better or worse than the actual serial killer who went around killing prostitutes. I thought about the events of the last month that had brought me to this low point in my life, wondering how it had all happened. I decided that it really started when I was fired from Smythe & O'Greeley and was forced to take a job as a telemarketer. If I had stayed in advertising everything would have been different.

Looking up, I noticed a woman standing in front of me, staring at me. I thought I might have been talking out loud, then I realized that the woman looked familiar, but I wasn't sure how I knew her. Then it hit me. She was Lisa, the woman I'd met at the bar that night.

When she saw my look of recognition, she smiled at me and I smiled back reflexively. The last thing I wanted now was to get into a conversation and yet I didn't know how to avoid it. I was about to get up to get out at the next stop when she sat down next to me.

In the bright fluorescent light of the subway, the ruddiness of her skin was apparent as were the dark circles under her eyes, and she wasn't nearly as attractive as she'd seemed in the dark bar.

"Long time no see," she said.

"I was thinking you looked familiar," I said. "I just didn't recognize you at first."

"No loss," she said. "So what happened to you?"

"Happened? Oh, I was in an accident. A car accident."

She didn't seem to care. I made sure to keep the part of the cast with the blood on it facing my lap.

"So what brings you to the West Side?" she asked.

"Work," I said, anxious to avoid the subject. "A lot of work. What brings you here?"

"Oh, just going to meet a friend," she said ambiguously. I realized that she was being intentionally vague about the sex of the friend, trying to make me jealous.

"Sorry I never called you," I said. "A lot came up after that night and I just didn't –"

"Don't worry," she said, "I wasn't exactly holding my breath. So what's in the bag?"

"The bag?"

"Yeah, what do you do, bring your laundry to work?"

I laughed tensely.

"Of course not," I said. "This is just garbage."

She looked at me, a combination of confused and disgusted.

"Just some things at the office I needed to throw out," I continued. "I didn't want to put them in the office trash."

I wasn't sure whether or not she bought the explanation.

"There's something weird about you," she said.

"Weird?" I said, feeling the prostitute's nose pressing against the bag. "What do you mean?"

"I don't know, there's just something about you I can't put my finger on. My girlfriend said it that night, after we left the bar. She said, you know there's something strange about that guy you were talking to and I agreed with her. But I really don't know what it is. I just had a feeling there was something, I don't know, I can't put my finger on it. Maybe it was the way you were dressed that night in that sweat suit, and the

226

way you kept staring at me. What I'm trying to say is you shouldn't feel like you lost out anything by not calling me because I wasn't going to go out with you anyway."

At the next stop, she got out. As the train pulled away, I saw her walking determinedly along the platform. I wondered if she somehow suspected that I had killed somebody. It seemed unlikely, yet why else did she say there was something weird about me? Then I decided that it was probably just a defense mechanism. Although she didn't want to admit it, she was hurt that I hadn't called her so she made up the excuse to herself that I was "weird," so she wouldn't feel bad about it. It was typical female psychology that had nothing to do with me.

I rode the subway all the way to 145th Street without any more mishaps. I'd never been to Harlem before so when I got out of the station I was disoriented and wasn't sure which way to walk to get to the river. I walked in a direction I thought would lead me there, then after I'd walked several blocks I turned back and walked in the other direction.

Most of the buildings in the neighborhood were abandoned or chiseled down to empty lots. Compared to the Upper East Side it looked like a war zone. Groups of people on street corners stared at me angrily as I walked by, as if they feared me or hated me or both. I realized how unusual I must look, the only white person in the neighborhood. They probably thought I was a cop.

Passing a housing project, a couple of teenagers started following me. I imagined what would happen if I got mugged. I remembered reading a story in the newspaper once about a girl who was dog-sitting for a rich

Park Avenue couple when the dog died. Afraid to leave the dead dog in the apartment, she put it in a suitcase and took it to the A.S.P.C.A. On the way there she was mugged and the suitcase was stolen. The article speculated on the expression the mugger must have had when he opened the suitcase and discovered the dead dog. I smiled, thinking about the expressions the teenagers would have if they stole the garbage bag and discovered the prostitute's head. Then I realized that this would be the worst scenario possible. The teenagers would be able to identify me to the police and I'd be arrested instantly.

Clinging to the bag tightly, I walked as fast as I could. The teenagers increased their speed also, then they veered off on a side street and left me alone.

Finally, I saw the river ahead. It was like discovering a pond in the middle of a desert. I walked faster until I was practically jogging. I crossed a playground and a baseball diamond and then I reached the railing to the water. To the right was the bridge where the subway passed on its way to the Bronx, so I walked left until I thought I was as out of view as possible.

From my briefcase, I took out the saw and put it inside a new garbage bag. I tied the bag tightly then threw it into the river as far as I could. It sank about fifty feet from the shore.

Next, I flung the bag with the head and the gloves into the water. It didn't sink, but this really didn't concern me. When the head was discovered, the police would simply think the serial killer had dumped it in the river.

I was about to walk away when I heard someone behind me. I stood still, hoping the person would leave me alone.

"What do you think you're doing?" the harsh male voice said.

Terrified, I turned around slowly. Then my worst nightmare came to life. A police officer was facing me, his right hand resting on his holster.

# 16

IDIDN'T HAVE time to think up a plan. I had to react impulsively and hope everything worked out.

"I'm sorry," I said. "Was I doing something wrong?"

"What the fuck are you doing here?" the officer said, still resting his right hand on his holster.

"Nothing really," I said. "Just taking a walk near the river."

"Up here?"

"Why not?" I said naively.

"What are you looking for?" he said. "Crack, heroin?"

"I don't do drugs," I said.

He looked at me closely. I realized that I'd lucked out – he hadn't seen me throw the bags into the river.

"You know where we are?" he asked.

"Yes," I said. "Near the Hudson River."

"This isn't the Hudson River, guy, this is the Harlem River. This isn't an area where people like yourself take walks."

"I'm new in town," I said. "I'm just kind of exploring the city."

"Where are you from?" he asked.

"Seattle," I said. "Bainbridge Island actually. Where I'm from we're kind of used to a lot of water."

This seemed to convince him. He took his hand off the holster.

"This isn't an area where you should be sightseeing," he said. "This is a drug zone. Get out of here before you get robbed or shot."

"Thank you, officer," I said, acting concerned. "I'll get home as soon as I can."

The officer went in one direction, I went in the other. I was terrified for what could happen tomorrow or the next day when the head was discovered in the river. If the police could estimate where it had been dropped and how long it had been in the water, then the police officer would be sure to remember me. The only thing I had going for me was that it had been very dark and I doubted the officer had seen me clearly, but I was still angry at myself for not weighing down the bag with the head to make sure that it sunk.

I hurried to the subway, knowing that to protect my alibi I had to get home as quickly as possible.

I took the 3 train to Ninety-sixth Street, then rode the crosstown bus through Central Park. By the time I arrived at my apartment it was nine-fifteen.

As I'd expected, Julie was very nervous.

"Where have you *been*?" she said. "I've been worried to death about you."

"Didn't you get my message?" I said.

"What message?"

"I left it on your tape this afternoon, it must have gotten erased somehow. I went to a movie after work."

"A movie?"

"Yeah, you know just to unwind from everything that's been going on. I feel awful that you've been worrying about me."

"There's nothing wrong with my tape at work."

"Well, I called," I said. "I'm not making it up."

I went to the bathroom and started taking off my clothes. Julie followed me.

"I can't stand this anymore," she said. "I just can't stand it. I mean I'm not making all of this up. I have a good imagination, but it's not *that* good."

"What are you talking about?"

231

"The affair you're having!" she was screaming. "Why can't you be a man and just admit it to me?"

"I opened my wallet and took out the ticket stub."

"Here," I said. "If you don't believe me, here. I don't know what's wrong with you lately, Julie? Maybe you should see a shrink or something."

She walked away into the living room, as meekly as an injured animal.

That was when I realized that I never truly loved her. If I loved her I would have left her right then and not gotten her more involved in my life than she already was.

But I was too worried about myself to worry about her.

When I came into the living room in my underwear she was waiting for me, crying.

"You killed him, didn't you?" she wailed. "I'm really engaged to a murderer!"

"What are you talking about?"

"I didn't want to believe it, but it's true, isn't it? I know he was going to fire you, that's what the detective told me, and I know how angry that must've made you. I still don't know why you'd kill him unless...unless there was somebody else involved, some woman. Maybe you killed your boss to be with this woman. That explains why you've been so mysterious lately."

"You're crazy," I said.

"I don't think so," she said. "I thought so yesterday, but now I know the truth."

"Please let's not have another night of fighting," I said. "If we do, we'll wind up regretting it."

"What's that on your cast?"

"I don't know, I guess it's some ketchup. I had a hamburger before the movie."

"It looks like blood. What's been going on, Bill? Have you been having rough sex with this woman? Is that how you got your fingers broken?"

"Listen to yourself," I said. "Just listen to yourself."

"What if I called the police right now?"

"The police? What the hell for?"

"I'll tell them all the things I didn't tell them yesterday. How I don't know for sure that you left the office when you said you did that night, how I think there's some woman involved."

"You better not call the police," I said.

"Why? You afraid they might find out about you?"

"There's nothing to find out," I said. "If you want to call the police, go ahead. The phone's right over there."

She waited a second then went to the phone and picked it up. Mascara tears were streaming down her face. She was shaking. Slowly, she started to dial. I counted six digits when she dropped the phone on the floor and started to cry uncontrollably. I put the phone back on the counter.

Julie didn't say another word to me all night. She just stayed in bed crying. I thought she might call her parents or one of her friends, then I decided this wasn't her style. She'd once told me how she felt alone in the world, how she felt she had no one to talk to about her problems. I told her not to worry, that she could always count on me. I realized how lonely she must feel now that I had broken that promise.

I was tempted to go into the bedroom and try to console her, to convince her one last time that I was the person she'd thought I was. But I knew it wouldn't work. I had deceived her too many times. The old Bill Moss had died a long time ago and she was just starting to realize it.

As far as I was concerned, Julie was more of a liability to me now than an asset. I didn't have any specific plan in mind, but I knew that if she continued to be suspicious of me I'd have to find some way to keep her quiet. It wouldn't be something I particularly wanted to do, but if I had to do it I would.

While Julie was crying, I watched television. There was nothing about a prostitute being murdered on the ten o'clock news, but by the time the eleven o'clock news came on, the story had broken. Reporters and police were on the scene at the parking lot and people were crowded behind the yellow crime scene tape, waving at the camera. The reporter said that the case was just developing, but that police believed that the serial killer had struck again. The decapitated body of a woman had been discovered by a janitor who was returning to his car. The identity of the woman had not been determined and the police were investigating whether or not the woman was a prostitute.

I smiled when they showed a police sketch of the man the police thought was responsible for the murder. He was a heavyset Hispanic man with a beard.

Before I went to bed, I washed the blood out of my briefcase. All of it washed out and I made sure all the excess blood went down the drain. Then, to make sure any blood residue didn't remain, I rinsed the drain with Drano.

The blood on my cast was harder to get out. After several minutes of scrubbing a faint pink stain still remained, and I finally had to slice off the stained layer of the cast with a razor blade and flush the material down the toilet.

I slept on the couch. In the morning, Julie was still in bed, wearing the same clothes she'd been wearing last night. I asked her if she was going to work today and she just kept staring aimlessly at the wall. I wasn't worried about her calling the police because I knew there was little she could tell them. She had no idea about the prostitute and she had no hard evidence that I had killed Ed. Besides, she was too depressed to get out of bed, no less make a phone call. It occurred to me that she might be capable of committing suicide. Although I knew I'd be sad if Julie ended her life, I also knew it would solve a lot of problems.

Approaching work, I watched closely for the black van, but I arrived at work safely, with no sign of the van or the pimp.

I spent the morning interviewing people for several telemarketing positions. In the afternoon I went to an off-site meeting at a project developer's office with Nelson and other company executives and discussed the possibility of expanding the Telemarketing Department at a new location. Although I was very busy all day, I didn't feel as involved in my work as I had on other days. I felt let down, like after a party when everyone leaves and you're suddenly all alone.

On the way home, I looked for the van again, and again it was nowhere in sight. I decided that if the pimp didn't come after me today, he probably wouldn't come after me at all. He probably believed what the police believed, that the serial killer had killed the prostitute, or he didn't care enough about her death to try to get revenge. To him, she was just a commodity, a way to make money, and while he would protect her while she was alive, she was useless to him dead.

My only remaining threat was that the prostitute's friend, the one she'd been with when she saw me leaving the office that day, would mention me to the police. If she put it all together, she might tell the police that I'd hit the prostitute, but the odds were she wouldn't think of it.

When I got home, Julie was still lying in bed. She still hadn't changed out of her clothes from last night, and from the way her hair looked she obviously hadn't showered.

"You can't just lie there forever," I said.

She moaned something incomprehensible. I ignored her and changed out of my clothes into sweat pants and a T-shirt and went out to the living room.

I looked at the T.V. schedule and saw that the Yankees and Indians were playing at eight o'clock. At seven I'd watch *Jeopardy*, then maybe I'd order some chicken wings or pizza.

There was a newspaper on the coffee table so I sat on the couch and started reading the sports section. The Mariners had lost again, but I was happy to see that Griffey had hit another homer, his forty-first of the year. I figured out that if he hit three homers a week for the rest of the season he'd break Maris' record. I hadn't seen the Mariners play in person all season long and I decided that the next time they came to New York to play the Yankees I'd go to at least one of the games.

At six o'clock, I watched the beginning of the news, but there was nothing new on the prostitute's murder. It wasn't even the top story anymore. A fire had killed fifteen people in the Bronx and a car bomb had gone off in Israel.

Before *Jeopardy* came on, the buzzer on the intercom sounded. I assumed it was the super or some kids playing around so I ignored it. But it kept buzzing and buzzing so I finally got up to answer it.

"Bill Moss?" the loud, crackly voice said.

"Who's this?" I said.

"Detective Figula. Can I please come upstairs?"

The police wanting to speak to me again didn't surprise me. I'd expected it at some point, whether they had any evidence against me or not. The only thing that surprised me was that they came to my apartment, rather than the office. What was so important that it couldn't wait until the morning?

I buzzed the detective up, then peaked into the bedroom and saw that Julie was still lying there, mumbling to herself. Quietly, I closed the French doors. The last thing I needed was for Julie to get out of bed and say something incriminating about me.

The doorbell rang. I let Detective Figula and a tall, heavyset black man into the apartment. They were both wearing gray business suits. Compared to the black man, Detective Figula looked even shorter and squatter than he had in my office.

"What can I do for you?" I said, acting as if their visit had interrupted something important.

"Sorry to come without any notice," Detective Figula said. "But there were some things I needed to discuss with you right away."

"Really?" I said.

"This is Detective Bryant, Homicide."

"Pleased to meet you," I said. "Sit down, make yourself comfortable."

"That won't be necessary," Detective Figula said. "I might as well give it to you straight. I still don't believe what you told me the other day in your office. I still think you killed your boss and I won't quit this case until I prove it."

"What the hell are you talking about?" I said.

"We're talking about murder," Detective Bryant said. "Two murders to be precise."

"I'd like to help you anyway I can," I said, "but now I'm getting fed up about this. I didn't murder anyone. Can I make that any clearer to you?"

"You're not surprised that Detective Bryant said two murders, are you?" Detective Figula said. "You know exactly what second murder I'm talking about."

"I have no idea what you're talking about," I said, "and maybe I shouldn't talk to you at all without a lawyer."

"You're gonna need a lawyer all right," Detective Bryant said. "You're gonna need a whole fucking team of lawyers."

"Where were you last night between eight o'clock and eight-thirty?" Detective Figula asked.

I paused to think.

"The movies," I said. "I was at the movies."

"Who were you with?"

"I went alone. But why do you need –"

"What theater?"

"I don't understand what the point of these questions is."

"It would help if you just shut up and answered them," Detective Bryant said. "You said you wanted to help us, didn't you?"

"What theater did you go to?" Detective Figula asked again.

"The Ziegfeld," I said. "Here, you want to see the ticket stub?"

I picked up my wallet from the coffee table and took out the ticket stub. Detective Figula examined it closely, then handed it to Detective Bryant.

"You always keep the ticket stub when you go to

the movies?" Detective Bryant asked.

"Will you please tell me what this is all about?" I said angrily. "This is really starting to piss me off."

"Can you tell us the last time you saw this woman?" Detective Figula asked.

He held up a small photograph of the prostitute. Her hair was brown in the picture and it looked like it was taken ten years ago.

"I've never seen her before in my life," I said confidently.

"You always forget the faces of the people you fuck?" Detective Bryant said.

"I don't know if you've been following the news lately," Detective Figula said, "but the woman in the picture was a prostitute. Her name was Denise Furguson. She was found decapitated last night in Chelsea."

"Are you talking about the serial killer?" I asked.

"You know what we're talking about," Detective Bryant said.

Detective Figula held up his hand to Detective Bryant like the stop sign.

"We don't believe Ms. Furguson's death was related to the death of the prostitute in Queens," Detective Figula said to me. "There were several inconsistencies in the manner she was killed. We believe it may have been a copycat murder."

"That's very interesting," I said, "but I still don't see what this has to do with me."

Detective Figula said, "We know that you picked up Ms. Furguson on the street a couple of weeks ago, Mr. Moss. We also believe that you may have been responsible for her death."

"I've heard enough," I said. "This is bullshit, that's all this is."

"Are you denying that you beat the shit out of Ms. Furguson last week?" Detective Bryant asked.

"Of course I'm denying it. What do you think I...I can't believe this."

"We have a witness, Robert Cantello Sr., who saw you go into the Royal Hotel on West Forty-third Street with her Monday, August sixth," Detective Figula said. "He said that you went up to a room with her for five minutes then you ran down the steps and left. He said that afterwards Ms. Furguson came downstairs with a badly bruised face. She said you were responsible for her injuries."

I laughed sarcastically.

"That sounds like me all right," I said. "I go around beating up prostitutes whenever I have the chance."

"We know you did it," Detective Bryant said. "So you might as well save us time and admit it."

"What do you think I am?" I said. "Some kind of lunatic? You think I go around beating up prostitutes, chopping off their heads for no reason at all?"

"No, we believe you had a reason," Detective Figula said. "We think she tried to blackmail you, or at least you thought she might try to blackmail you. You see, her death was just a little too coincidental for me to swallow. The other day I questioned her about Ed O'Brien's murder. I was asking around the neighborhood to see if anyone saw somebody leave the building that night between six-thirty and seven. Ms. Furguson claimed she was across the street from the building that night but that she didn't notice anything. I had a funny feeling she was holding out on me about something, but I didn't know what it was. Then she turns up dead and lo and behold we discover that you'd beaten her up a week before you murdered your boss."

"I didn't murder my boss," I said.

"Well, you have to admit it's quite a coincidence the way events unfolded."

"I don't find anything coincidental about it," I said, "because like I'm telling you, I never saw that prostitute before in my life."

"Tell him about that guy Jacobson," Detective Bryant said. "The one who saw him putting the head in the garbage bag."

"We have another witness," Detective Figula said to me, "claims he saw you in the parking lot on West Seventeenth Street, putting something into a large garbage bag. Of course he didn't know what the object was at the time, but he gave us a complete description of you."

I sensed it was a trick, that the detectives were inventing this Jacobson person, but I wondered how they'd found out about the garbage bag. Had the head turned up somewhere?

"I still can't believe you're accusing me of this," I said. "Mr. Jacobson, whoever he is, must be making a mistake. I had absolutely nothing to do with any murders. I don't know how I can make that any clearer to you."

"What was the plot of this movie you saw?" Detective Figula asked.

"The plot?"

"You remember it, don't you? After all, you just saw the movie last night."

Fortunately, I had read a review of the movie a week before and I was able to give the detectives a full account of it, including what I'd thought were the strong points and weaknesses. Finally, Detective Bryant interrupted me and said:

"This doesn't prove anything. He could have seen the movie some other time or heard about it. Why did you dump Ms. Furguson's head in the Harlem River?" he asked me.

"I didn't dump her head in the Harlem River," I said.

"Then where did you dump it?" Detective Bryant asked.

"I didn't dump it anywhere," I said.

"So you took it home with you first?"

"I never saw the goddamn head," I said.

"Well, the head got into the river somehow. It turned up today in a garbage bag and it didn't get in there all by itself."

"Did it ever occur to you guys that maybe the serial killer killed this prostitute, and maybe you're wasting a lot of time harassing me about it?"

"The serial killer didn't kill Ms. Furguson," Detective Figula said.

"How can you be so sure?"

"The pattern doesn't fit. In the other murders the prostitute had been picked up first and the murderer had sex with her. We don't believe the prostitute was working when she was killed."

"Then you're going to have to work on some other theory," I said, "because you're way off base thinking I had something to do with it. And I was serious about what I said before about calling my lawyer. There has to be something illegal about what you've been putting me through the last few days, even going to my fiancée's work and harassing her."

"Do you mind if I take a look around the apartment before we go?" Detective Bryant asked.

"You wouldn't find anything anyway, but unless you have some kind of search warrant I'm not going to let you spend another minute here. You've put me through enough hell already."

The detectives looked at each other as if they realized they had nothing left to accomplish by questioning me.

"I'm sure we'll be talking again," Detective Figula said to me. "Sooner rather than later."

I let the detectives out and locked the door.

They'd left because they didn't have enough evidence to arrest me, but I knew that wouldn't be the case for long. Already, they'd put most of the case together and it was only a matter of time until they figured out the rest of it. The cop who saw me in Harlem was going to come forward soon and then the prostitute's friend would come forward, confirm that I was indeed the person who had beaten up the prostitute in the hotel. That could be enough for the police to press charges, and then when Lisa came forward and claimed she saw me on the subway with the garbage bag and after the police dredged the Harlem River and discovered the saw and the gloves, I could count on spending the rest of my life in a ten-by-ten cell.

I suddenly realized that I had been deluding myself all along. There was no bright light waiting for me at the end of the tunnel; the tunnel I was in led to nowhere. The murders were sloppy. They'd been committed impulsively, without any real planning as to how I'd get away with them. I'd left behind so much evidence and so many clues that it was a miracle I hadn't been arrested already.

I knew my only hope was to run. I had no future in New York or Seattle or anywhere else in the United States. My only chance was to get to Canada or Mexico and start from scratch. I'd have to change my name, invent a past. No one would hire me to work in a management position without experience, so I'd have to get another low-level job somewhere and try to work my way back into advertising. Actually, not having a past wouldn't be so bad. I wouldn't have to worry about personnel directors popping up and revealing old skeletons. People who don't exist don't have skeletons.

I started packing. It might explain my mental state at the time to mention that I had no idea how my escape plan would work. It didn't even occur to me that the police would be watching my every move now and that there was no way I could make it out of Manhattan, no less to Canada or Mexico. In a matter of a few seconds, I had managed to delude myself again into thinking that everything was going to be all right.

After I'd stuffed as many clothes as possible into a suitcase, I checked my wallet to see how much cash I had on me. I only had about a hundred dollars. In my bank account I thought I had another hundred. It wouldn't be enough to get me to Mexico, but it could be enough to get to Canada. I figured I'd take a bus somewhere, then try to hitch a ride. The plan was very vague, but at the time it made perfect sense to me.

I turned around and saw that Julie was sitting up in bed.

"Are you leaving me now?" she asked.

"Yes," I said and I walked out of the bedroom.

I gathered a few more things in the living room that I thought I might need in my new life – my watch, my sunglasses, my Seattle Mariners baseball cap – then I went into the bathroom. When I came out, Julie was waiting for me in the kitchen. She looked completely deranged and I guess I should have been more worried about it than I was. Her hair was a wild mess, she had deep blue circles under her eyes, and there was more red in the whites of her eyes than white.

"Can you just tell me why," she said, "why you had to do this to me?"

"Do what to you?" I said. "I have no idea what you're talking about."

"Ruin my life," she said. "Make such a fool out of me."

It was like talking to a crazy person. I had no idea what she was talking about and I was getting tired of listening to her.

"Is that what you really think happened here?" I said. "If you do, you have more serious problems than I thought."

"You're a murderer," she said. "I can't believe I got engaged to a murderer."

"You don't even know why I'm leaving," I said. "You think it has nothing to do with you, right?"

"I never did anything wrong," she said defensively.

"That's what you think," I said. "But the truth is you're paranoid, you sabotage relationships. You just can't believe that I'm a good man so you invent all these problems I have. You accuse me of cheating on you, lying to you, murdering people. If you could just see how crazy you are maybe you'd really try to get some help."

"For a telemarketing job, Bill?" she cried. "That's what this is all about? Some stupid telemarketing job? That's why you killed a man? That's why you ruined our lives?"

I didn't want to hear it anymore. Pushing her aside, I headed toward the door. That's when the pain came. It started in my neck and seemed to extend inside me. My legs buckled and a general weakness overcame my body.

Then all I felt was tingling.

I was on the floor, a few feet away from the door. Julie was crying and yelling. I didn't know what had happened to me, how I had gotten this way. All I wanted was for time to stop, to be back in Bainbridge Island and to be ten years old. I didn't know how I would change my life, but I knew I would. I was crying. The red puddle near my head was getting bigger.

## 17

WHEN I WOKE up three days later I was facing a white ceiling. I couldn't move my head and there were tubes coming out of my mouth. My throat was very dry. I tried to scream, but the only sound I could produce was a faint gurgling noise. The face of a woman appeared over me. She was smiling the way people lean over strangers' baby carriages and smile.

"Nice to see you up," she said.

I tried to say "water."

"It's okay," she said. "It'll be hard to talk for a while. Do you know where you are? You're in Lenox Hill Hospital in Manhattan. You've suffered a serious spinal cord injury."

That's when I realized that I couldn't feel anything below my neck. I prayed that I was asleep, having a nightmare.

"I'm afraid things aren't going to be quite the same for you anymore," the woman said.

I got the technicalities from the doctor the next day. The C4 vertebrae of my spinal cord had been severed, which is just about the worst type of spinal cord injury a person can suffer. I had been stabbed in the neck with a four-inch knife.

I had already undergone three operations and the doctor said more surgery could be necessary. For at least a few weeks I'd be hooked up to a ventilator. Because I had been in a coma, there was a chance I had suffered brain damage.

During the next few weeks I was near death several times. I had a severe case of pneumonia and I needed an emergency operation when scar tissue from a previous operation restricted my breathing. A stream of doctors and nurses came in to monitor me, drug me, feed me intravenously, and change my bedpan. Since the bone in my neck had been fractured I had to continue to be stabilized by a halo which was screwed into my forehead. I could only talk when a nurse stood by to suction the mucous from my mouth and from the tube which had been inserted into my throat. I was so out of it from the medication that I spent most of my time asleep. Even asleep I was depressed. I dreamt I was able to pick up a knife or gun and kill myself. Then I'd wake and realize with horror that from now on even suicide would be impossible. I'd have to live out the rest of my life in misery whether I liked it or not.

When Julie hadn't come to visit me after the first few days, I knew she was probably out of my life for good. I was happy for her. As crazy as it may seem, I didn't blame her for my injury. Although no one had said anything to me about it, I was fairly certain that she had stabbed me. While I wished she hadn't done it, I knew she had acted out of desperation, and anyone in the same position probably would have done the same thing.

During this period, Detective Figula came to my room several times. I heard him asking the doctor whether he could question me, and each time the doctor told him that I was too weak to talk. To be honest, I didn't care one way or another. The murders I'd committed were my least concern and at times they didn't seem to have anything to do with me. My entire life seemed to be someone else's life that I could view like scenes in a movie. I could rewind it and repeat certain events and none of it was real.

One afternoon I was having another suicide dream –

I was about to jump into a volcano – when I woke up and saw Detective Figula staring down at me. I closed my eyes and pretended to fall back asleep.

"Come on, Bill," he said. "The doctor said I could talk to you today. Let's not make this any more difficult than it has to be."

He waited until my eyes opened.

"You've been quiet for long enough. I need to know the truth."

I was more alert, but I hadn't regained any movement below my shoulders. My voice was a hoarse whisper.

"Leave me alone," I said.

"Sorry, but I can't do that," he said, "not until I get that confession out of you I won't. You did it, didn't you? You killed your boss and you killed that prostitute to cover it up, right?"

There was only one reason why I didn't confess to my crimes and it had nothing to do with me. When you're paralyzed it doesn't seem to matter whether you spend the rest of your life in jail or on an island in the Bahamas and I had no plans to go to the Bahamas. But I didn't want to hurt Julie. I realized how humiliating it would be for her if it came out in the news that her fiancée had been a ruthless murderer. After all the ways I'd disappointed her, lying to the police this last time was the least I could do to repay her.

"I didn't do anything," I said. "Why won't you believe me?"

"I'm giving you a chance to clear your conscience," he said. "Do you want to just lie here thinking about the lives you ruined?"

I tried to speak. A nurse had to come over and suction my mouth and wipe the saliva off my chin.

"If you have evidence I did something," I finally said,

"why don't you just arrest me...stop bothering me."

Detective Figula took a deep breath.

"The fact is I don't have any evidence against you," he said. "No substantial evidence anyway. I guess you did a good job cleaning up after yourself that night."

"I was at the movies," I said weakly.

"I checked up on that. The ticket taker remembered seeing you. She identified the cast on your hand and the scar on your forehead."

"So," I said. "That proves it."

"I'm afraid it proves nothing," the detective said. "One of the ushers remembers seeing someone getting up about halfway through the movie and going out one of the side entrance doors. He said it was dark and he couldn't identify the person, but I have no reason to think that the person couldn't have been you."

"It wasn't," I said.

"What about this knife in the back?" he said. "Do you remember how it got there?"

I hesitated. I knew that Julie must have made up some story to protect herself or he wouldn't be asking me about it now. I didn't want to say anything that would make the police suspect Julie, if they didn't suspect her already.

"I was in my apartment," I said. "Then I...I woke up in the hospital. I don't remember anything else. Honest to God."

"You don't remember fighting with a black man who had broken into your apartment."

"A black man?"

"Actually, your fiancée claimed he was Puerto Rican."

"I only know what the doctors told me," I said. "I don't know how much longer I can talk."

"I understand your fiancée hasn't been here to visit you," he said. "Did you have some fight about something?"

I tried to shake my head, forgetting for a second that my head was still held steady in a halo.

"My life isn't the same anymore," I said. "That changes things in a relationship. I guess I'm just too much trouble for her now. That makes sense, doesn't it?"

I could tell that I had affected Detective Figula and that he was beginning to feel sorry for me. After that day, he returned to interview me several more times, but I never budged on my story. Fortunately, the cop in Harlem never came forward about seeing me near the river that night. I assumed this was because it was dark and he didn't recognize me, but I never found out for sure. Since I didn't get any publicity in the press as a suspect, Lisa didn't come forward either with her story that she'd seen me on the subway with the garbage bag. Although the prostitute's friend had identified me as the man who had beaten the prostitute up, the police were never able to prove that the prostitute had been trying to blackmail me or that I had any real motive to murder her.

Finally, the police stopped coming to question me. There was a T.V. in my room on just about twenty-four hours a day and I saw no new reports on the news about either of the murders. There had been another murder of a prostitute in Queens and, according to one report I saw, the police were still considering the possibility that Denise Furguson's death was related to the other murders.

I realized that, barring any new developments, the police had probably given up the case against me.

Personally, I didn't care one way or another, but I was happy for Julie. Now she could live out the rest of her life peacefully, without fear that her past with me would come back to haunt her. As it turned out, I didn't see her again until six years later. It was a sunny spring afternoon and I was in Central Park, travelling along a path in my motorized wheelchair. I controlled the chair with a sip 'n' puff mechanism, which required me to blow air into a straw device. At first I didn't recognize Julie. She'd lost weight and she'd stopped dying her hair blond. She looked much fitter and healthier than she'd ever looked when I'd known her. Standing next to her was a tall, slim, professional-looking man whose hands rested on the handle of a baby stroller. Sadly, I realized how that could have been me standing next to her. She saw me staring at her and the way her gaze stayed fixed on mine I knew she recognized me. There was a long awkward moment during which I felt very embarrassed and ashamed. I smiled at her. She seemed uncertain for a moment, then she turned away. I watched her walk away with her husband and child, hoping she would look back at me. She didn't.

It took me a long time to get my life back together. After two months had passed since my injury, I was moved to Mount Sinai Hospital for rehabilitation. I had daily appointments with doctors, nurses and therapists. Despite the rigorous training program they put me through, after another month I didn't show any sign of improvement. The only good news was that I hadn't suffered any significant brain damage. The psychologist said my mind would always be healthy.

My body had begun to shrivel away. The doctors said this was normal with quadriplegics, that I shouldn't be afraid to look at myself. I still had dreams of suicide.

A couple of months went by and I hadn't gained any new movement. There was talk of sending me home, but I told them I didn't have any home to go to. I couldn't go back to my old apartment – I didn't even know whether Julie was still living there – because it was a fifth-floor walk-up. They said my only other option was to go to a nursing home. I said that was all right with me and it seemed as though the rest of my life had been decided. I'd be fed and changed and taken care of like a baby until one day I'd drop dead and they'd bury me in some anonymous cemetery. I had absolutely nothing to live for.

Then one day something happened that would change the rest of my life.

A pretty woman with dark curly hair visited my room. I had seen so many doctors and nurses and psychiatrists and other hospital officials that I didn't even pay her any special attention. I hoped she would just go away and leave me alone in my misery. She asked me questions about myself and my life – where I was from, what I'd done for a living, things like that. I ignored all her questions and it seemed as though she was fed up with me and about to leave when she asked me if I wanted to talk about returning to work.

I thought it was a cruel joke. Since I'd been in the hospital, work had been the last thing on my mind. No one from A.C.A., not even Nelson, had come to visit me, and I assumed this was because they all still suspected that I'd killed Ed. I didn't think there'd be any way I could continue my job there, and I didn't see why anyone anywhere would hire me.

"Leave me alone," I said. "Stop fucking with my head."

She didn't leave. Instead she told me about all the

technology and services available to help paralyzed people and she said when I was ready I could go to her office to meet with her.

Out of curiosity, I went the next day. It turned out she'd been telling the truth. She taught me how to use a computer which I could control with a mouth stick, and she said that at some point I could learn to use a voice-activated computer. Although it took me a while to catch on, I was thrilled to be actually using a computer again. In some ways, it was better than if I had risen from my wheelchair and learned to walk again. Life without work had always been inconceivable to me, which may have been the main reason why I'd been so depressed. If I could work, it didn't seem to matter to me whether I was paralyzed or not.

I met with the woman two times a week. After each visit I became more and more convinced that I could actually return to work again. The question was what type of job I would try to get. I knew returning to A.C.A. was probably out of the question and even before my injury it had been nearly impossible to get a job in advertising. My only other skill was phone sales so I decided that's what I'd do.

With my Social Security Disability Insurance I was able to move into a small, specially equipped apartment on the ground floor of a high-rise apartment building on the Upper East Side. It was exactly the type of building Julie had always dreamed of living in, complete with a doorman, health club and swimming pool. A state agency sponsored me for evaluation while I tried to return to work. Medicaid paid for a twenty-four hour home attendant who fed me and moved me periodically to make sure I didn't get pressure sores. I obtained a voice-activated computer and I learned how to use it as well as I'd ever used a manual computer.

It took me a few months, but I finally got a telemarketing job, selling computer hardware to small and medium-size businesses. It was a large office with about twenty telemarketers a shift. Every day when I arrived the Floor Manager would rest the headset on my head then I'd log on to the computer and start calling. I was happy to discover that my old sales skills were still intact. My first day at the job I set a company record, selling nearly ten thousand dollars worth of equipment. With the voice-activated computer I became a virtual selling machine. I could make nearly twice as many calls as the other workers, which meant I was twice as effective. All I had to say was "dial" and I'd be back on line, making a pitch to another prospect.

I was earning about a thousand dollars a week. I was so thrilled to be back in the working world that I rarely thought about my injury anymore. I actually found it convenient to come home from a day at the office and have someone bathe me and feed me. On weekends, I sat by the pool reading newspapers and magazines. During the week, I was completely focussed on work, thinking about new sales strategies and ways to improve my performance. In many ways I was living a perfect life.

But as time went on, I started to feel limited at my job. I knew that I had more in me than to be a lowly telemarketer. I started to dream about returning to a job in advertising. The problem, of course, was that I needed to have some recent management experience on my resume. If I could get promoted at the telemarketing job, perhaps work my way up to running the department, I could use it as a stepping stone for getting my career off the ground again.

The only trouble was my boss was young and he had no plans of leaving the company. The only way I'd ever get in charge of the department was if I could somehow get rid of him. Sometimes I imagined myself rising up from my wheelchair, walking into his office, leaning over his desk, and strangling him. It was so clear – the sensation of his neck caving in, his body falling limp, his power becoming mine. It was a beautiful thing to think about.